D1606326

What Reviewers Are Saying About Secrets and
Sacrifices

Diane M. Wylie

Secrets and Sacrifices

Diane M. Wylie

Diane M. Wylie

Vintage Romance Publishing

Goose Creek, South Carolina

www.vrpublishing.com

Diane M. Wylie

Secrets and Sacrifices

ISBN: 0-9785368-5-1

PUBLISHED BY VINTAGE ROMANCE PUBLISHING, LLC

www.vrpublishing.com

Dedication

For Ed, Elaine, and Scott. I will love and cherish you always and forever.

Diane M. Wylie

Chapter One

Late Fall 1861
Allegheny Mountains

Charlotte "Charlie" Garrett, crouching uncomfortably behind a boulder, swallowed the lump of fear in her throat, adjusted the position of her beloved army-issued Springfield, and waited. All snipers had been ordered to come before the main body of the regiment and pick off any Yankees they could. The moment of truth had arrived. Since disguising herself as a young man to join the Twenty-Fifth Virginia Infantry, following her husband Joshua into war, Charlotte had never shot a man. She was now a sharpshooter for the regiment, having been ordered into this maligned group of men due to her ability with the weapon she clutched tightly in her hands.

From where she was hidden she could see Clarence, the older man who had taken her under his wing, and a few of the other soldiers selected for this job. He was lying on the ground behind a huge log, and two of the younger snipers were up in the gnarled oak trees that overlooked the ground below. The others were invisible through the falling snow.

The weather had gotten progressively worse up in the mountains, and the soldiers had been growing more and more discontent. The Confederates held this part of the Allegheny Mountains and were to defend Staunton-Reidsburg Pike from Union forces who hoped to take the summit from them.

The idea that the officers were counting on her and the rest of the sharpshooters to draw the enemy out from behind their artillery made her stomach feel as though it were full of nervous butterflies.

Taking off her spectacles, she looked down at the valley while she polished the smudged glass ovals on her shirt. No Bluecoats were visible at the moment. Charlie's stomach twitched. *Where are the damn Yankees?* Smoke belched out of the slightly raised tree line, and a loud boom echoed across the ground.

All of the time spent drilling and marching had not prepared her for the mind-numbing terror beginning to claw its way up her spine. Today something was going to change…her life was going to change…history was going to change. Two armies were going to clash, and people were going to die just like they had already died in the time since Fort Sumter and Bull Run.

Oh, God! She was starting to tremble at the very idea that she was here doing this! She wished she had not joined the snipers. It came as a surprise when she found out most of the other foot soldiers didn't like them. Jeers of "sneak" and "murderer" were sometimes directed toward her group. The soldiers who fought out in plain sight didn't appreciate the skill of those who perched in trees or behind rocks to pick off their unsuspecting targets. Many considered the sharpshooters to be coddled or even cowardly when they were allowed to shoot behind cover while the others marched headlong into battle.

It would have been so much easier to stay with her husband. If she were beside him, with his comforting presence to draw strength from, she was sure her heart would not be pounding as hard as it was. Joshua seemed to have gotten over the rage she had seen him display on the practice field when he recognized her, despite the baggy uniform, dirty slouch hat, short hair, and glasses.

* * *

All during training camp in Virginia, Charlie had managed to avoid direct contact with Josh. They were in the same company and, with Josh's natural ability to cultivate new friends, she knew it would only be a matter of time before he made the rounds of the entire regiment and knew each one of them by name.

She had carefully studied the actions and habits of the men around her and had gotten very adept at burping, spitting, and scratching when the time seemed right. By acting like a man, dressing like a man, and keeping her hat pulled low, Charlie had managed to avoid detection. Even Clarence, who kept a close eye on his "adopted" son, had not picked up on her gender. Fortunately, he respected her need for privacy whenever she could get it.

Then one day it happened. Charlie lined up with the rest of the troops on the practice field as usual. Standing beside Clarence at attention, she waited for the officers to give orders. She remembered looking around and searching for Josh, as usual. Her husband was the whole reason she was here after all. She just couldn't bear to be so far away from him. All she needed to get through the day was to see his handsome face, but she had to make sure he didn't see her. He was somewhere in the ranks of soldiers that had gathered on the muddy field.

"At ease, men," Captain Weaver had yelled. Then he'd moved closer to the rank and file. "Tomorrow we march to our destiny, gentlemen. We must rise above the oppression of the Federal government and, with your help, we will persevere against the Northern aggressors."

A chorus of whoops and catcalls had erupted all around and swelled to a thunderous noise.

"Hear that, lad?" Clarence had clapped her on the back hard, almost knocking her over. "We're gonna whip them Yankees. We are gonna whip 'em and send them running with their tails 'tween their legs." He had grinned at her from under his grizzled, scraggly beard.

"We sure are, Clarence, we sure are!"

Suddenly, the trumpet had blown, and they had all settled down and stiffened to attention again.

Captain Weaver had been trying to speak once more. "Everyone has done a bang-up job these past weeks. Some of you have never handled a rifle before, while others have obviously been hunting many times and know exactly how to handle a gun. One such young man has proven himself to be a very good shot. He will be part of the sharpshooters in our regiment. Charlie Garrett, please step forward!"

With no choice, Charlie had come forward then turned and, with a start of surprise, she had found herself locking eyes with Josh in the crowd. That was the heart-stopping moment when she knew her husband had seen her, really looked closely at her.

The thunderous cloud appearing on Josh's face the moment he realized the real identity of "Charlie" Garrett had been obvious to her, even yards away from him. She had watched him reach for his powder charges and prepare to load his rifle. Terror had swept through her. He'd glared angrily at the soldiers all around him The other Augusta County boys had seen Josh's strange reaction, encircled him immediately, and Billy Kaufman, the largest man in the regiment, had taken Josh's gun away with one massive hand, then pinned Josh's arms to his sides. As soon as she had the opportunity, Charlie had escaped the practice field. She just hadn't been able to face him.

Joshua had not come anywhere near Charlie when the regiment marched into the Allegheny Mountains, which was fine with her. She had really needed the time to think.

Then, just this very morning, Josh had just walked up to the cook fire, introduced himself as her cousin, and they walked off to talk.

"You need to go tell Captain Weaver you're my wife and that you joined up without my permission or knowledge. I'll give you my wages, and you can buy passage home," Josh had said as soon as they were out of the other soldiers' earshot.

Startled by his blunt command, she'd nearly tripped over an exposed root. He had not considered for a moment what she wanted or even why she was here. Fighting tears she had quickened the pace, leading him down a ravine to a spot where they might have a little privacy.

"Stop, Charlie." Josh's hand had landed on her shoulder gently but firmly. "You heard what I said, but I will not be the one telling the Captain anything. You will."

"Oh, no, I won't." Facing him squarely, she had raised her chin and crossed her arms over her chest. Clenching her jaw, she'd given him her best stubborn glare. Only he hadn't blustered and blown as usual. He hadn't even huffed. Not once. The sad expression on his face had been thoroughly confusing to Charlie. It was so unlike her husband to react this way. His hand had come up toward her face, and she had flinched involuntarily. Josh's woeful expression had deepened. "Charlie, oh my darling, is this what you think of me now?" He'd dropped his hand. "Do you think I would raise my hand in anger to the woman I love? Though it seems plain you no longer love me."

"What? Why do you say that, Josh? I joined this army because I love you. It is the only reason I am here."

"If you love me, why are you sleeping with all of these men?"

"Josh! No one has touched me! They think I am a man, like they are!"

"If it weren't for big Billy, I would have shot them all! What about your parents? Where do they think you are?"

He had moved closer then. Slowly his big hand had come up and gently removed her hat and glasses. "There now, you look more like yourself." His fingers played with the short, dark curls. "I miss your long hair."

"It will grow back," she had informed him tersely. "I told my family I was going to visit Aunt Betty in South Carolina. I told them I couldn't bear to stay at the farm without you…and it was true. I couldn't, Josh." She had needed to pray for control and the right words. "You have to understand...I like it here...where I know you are close. I like the army. It's like camping out. I always enjoyed the hunting trips we went on with my brothers."

He had frowned even more sternly, if that was possible. "You liked hunting? Why did you refuse to kill the doe on the last trip we made?"

Fiddling nervously with a button on her uniform, she had watched Josh lower his long-limbed body to a moss-covered log. "That was different—uhh!" Josh had yanked her down onto his lap. "—That was different. It was a beautiful animal with two young ones. They were so darling. I just couldn't kill their mother."

Josh hadn't looked at her face. He had kept his eyes down in the vicinity of her chest. "Honey...those Yankees may not be beautiful, but chances are good that some of them will be daddies to young ones, too." He'd raised his face then, so handsome and so familiar, and had looked at her somberly. "Are you prepared to shoot somebody's daddy, somebody's husband, or somebody's child?"

* * *

His words came back to her now as she looked down on the scene below and waited for a glimpse of blue. She put on her glasses and wiped her perspiring hands on her gray woolen pants. Was she prepared? Could she shoot somebody's husband?

"Clarence," she called softly.

He didn't turn around. He too was busy scanning the ground below. The spyglass glinted in the sunlight. Would the Yankees see the reflection off the glass? Her heart jumped into her throat, choking her and increasing the trembling of her hands. How could she shoot now?

"C-Clarence?"

The grizzled face swung around to face her. "Charlie? You okay, boy?"

She motioned with her hand and, after a quick look around, Clarence came in a crouching run to join her.

"Whatsa matter? You got a case of the jitters?" he asked amiably. Then he glanced down at her hands and up again at her face. "Yah sure are jumpy, Charlie. Yah gotsta calm down and keep your mind on one thing at a time. Jus' remember what I taught you. Tear open the cartridge, git the powder down the barrel, put the bullet in — don't forget that part," he gave a short chuckle, "then ramrod it down, put the cap on the nib under the hammer, and ya'll is ready to go again."

"Sure, I remember it all," Charlie retorted indignantly. "I'm not stupid, you know, just scared."

Clarence chuckled again. Reaching down at his side with steady hands, he offered his canteen. She looked at it, puzzled. "I have my own water, Clarence, I don't need to drink yours."

"Mine is special. Have a drink, boy," he insisted, thrusting it at her.

"Okay." She took the canteen and tilted it up for a large mouthful. "Gak!" She choked and finally swallowed the stuff that burned all the way down. Tears sprang to her eyes, and she pulled out a blue bandana to wipe under her glasses.

Clarence laughed softly again. "Ain't you never had no strong drink befo'? A little shot of courage, that's all.

My grandma set a great store by her own shots of courage. Said they were the reason she lived so long…my grandma was ninety-seven when she passed on."

A shot rang out. They threw themselves into position. The other snipers were taking shots at a group of Bluecoats picking their way through between the rocks and scattered trees. A cry echoed up the mountain, and Charlie saw one man fall, holding his hands up to his neck as a stream of red appeared, visible even from this distance.

Clarence sighted down the high-powered scope of his special-issue Whitworth rifle and easily picked off another soldier from a distance of almost four hundred yards. He turned away to reload with a precious .45 caliber bullet then took down another man before Charlie could squeeze the trigger of her ordinary rifle once. The Yankees were running back in the direction they had come. One man was lagging behind the rest, having a more difficult time maneuvering the natural landscape. He would be so easy to shoot. The snipers continued to fire all around her. She took a bead on the clumsy soldier.

"Shoot, Charlie! Every man you take could save the life of one of ours."

Taking a deep breath, she closed her eyes and pulled the trigger. Opening her eyes again, she saw the man fall to the ground. She'd killed a man! No…wait…the man sprang up and began running again. He had only tripped and fallen.

"Come on, boys!" Clarence called to the sharpshooters. "Stay sharp now. The real fighting is about to start. The snow is lettin' up!"

Sure enough, no sooner had the words left his mouth than the now-familiar Rebel yell sent goosebumps skittering along Charlie's arms. With an explosion of noise, the army in gray erupted from somewhere below them. Hoards of men came screaming out into the open—some falling over their own feet in their haste and others nimbly leaping over the obstacles in their path. The Confederate flag, like a beacon of light, drew them toward their enemy in a stream of humanity.

"Here they come!" Clarence shouted. "Pick off as many Yankees as you can before they reach our men!"

As if they were magically summoned, the tide of blue flowed out of the trees heading directly for a clash with their boys. Spurts of gunfire now accompanied the war cries of the Rebels and the screams of men being hit.

Charlie hurried to reload, tasting the powder as she ripped open the cartridge to put it down the barrel. *No time to waste. Josh is down there! Don't think. Just aim and fire.* She listened to the voice in her head directing her to pick out a Bluecoat through the pall of smoke, pull the trigger, reload, pick another one, fire, and load again. There was no time to watch them fall, no time to see how she had put a bloody hole in a living, breathing human being. A strange kind of trance fell over her, and her actions became mechanical, repetitious, and unthinking. Over and over she hit her mark.

But gradually, confusion began to mount, and her anxiety grew. It was getting harder and harder to sight her targets. She could no longer see the Bluecoats clearly! Pulling off her glasses, she flung them aside and continued to peer down the gun barrel. Nothing! A quick rub of her eyes…still nothing. What was the problem?

"Charlie! Charlie!" Clarence was tugging at her arm. "We have to go down! The smoke is too thick to see from here anymore!" Grabbing up her wire rims again, she followed the angular figure of her mentor as they made their way down to join the fighting below.

Sliding down the steep incline with rocks rolling under her brogans, Charlie strained to see what was happening. The noise was horrendous. The high-pitched whine of bullets, the lower booming of the cannon fire, and the screams of injured and dying men filled her ears, blocking out sensible thought. Everywhere, soldiers were running, stumbling, and crawling in the opposite direction.

A bugle's faltering tones rang out, sounding the retreat. "Back! Go back!" An officer on horseback gestured to their group. "Retreat! No use, boys. There are too many of them!" The captain had lost his hat, and blood ran from a rent in his sleeve. The distinctive whine of a cannon ball grew louder, and Charlie dove for the ground. It hit behind the horseman. He was gone in a shower of dirt and debris that exploded up then came down on her head.

Quickly scrambling to her feet again, fear gripped her with a horrible force, and she forgot to follow Clarence. She had to find Josh! Where was he? Charlie began to run.

"Charlie, come back! We have to retreat!"

Clarence was calling after her but she paid him no mind. The smoke lay in a thick blanket over the valley. Soldiers appeared out of the fog, stumbling and staggering past her. Searching and searching, she ran, tripping and jumping over obstacles. Some of them appeared to be human. Bile rose in her throat as she peered with dread at each torn and bloody man who lay on the battleground or crawled past. Some plucked at her sleeve and pleaded for help, while others were beyond helping. There was no time to spare for any man, no matter their rank or need.

"Joshua Garrett! Have you seen Josh Garrett?" she pleaded with the soldiers who ran, hobbled, and crawled past her. But they ignored her frantic words in their quest for safety. Bullets whined past Charlie's head and plucked at her clothing as she made her way deeper onto the smoky battlefield, but she cared little.

Chapter Two

"Mop up some of this blood! Get some straw to soak it up!"

Captain Daniel Reid and the other surgeons were busy, extremely busy. Casualties were pouring into the hospital tents as fast as the stretcher-bearers could cart them in, put them down, and go out to get more.

Daniel turned his attention to the next patient, a case he would not have bothered to treat a month ago. Daniel, as well as most of the army's surgeons, was initially unprepared for the extent of the injuries inflicted on a body by war. The first battle at Bull Run had introduced him to spectacles he would never forget for the rest of his life. Since that time, he had made it his mission to learn the best way to handle the horrifying injuries. He experimented with new theories each time he faced the battlefield injuries.

The man on the table before him had taken a minie ball in his shoulder and head. The shoulder would heal, but the head wound was an injury that was often fatal, either immediately or later. Daniel had wondered whether such a patient might be saved if dealt with as soon as possible.

"Be very careful with the chloroform, Joseph. Watch his breathing. These head injury cases can stop breathing with little warning. They seem to be more sensitive to the stuff."

"Yes, sir," Joseph Hill replied as he dripped the liquid onto the cloth over the man's mouth and nose, while holding the patient's bearded chin with his other hand.

Normally, Joseph, as his surgical assistant, would be standing at the end of the table, but this time Daniel needed access to the man's head. Using his own shaving razor, he shaved the hair around the man's entry wound quickly, and poured a generous amount of carbolic over the area. With a pair of bone forceps, he located the ball and removed it. The amount of gray brain matter damaged was relatively small. Carefully, Daniel replaced the pale bone fragments, pressing a piece of cloth over the wound to hold everything in place. *This is like assembling the pieces of a rather grizzly puzzle.* He left it to Joseph to bandage the man's head.

Daniel moved to the second table where the next patient lay waiting, writhing in pain from a shattered ankle. *Damn, another amputation.* Although most of the soldiers did not believe it, Daniel, and most of the surgeons, hated it each time they had to do one. The joy of this occupation came in being able to help restore people back to normal, to help them regain their former selves. But this was not always accomplished. The surgeons had learned early in the war that a quick and efficient amputation was most often the only way to save a life. He signaled for the application of the chloroform and picked up the bone saw.

It was deep into the night before Daniel was finally able to walk wearily out of the hospital tent. He barely missed stumbling over the rows of blanket-shrouded bodies, lined up neatly in the faint glow of his lantern.

Pausing for a moment to cross himself and say a

quick prayer, he stared with burning eyes at the remains of the men who had died that day...men he could not save. A hand, pale and stiff, lay palm up, fingers open beseechingly. The sight gave him a sick feeling deep in his stomach. Then he saw something that made him even more heartsick. A gold wedding band reflected the dim light of the lantern. *A widow has been left behind, and she doesn't even know it yet.* Bending down, he looked at the piece of paper pinned to the soldier's uniform. Daniel pulled his tattered notebook from his pocket and noted the name. Then, removing the ring, he placed it in his pocket and tucked the cold appendage under the rough army blanket.

More husbands and sons would perish in the days and weeks ahead due to fever or pneumonia or any one of a number of problems that could arise even after he had sewn them back together.

I hate this war. The killing and maiming of perfectly good human beings is such a terrible waste. But here he was, doing his duty for the Cause, helping to defend his adopted state of Virginia from the Northern invaders and put back together the shattered bodies. It was the right thing to do...to help his fellow countrymen with the only skills he had to bring, the knowledge and techniques he had learned while studying at the College of Physicians of Philadelphia.

"Captain Reid?" The voice of an older man finally got his attention. He turned slowly to face Corporal Blackwood.

"Blackwood." The sad-faced officer saluted, and Daniel wearily returned the salute. "What is it...and can it wait until tomorrow? I'm dog tired."

"Sorry, sir, but General Smith wanted me to tell you to keep the ambulance wagons here. We ain't done fighting yet." Daniel nodded. "We have some men missing too, sir. Five."

With a deep sigh, Daniel ran a hand through his hair. "All right, Corporal, get a detail together to bury these poor souls as soon as dawn breaks."

"Yes, sir." He saluted again and was gone.

Now Daniel was alone again with the moths flitting around the lantern in his hand and the silent corpses. Straightening his back and stiffening his arm, he gave them a crisp military salute. "You men are better off than most would think. This hell on earth has only just begun, I fear. Rest in peace, fellows…the war is over for you."

* * *

A pale crescent moon still hung in the pre-dawn sky when she sighted the flickering torches bobbing across the clearing. Charlie lay on her belly in the underbrush, with the smell of damp earth and decaying vegetation in her nose, watching the burial detail arrive. Ned Hagan from their hometown was there, and the redheaded young man, Victor Marshall, along with Billy Kaufman. The only Augusta County boys missing were Victor's brother and Joshua Garrett.

It wasn't long before there were thirteen rectangular holes in the soft dirt. She watched them bury the soldiers, carefully lowering each man, one-by-one. Josh was the last man. She knew his long, lanky body, even from a distance, and was grateful for the loving way Ned and all the county boys handled him.

A sob rose in her throat. *This cannot be happening!* But she knew it was true. Her husband was dead. She could hear Victor's pitiful gulping sobs from where she lay, as he helped put his brother, Oliver's, body in the grave. The sound made her chest ache with renewed anguish. Finally, each man removed a tattered hat and stood with bowed head over the fresh graves.

How she longed to stand with them and say goodbye properly. But the tears had wracked her body nonstop since she had found Josh on the battlefield. Even now, her breath came in trembling shudders at the memory of finding him mortally wounded. She said her own agonized and personal goodbye to her beloved husband before the soldiers came to retrieve his lifeless body. If she came out of hiding now, it would be the end of Charlie Garrett and the end of her time in the army.

She had no intention of leaving the fight now! The damned Yankees had killed her husband! They were trying to destroy everything she and other Southerners held dear!

All her life Charlie had felt vaguely discontented and unsettled, as if there was something she had forgotten to do. But since she had mustered in and become part of this honorable group of men, the feeling had gone away. She had a purpose now…and it was to kill Yankees…as many as she could!

The Twenty-Fifth Virginia would march again. There were unmistakable signs that they were leaving. The next day, she found a new hiding place so she could watch Clarence and her tent mates. All of the soldiers were scuttling to and fro, striking tents, dousing cook fires, and packing kits and wagons. Charlie wanted to be with them, but the overwhelming sadness had such a hold on her all she could do was lie under the leaves of the rhododendron, sobbing and allowing the bugs to bite her skin and crawl in her hair. Would she never stop crying? *Charlie wouldn't cry. Charlie is a man. I am Charlie. Charlie has to go back and fight and…stay alive.*

Chapter Three

She woke early in the morning with a pounding headache and an upset stomach. The dew lay heavy on the grass, dampening her brogans and making her skin clammy as Charlie stumbled away from Clarence and the other sleeping men in the tent.

Overnight, the weather seemed to have turned unseasonably warm, melting all of the snow. Forcing her legs to move, she waded through the early morning fog toward the river, functioning on instinct alone. Sorrow choked her hopelessly, rendering her barely able to eat or speak.

Oh, she knew very well that Clarence and the Augusta County men watched her closely since she had come back two days before. They were wondering, no doubt, why a lad would grieve so for the "cousin" he had only just met. But she could not bother with them right now. It was all she could do to move from one day to the next, from one breath to the next. In fact, there were times she didn't think her heart would take the next beat, so badly did the pain squeeze her chest each time she thought of Josh.

Joshua! Gone…dead! A fresh onslaught of black grief gripped her, stealing away her breath and taking the strength from her limbs. Her knees buckled and down she went, rolling down the riverbank and sliding on the wet grass until she slid to a stop at the base of a scrubby bush, collapsing in a shuddering, sobbing heap on the ground.

25

Tears streamed down her face uncontrollably, and Charlie gasped for air. Suddenly, her stomach convulsed, and she wretched until nothing was left. The rancid taste of sickness filled her throat. Pulling off her glasses, she tucked them carefully into her jacket pocket and raised her canteen to her mouth. Taking a mouthful of tepid water, she rinsed her mouth and spat. Then she took a tentative sip. Her stomach still rolled with nausea.

Closing the canteen and curling up into a ball, she closed her eyes. She wondered if it were possible for a person to go insane from grief and loss. Images of Josh kept dancing across her mind. The dark thunderous look on Josh's face when he recognized who she was, the light of passion in his eyes when they made love, and the gentle love shining in his eyes on their wedding day.

Once more she began to cry, sobbing uncontrollably until exhaustion took over, and she fell asleep again.

* * *

The sound of men's voices filtered through the trees and reached Charlie's ears. Her eyes flew open, and her heart leaped into her throat. How long had she been asleep here under this bush? Had she missed the call to march? Were they breaking camp already? Then she heard the voices coming closer to her hiding place.

"Did y'all hear we is gitting a chance ta rest today?"

"Sure did," came the reply. "Captain Reid didn't waste no time making us come down here and take a bath in this here river." The speaker let out a grunt of annoyance. "Don't know what fur. We'll jus' get dirty again. 'Sides, it's too cold."

"Quit yer bellyachin', Roy, a good dunk in that there

river might wash some of them lice off you." The speaker laughed heartily at Roy's expense.

The laughter faded as they moved past Charlie's spot.

A bath! Oh, how wonderful it would be to have a bath. Sitting up, she rubbed her face, feeling the dirt and oils that had accumulated for so long. Lifting her arm, she gave herself a sniff. *Sakes alive!* The odor wafting out from the wool jacket was horrendous.

Crawling on her hands and knees, she came out from under the bush and pushed to her feet. Her back hurt, and her belly growled, letting her know she had missed breakfast. *Breakfast and a bath...take it one step at a time, Charlotte Elizabeth Garrett. Just concentrate on those two things and nothing else. You cannot just crawl under a bush and die. Josh would not want that... No! Do not think of Josh now...food and a bath...food and a bath.* She repeated it silently, like a mantra.

Hearing splashing, shouts, and laughter coming from further down the riverbank, her feet automatically led her in that direction. Somehow, the sounds of life and thought of getting clean pulled her irresistibly. By habit she groped in her pocket, pulled out her glasses, and put them back on her face as she walked on unsteady legs, slipping in the mud and wet grass.

The sight meeting her eyes brought her to a sudden stop, realizing immediately the foolishness of her actions. Below her, in the calm waters of the slow-moving creek were naked men. Many, many naked men...probably more than half of her company was there. There were tall men, short men, young unblemished men with rosy pale skin, and wrinkled older men with permanent farmers' tans. Some of the soldiers were totally naked, and others wore grimy undergarments.

Uniforms, shoes, and guns littered the riverbank, dumped where they were shed.

A group of young men were frolicking together, pushing each other down into the cold water with whoops and shouts. Charlie stood, rooted to the spot, staring at them. Never before had she seen such a sight!

Oddly drawn to watch the sight she should, by all rights, be turning away from in horror, she continued to stare in fascination. This was a world she would never be allowed to glimpse as a female, but they allowed her to stay because they thought she was one of them.

She was one of them…a soldier too. An odd feeling of calm settled over her. Charlie Garrett belonged to this group of honorable, brave men and they accepted "him" without reservation.

Her gaze swept over the joyful scene. The men called out to the ones standing fully clothed along the edge of the water.

"Captain Reid! Aren't you going to follow your own orders?"

"Y'all gotsa ta git in this here freezing water, too!"

Twisting around, she looked to see who they were talking to. A tall man stood on the bank, still fully dressed in his gray uniform and boots. He was hatless and his tawny hair shown golden in the sun. The light reflected off his shiny captain's bars set on impressively broad shoulders. It was the regimental surgeon, the man who had tried so hard to save the lives of the soldiers.

"Wash that grime and lice off yourselves, boys! It's a fine day today for swimming…not bad for a mountain winter day," he called to them.

* * *

Daniel laughed as he watched his fellow Rebs frolicking in the water. Some of them were actually using soap to get themselves clean. The medical team struggled continually with the issue of hygiene. They had to remind the men again and again that they must take care of their bodily needs downstream of their drinking water.

More and more men were stripping off their uniforms and jumping into the cold water. The day was a freakishly warm one for this time of year.

For a few minutes, Daniel watched them, wishing he were able to leave his burden of responsibility behind and just go for a nice long swim. But he had patients who needed tending. Turning to leave, he came face to face with John Dunn.

"Go on, Captain, I know you want to. It's written all over your face. Everything is under control. Joseph and I are perfectly capable of handling everything for a few hours." He grinned and gave Daniel a shove toward the water. "If you don't take off your uniform and get yourself in the water, I think I can get a few of these fellas to give you a hand!"

"Come on in, Captain Reid!" someone shouted. "The water's colder than a witch's tits!"

A fleshy fellow climbed out of the water wearing nothing but his skin. He advanced on Daniel with a grin and a gleam in his eye. Putting his hands up in surrender, Daniel backed up a few steps.

"Okay, okay, I'll do it! You men have no respect for an officer, do you?" He laughed and began to remove his jacket, then peeled off his shirt. But he kept an eye on the big soldier. The man turned his attention to someone behind him just as Daniel was folding his shirt.

"Charlie!" the man called jovially. "Charlie Garrett, you're next!" He laughed and began to move past Daniel, the big soldier's bulk rippling and jiggling as he walked ponderously up the riverbank.

Daniel turned to see who this Charlie Garrett was. The name sounded so familiar…Garrett.

What he saw behind him was a small, pale figure frozen in place with big startled eyes, like a deer poised to flee. The young boy was clearly frightened by the huge naked man advancing toward him with beefy arms outstretched.

"Hold it, soldier!" Daniel commanded. The giant froze in mid step. Still holding his shirt in his hand, Daniel walked around him and stood in front of the boy.

"Are you Charlie Garrett?" he asked.

The boy nodded, wide-eyed with fear.

"Do you want to go into the water?"

Charlie shook his head negatively, making the sun glint off his spectacles.

Daniel took in the badly soiled uniform with dark bloodstains on both sleeves, his chest and on the boy's belly. This boy had held an injured soldier in his arms. He badly needed a bath. His face and hands were blacked with powder residue, and his short hair hung in greasy strings under the filthy slouch hat. But this was not the way to do it. This boy was still badly traumatized by the recent battle.

"Garrett…one of the soldiers we buried was a Joshua Garrett. Are you related to him?"

Suddenly, the boy's eyes filled with tears, and he turned his head away. "It's okay, son," he said, putting his hands on the thin shoulders. "You don't have to do this now…"

All he got in answer was a quick nod and a half salute before the boy bolted, stumbling up the bank and out of sight.

Daniel turned back toward the large young man. The grin was gone, and a sad, worried look filled his face. "I'm sorry, Captain. I only wanted to help."

"What is your name, soldier?"

"Billy…Billy Kaufman from Augusta County."

"Well, Billy, tell me about your friend, Charlie."

"His cousin, my friend Josh Garrett, died in that battle, sir. Charlie didn't come back for two days. We done asked Charlie's friend and him to join our campfire since we lost Josh and Oliver Marshall. Charlie—he's one 'o them sharpshooters, ya know—snuck back in the middle of the night and ain't said nothin' since…and he don't eat none, either. I think he's sick or maybe just real sad. Maybe you can help him, sir?"

"Of course, I'll try to help anyone I can, Billy." Putting his arm around the big man's hairy shoulders, Daniel led the way back to the river. "How about we get ourselves a bath first, and we'll worry about Charlie Garrett later, okay?"

* * *

It was almost evening by the time Daniel had checked on all his patients, cleaned and boiled his medical instruments, and packed them carefully away again. He wasn't exactly sure why he felt as though he had to boil the instruments. None of the other surgeons did this kind of thing. Maybe it had to do with his mother. She had been such a fanatic about cleaning and boiling their eating utensils when anyone in the house came down sick. It seemed reasonable that he should boil these metal utensils as well—after all, these men could easily be sick—many soldiers under a surgeon's care did come down with all manner of illnesses.

Perhaps he would stop this strange practice of cooking his instruments. The other surgeons often mocked his actions as foolish. Shaking his head, he gave a soft grunt. It was no use...he knew he would boil them again out of habit.

Actually, he was quite pleased with the progress the men were showing. The patient with the head injury was now able to take a few tottering steps, and his speech was fully functional.

Someone called his name, breaking him out of his thoughts.

Looking up, Daniel saw dozens of smoky cook fires flickering in the half light. Dark shapes of the soldiers moved around them. The air smelled of bacon and coffee. His stomach growled.

"Captain Reid, sir?" A soldier detached himself from the circle of light around the fire and moved toward him with the hitching gait of an older man who had been in one position too long.

"Yes, is there something I can do for you?" Daniel hadn't realized how hungry he was. He swallowed the liquid gathering in his mouth.

"My name is Clarence, Clarence Stoner." The man offered a hand, and Daniel shook it. The hand was callused and rough, a hand that had seen hard work.

Catching a whiff of soap on the shorter man walking beside him was a pleasant finding. This man was clean; he had apparently been down to the river to bathe. "Go on, Private Stoner. How can I help you?"

"Not me, Doc, there's a young boy what's part of my sniper group who's not himself no more."

"Did something happen to the boy? Is he sick?"

"His body ain't sick…yet…it's his mind that ain't been working right." Clarence heaved a deep sigh. "Poor Charlie. His cousin died back there, and I think the lad were with the man when he passed, and it uncorked his brain."

Daniel stopped and peered at the old soldier. "What makes you think so?"

"Well," he rubbed a hand over his long, grizzled beard, "he don't talk, not a word since he saw the elephant."

"The 'elephant'?"

"Ya know, the fight. I cain't barely git little Charlie to eat anything…just a bite here or there. Plus he's filthy as sin. He's a kind of odd guy, real private-like. Won't undress 'round any o' the other boys." Clarence took a deep breath. "The other men are complainin' about Charlie's stink. Now that the rest of us are cleaned up, well, his smell stands out more prominent like."

33

"Are you talking about a small young man with eye glasses and short dark hair—Charlie Garrett?"

"Yup, that's the lad." The graying head bobbed up and down agreeably.

"Yes, I saw him earlier today. He refused to go into the river with the rest. He seems very much affected by his cousin's death and the recent battle."

"I cain't get him to take off his blood-stained uniform even. Turns my stomach. Can you help, Captain?"

"Does he trust you, Clarence?"

"I suppose."

Daniel knew he was no expert in problems of the mind. The boy needed some time to recover from the horrors he had witnessed. The need to escape, whether physically or mentally, was something he understood well.

"Clarence, here's what you can try…"

* * *

Charlie floated face down in the cold water, spreading her arms and legs out. She allowed the water to hold her body in its embrace, cradling her like a gentle lover. Exhaustion of mind and body rendered her powerless in the face of Clarence's impassioned pleas. He convinced her to come here during the night to wash. It felt indecently wonderful to slip under the water, even as cold as it was, then remove the altered corset binding her breasts, and allow them to float free.

She walked into the water fully clothed, only removing her shoes, hat, and glasses before entering the water, not trusting the Augusta County men to keep watch against interlopers without watching her, too. Armed only with a bar of homemade soap, Charlie totally submersed her entire body. With only her head above water, she gradually undressed, pushing her clothing under the water and standing on the articles to keep them from floating away.

First she scrubbed her skin until she tingled from head to toe. Then she dunked her head in the water and washed her face and her hair, rubbing her fingertips into her scalp.

She scrubbed her clothing, thankful that the night hid the awful bloodstains—Josh's blood. Sadness, her ever-present companion, cloaked her mind once more, having temporarily lifted with the bliss of cleanliness.

Dropping a big stone on the garments to hold them, she allowed her body to float and drift on the shallow water. Somewhere an owl called, a lonely kind of sound. *Wash away my inequities, Lord; cleanse me from my sin.* The words, translated from the Latin mass she had attended as a child echoed through her now. Could she really be cleansed from her sins? Lying, killing, and deceiving her husband—were those sins that could be forgiven?

Lifting her feet and rolling onto her stomach, she put her face into the water and allowed her body to drift again, closing her eyes. How easy it would be to just blow out her breath and slowly fall gently to the bottom of the river. She was just so very tired.

A shout went up from the riverbank.

"Charlie! Where are you, boy?" Clarence sounded panicked.

With a sigh, she answered him before he came

splashing into the water. "I'm here, Clarence."

Suddenly, Charlie was quickly pulling on her sodden clothing. With no time to spare, she jammed the corset up under her shirt. She would have to put it on later. Yanking on the wet trousers was not easy, but they were on. Thank heavens it was pitch black out here.

"This way, lad! Time to get out now befo' ya freeze your parts off. Ya done enuff getting clean for one small person."

The water dragged at her legs as she slogged to the water's edge. A big hand grasped her arm and pulled her to dry land.

"Charlie! What kind of strange boy are ya—going bathing with all your clothes on?" She didn't answer. He wouldn't expect conversation by now, and she knew he wouldn't press her about it. He threw a blanket over her and gave her the glasses, shoes, and hat she had left on the bank.

They went back to the tent, gathering the rest of the Augusta County boys along the way. "You fellas wait outside whilst he gits them wet clothes off." He gave her a shove into the tent. "I'll come git your uniform and dry it by the fire after you snuggle down into the blankets, son."

A few minutes later, Stoner was back inside to gather up the wet things, mumbling and grumbling about people being forced to bathe in the middle of winter and causing them to come down with the consumption.

Charlie burrowed under the covers and closed her eyes, allowing her friend to take care of everything else. He would respect her need for privacy. He was a good friend…and now he was all she had.

Chapter Four

January 1862

The Twenty-Fifth Virginia infantry had been on the move for some time now, giving Daniel much to contend with. The horrendous weather in the Allegheny Mountains and the sporadic, unorganized fighting had left the men demoralized and unable to claim victory.

Daniel was proud to note that he and John Dunn had not lost one more soul after the initial casualties. Now, as he rode shivering with cold beside the columns of men marching toward the next engagement, he worried that the entire army would freeze to death before they reached their destination. A howling wind blew from the northwest, and the temperature had dropped alarmingly. Snow was beginning to fall steadily, sometimes turning into stinging sleet, which forced him to turn up his collar.

Gently tugging on the reins, he slowed the horse to a walk then stopped the animal beside the road. He carefully scanned the soldiers trudging by, observing faces and body language, looking for signs of weakness or infirmity.

Canteens and gear rattled and clanked as they walked. The packs were heavy and some of the weary soldiers had started to discard personal items in favor of a lighter load. Daniel sincerely hoped they had not dropped their bedrolls, blankets, or tent canvases as they marched. If the soldiers had no shelter and nothing to keep them warm, sickness was sure to follow and spread from man to man.

As hard as he tried to prevent it, he was starting to like many of these men. It was a dangerous thing for an army surgeon to become friends with the men whose arms or legs he might be forced to remove in the near future.

Rubbing his burning eyes, he forced himself to recognize the men he had seen several times already. The big man, Billy Kaufman, trudged past dragging his toes in the snow. Shoulder to shoulder they came past him. There was the older gentleman, Clarence, and right beside him was the young man, Charlie Garrett. He watched Clarence lower his head to the lad's ear and speak to him. The brim of the soiled slouch hat, tied on his head, hid most of the boy's face, but Daniel saw him take a deep breath and straighten his snow-dusted shoulders just a bit.

"Come on, boys, just a little further now. We'll be making camp soon," Daniel shouted over the wind with his eyes still drawn to the Garrett boy. There was just something very compelling about the lad and his burden of sorrow.

The sound of an approaching horse drew his attention away just as the small form of the boy soldier shuffled away, lost in the masses of gray and butternut uniforms and swirling white.

"Reid, we've lost some of the supply wagons...they've fallen hopelessly behind." Captain Weaver leaned close to Daniel to avoid shouting the news to the already disheartened soldiers.

"My God, Weaver! We've been marching them

through a damned blizzard and now we have no food or medical supplies?"

"General Jackson has ordered us to keep moving. Colonel Fulkerson's mad as an old wet hen. Fulkerson wants to set up camp and not move until spring, but Jackson's set on catching the Federals holding Bath." Weaver shook his head, "We have no choice, Reid."

Daniel started to dismount when Weaver grabbed his arm. "You aren't walking are you?"

"If they walk, I walk."

The pressure on his arm increased. "You fool, Reid, these men need you! What good are you to them if you're exhausted? This is no time to play the martyr."

Reluctantly, Daniel shifted back into the saddle and nodded. "You've made your point. Have you seen John Dunn?"

Weaver took off his hat, knocked the snow off against his knee, and replaced it firmly on his head. "Up front!" he shouted then rode in the opposite direction.

It took Daniel an hour to locate John Dunn, who was found plodding blindly through the snow at the head of the column. Dismounting, despite Weaver's earlier protest, Daniel walked beside John, leading the horse.

"The supply wagons are too far behind to catch up with us tonight, John. I have some medications and bandages in my saddlebags but not much. Any sickness in the men?"

"We've got a few with coughs, Captain. But I'm more worried about men losing their fingers and toes in this cold. I can hardly feel my feet myself."

Reflexively, Daniel glanced down at Dunn's feet. Did

he expect to see them gone? Rubbing a hand over his eyes, he realized how tired he was to be thinking such silly thoughts. "We have to stop soon. Make sure you pass the word that every man is to dry out their socks immediately and warm their appendages, too."

"Their what, sir?"

"Fingers and toes. If anyone has fingers and toes turning white, bring them to me immediately."

"Yessir," Dunn replied. Then, being a very talkative type, he continued to expound on their problems and bemoaned his various aches and pains.

Daniel tried hard to concentrate on what John was saying, but suddenly, he was shoved in the back. Stumbling forward, he barely avoided a fall in the snow. Quiet laughter erupted from the soldiers behind him. But before he could turn around to see who it was, Daniel was butted in the rear and sent forward again, slipping and skidding on the icy ground.

Now the men were really laughing. Daniel finally gained his balance and turned to see the perpetrator.

"Galileo!" A red-brown face with big brown eyes looked back at him. A lock of black hair hung rakishly over one eye, giving his horse the look of a scalawag. Snow and ice coated the horse's coat and mane. The animal shook it off with a loud whinny.

"Captain! What kind of games are you playing?"

A strange stillness came over the regiment as every man came to a complete halt at the sound of the high-pitched voice. Immediately, they stiffened to attention. Daniel, already knowing this was not going to be good, looked around to see a scruffy figure, in a faded uniform astride a small sorrel. The man's large feet in flop-top boots were stuffed into shortened stirrups. The eyes glittering out of his humorless, bearded face held no trace of friendliness or tolerance.

Feeling his face burn despite the cold wind, Daniel straightened his spine, transferred the reins to his left hand and saluted the commander of the First Virginia Brigade.

"Sorry, sir. No games, General."

"I would expect better of one of our military surgeons. Let's keep these men moving before they freeze!"

"Yes, sir!" Daniel saluted General Thomas Jackson, swallowed hard, and turned to the column of waiting men. He caught sight of the amused pale face of Charlie Garrett in the crowd, standing as straight as the rest of the men. "All right, men, move out!"

Without another word, the General turned his little horse and moved away until he disappeared into the swirling whiteness.

Mounting his horse again, Daniel took up his position at the head of the column. The afternoon was waning, and visibility was growing worse. He was certain that even the ambitious General would soon be forced to call a halt to their march and allow the men to get some sleep.

A smile crept over his face as he remembered the look on young Charlie's face…it was worth getting into trouble if he had been able to lighten the poor boy's terrible sorrow for at least a few minutes.

* * *

The winter days were short, and the going was rough as the Confederates struggled toward the town of Bath, finally reaching the outskirts by dusk.

"Stoner!" Captain Weaver came riding up to the brigade. "Get your snipers and follow me. We're going around the mountain for a surprise attack."

Charlie struggled to keep up with the snipers and militia. They slipped and slid on the ice, climbing down and up steep ravines, and struggling through the wooded mountainside.

"Go!" came the command. The company ran through the trees, rifles loaded and yelling at the top of their lungs. Pine needles and snow crunched under her brogans. She hated those Yankees. *They were the invading army, and they had killed Josh! They would die now for what they did!* She repeated this vow each time they encountered the enemy.

More fallen maple and pine trees blocked their way up ahead. She could see the gray and butternut uniforms scattered on both sides of her, all of them running toward the enemy.

Shouting and gunfire ricocheted through the trees. Puffs of gun smoke and the men's steamy breaths could be seen easily in the frosty air.

Suddenly, she saw the Bluecoats as if conjured up by magic. They leaped up from behind the fallen logs with rifles blazing. The shots ripped through a soldier on her right, and he went down screaming. Charlie threw herself to the ground and fired. A Yank fell back, holding his shoulder as bright red blood streamed down his chest. Her fear of the dreaded enemy vanished in the next heartbeat as she saw the pain and fear on the man's pudgy face seconds before he fell. He was just a man.

There was no room for second thoughts, no room for doubt now! Ripping a paper cartridge open, she poured the power in and reloaded her rifle. Screaming and yelling filled her ears, and she wanted to jump up and run away. Gritting her teeth, she clamped down hard on the primitive flight instinct and took aim. Again she hit her chosen target, and he went down on the hard frozen ground.

Bullets whistled by her ears, plowing long furrows in the ground. A gray pall of smoke began to gather in the low-lying hollows. Spying a large tree, Charlie ran behind the gnarled oak and crouched low behind it. Using her teeth, she tore open another paper cartridge, tasting the black powder before loading once more.

Load, aim, shoot. Load, aim, shoot. Where was Clarence? It hit her suddenly. No Confederate uniforms were in her field of vision. Union soldiers were in front of her, advancing through the trees with guns spitting fire, stepping over dead bodies lying in the snow. Panic swept over her. Her heart pounded so hard that she expected the Yankees to hear it. *Dear Lord! Where did they all go?* Was she the only Reb left? There was no denying her instincts this time.

Clutching her rifle to her chest, Charlie ran.

Chapter Five

June 1862

The soldiers were grateful the winter's harsh grip had finally passed. There had been no letup in the fighting for the Twenty-Fifth Virginia all winter, despite the freezing temperatures.

Daniel treated men for diarrhea, fevers, vomiting, rashes, blisters, and boils, in addition to the injuries inflicted upon them. To say that he was busy was an understatement. Most days there was no opportunity to do much more than work, eat, and sleep. Sickness had swept through Jackson's army more than once, and the surgeons were forced to send many of the soldiers to the army hospitals away from the battlefields. Sometimes they returned to the regiment; sometimes they didn't.

Thankfully, the tide of the war for the regiment had turned with Jackson's success in the Shenandoah Valley. Coming down out of the mountains and heading to the valley had been the true saving grace for the soldiers surviving the battles. Food and supplies were plentiful in this pretty place during the first blush of spring.

But even this happy occurrence would not last. As time went on, the bountiful valley began to suffer the consequences of its use as a battleground. The land was pockmarked with torn earth, trampled vegetation, and broken tree stumps.

With a feeling close to desperation, Daniel walked along the dirt road leading away from the acres of army tents. He had to get away from the constant needs of the men for just a short while or he was sure to start yelling!

The day was warm. As he walked, he unbuttoned the top buttons of his white shirt and rolled the sleeves up above his elbows. He owed Lucy a letter and was determined to get one off to her today. For too long now he had been neglecting his duty to his sweetheart.

What was the family was doing on this beautiful day? Most likely they would be sitting out on the front porch, drinking lemonade and discussing the war.

Havre de Grace was a quaint little town in the politically divided state of Maryland, so it was not uncommon to have both Southern and Northern sympathizers in the same household. The Reid family was no exception.

Mother and his younger brother, Bradford, would most likely be arguing the side of the South. Father and his sister, Nora, would be pro-Union, while lovely, fragile Lucy Masterson always sided with Daniel. If Daniel switched loyalties tomorrow, Lucy would change hers right along with him.

He was not sure whether he should be happy she did this or not. One time, irritated by her puppet-like behavior, Daniel tested the depth of her devotion by arguing first for the succession of the Southern states, then immediately defending the need for a united nation. Lucy had bobbed her head agreeably no matter which way he took the discussion that day. He liked her loyalty to him but sometimes really wished she would speak her own mind.

Daniel had come to like and respect the Southern

way of life…so honorable and genteel. He liked the people he met in Augusta County when he went there to live and help with Uncle Cornelius Reid's practice while Uncle Corny recovered from a bad case of the gout.

Once he had even brought Lucy out to his uncle's home once for a visit. Uncle Corny and Lucy seemed to get along fine. He was surprised to find out later she was not comfortable with his uncle or the people of the community who had come out to greet them.

He learned a little more about his betrothed then. Lucy Masterson privately confessed to Daniel that she "…could not abide living around such backward types as she encountered in Virginia."

"It is the duty of the more cultured, refined people of the northern part of the country to take these people in hand," Lucy further declared. "However, letting them go their own way would not hurt us in the least. It would make life much easier."

When he decided to enlist in the Twenty-Fifth Virginia, Lucy had been severely distressed. For once she had not thought he knew best and tried to gently dissuade him from joining.

There were times now when he questioned his own motives. Perhaps he had done it just to be contrary? Or perhaps it was to delay setting a date for their wedding? He couldn't be sure, but Daniel was absolutely certain he would support the Confederate army whether in his capacity as a surgeon or as a soldier. No government had the right to tell a state what they could or could not do.

Rounding the bend, he scuffed his feet along, watching the dust rise up from around his booted feet in little clouds. It bothered him that the clothing and shoes of the soldiers were beginning to look very worn. He pondered the problem of obtaining new shoes and uniforms for his men. Where could he get them? The North had managed to gradually increase their stranglehold on the waterways and railroads, making supplies harder and harder to get.

The valley was being stripped bare of food and livestock the longer the army stayed here. The people of Virginia were doing the best they could to feed and clothe their soldiers, but they were running dangerously low on what they could spare without starving themselves.

A small path veered off to the left of the main road. Daniel ducked down and followed the path leading downhill. Pebbles skittered under his boots, causing a momentary slide, but he regained his footing easily.

With a bit of searching, he found the perfect place for his letter writing. A dry log beside the small trickling stream made just the right seat. He settled down and smoothed the paper out on his lap. A dragonfly buzzed across the water, flitting back and forth erratically.

Retrieving his penknife from his pocket, Daniel shaved a sharp point on his pencil and poised it over the paper. *Hmmm…where to start?*

Dear Lucy, he wrote and paused. He supposed he should try to keep the letter light. It was best that he not provide too much detail. Lucy was the sensitive type and easily upset. In other words, he couldn't tell her the whole truth. He couldn't tell her of the pain and suffering, the loss of limbs both deliberate and accidental.

There was no way to share with her his frustration at being forced to try and piece these men back together again after they were torn apart. Like Humpty Dumpty, they were broken and all the King's soldiers and all the King's men couldn't —

Daniel dropped the pencil and put his head in his hands. God...he was so tired. With a sigh he closed his eyes and rubbed his temples. A bee buzzed around his left ear, but he didn't move. Breathing in and out slowly, he became aware of his own stink. Lucy's delicate senses would be offended if she could smell him now. The sound of the creek water, burbling over scattered rocks, seemed to wash over him, soothing his jangled nerves.

Somewhere a whippoorwill called to its mate. He could hear the sounds of nature now that his anxious thoughts no longer blocked them out. Sweat trickled slowly down his back All of his senses became gradually more alert. Some sound was trying to make its presence known. Lifting his head, with his eyes still shut, he cocked his head.

Someone was crying. It was the unmistakable sound of sobbing.

Of course...he couldn't get a minute alone! Opening his eyes, he picked up the pencil and held it over the paper again, trying to ignore the sound. He was going to go insane if he didn't have a few moments of privacy.

But the sound persisted...so low and sad. Daniel took a deep breath. He could barely hear it now, but still it called to him. Putting down his pencil and paper, he stood and stretched, feeling each vertebrae pop and his muscles lengthen.

There was no help for it. Turning, he followed the noise. Several times it stopped for a few moments before beginning again, soft and keening…someone in distress. This he could not resist. Daniel shoved his way through the heavy summer growth.

He caught a glimpse of gray cloth between the leaves. Carefully and slowly, he made his way closer. The crying had stopped. Pushing aside the green curtain, Daniel came to a halt, momentarily frozen by the sight beyond. It was a barefoot young soldier in a filthy slouch hat and glasses. He was hunched over, resting his elbows on his knees. One arm came up, and the boy wiped his nose on his uniform sleeve.

"Hello," he called softly.

The young man leaped up, bringing his rifle level with Daniel's chest, eyes wide with fear. Slowly the boy backed away, ready to run.

"No," Daniel said softly, putting out a hand, palm up. "Don't run away. I won't hurt you. Maybe I can help you."

He dashed a hand across his reddened eyes and lowered the rifle. "Sorry, I thought you might be a Yankee."

"No," Daniel smiled, "I'm not the enemy. I'm Captain Reid."

The boy's eyes widened even further behind the lenses, then he stiffened to attention and saluted. "Sorry, sir, I didn't recognize you…aren't you the regimental surgeon for the Twenty-Fifth?"

Daniel moved a few inches closer. "At ease, soldier. Yes, I am." He smiled, trying to get the boy to relax.

There was something very unusual about this young man with his small pale face and dark, sable-colored hair. The boy looked around behind him nervously as if he were going to flee.

"Uh, sir, if you don't mind, I have to be going...I-I have to...ummm...I have to report to Captain Weaver for picket duty."

Daniel stopped in his tracks. He knew the lad was lying. It was all the boy could do to keep from running away immediately.

"Before you leave, Charlie, I want to tell you that I am not just a doctor...I am a good listener, too. Any time you need to talk just come on by my tent." He smiled again, hoping to reassure him.

"H-How did you know my name?"

"I remember you, Charlie Garrett, right? You are the sharpshooter in Clarence Stoner's group...am I right?"

"Uh...yes, sir." Charlie started backing away. "I have to leave, is that okay, Captain?"

"Yes...sure...go ahead."

No sooner had the words left his mouth than young Garrett turned tail and crashed through the brush. Immediately, the stalks and leaves covered his path as if he had never existed.

* * *

Charlie stumbled and staggered clumsily through the plant life, which seemed to be reaching out deliberately to scratch her face and hands.

Of all the people to find her, it would be HIM! Captain Reid was the last man in the entire regiment she wanted to stand anywhere near. As a medical man he might look at her just a little too closely and see past her disguise. She may not be the only beardless soldier in the Twenty-Fifth, but she was fairly certain she was the only one with a pair of breasts...although...Billy Kaufman came fairly close. But even his excess flesh was melting away from the constant exercise and bad food they were all forced to endure.

Her lungs burned, and her feet hurt, but Charlie didn't stop running until she burst out of the tree line and onto the bare earth with its deep cannon holes and furrows.

She pushed a pebble off the bottom of her bare foot and wished she had not left her shoes in the tent to save them further wear. A fly buzzed around and landed on her hand, tickling her with its tiny black feet.

The captain was a very nice-looking man, she had to admit, and her pulse raced out of control whenever she caught sight of him. Plus, he had this most disturbing way of looking at her with those clear blue eyes. It made her feel as though he could see into her innermost thoughts. She shivered just thinking of the man. He had a way about him that made her feel like a woman again.

Most of the time she could actually forget she was a woman. She was just a soldier like the thousands of other soldiers all around this valley. Except...except when Captain Reid appeared with his thick blond hair, neatly trimmed beard, and handsome face.

Charlie stopped dead in her tracks and covered her face with her hands. *My beloved Josh is dead...dead for only a few months and here I am already thinking of another man!*

Perhaps she should give up being a soldier and head

home to Mama and Papa. More and more thoughts like that began to creep into her head making it ache with confusion. It would be so easy to do, just go up to an officer, tell him she was a woman, and they would send her home in a flash.

To go home to food and shelter and a feather bed...it would be wonderful...it would be awful. To walk in the door of her house and know Joshua was never coming back again. It was unthinkable.

Chapter Six

Charlie was well aware she was just moving through her days, doing what she was told to do. She walked when she was told to walk. She ate when she was told to eat and slept when she was told to sleep. She also killed when told to kill, which was the worst part of all.

There was no doubt she was good at what she did. Her ability as a sharpshooter allowed her to pick off many Yankees with just one shot in the head. On some level, she realized that she was killing a fellow human being — someone who had been a mother's precious baby at one time. But she didn't allow such thoughts to creep into her consciousness. If that happened, she might actually be forced to make a decision, and she was not ready to do that.

The Seven Days Battle, fought between the end of June and beginning of July, had brought the loss of Colonel Fulkerson, who had been reconnoitering at the battle of Gaines Mill. Losing their colonel was a blow to the Twenty-Fifth but didn't diminish their desire to win this war.

When September came, bringing with it cool winds and autumn leaves, the dirty, ragged army was ordered by General Robert E. Lee to march into the border state of Maryland.

Charlie was hungry again. The only food she had in her haversack was apples. She knew no one else had anything any better. Sighing, she retrieved the fruit, picked out a worm, flicked it away, and began to eat.

The regiment was getting smaller. Louis Sampson had dropped by the wayside several miles back. He had simply stopped in the middle of the road, forcing others to walk around him while Ned Hagan and the other Augusta County men gathered around with Charlie looking on. Poor Louis no longer had any shoes, his face was drawn and gaunt, and he was suffering from a bad case of lice, despite Captain Reid's best efforts to combat the pesky vermin.

"What are you doin', Louis?" Ned demanded. "Y'all cain't just stop here."

"Just go on without me, Ned. I just cain't go no further. I'm going home. I know it isn't close, but I cain't take it no mo'. I'm goin' back."

"Hush," Clarence growled. "You don't want no officers to hear that you is gonna desert!"

"Then y'all jus leave me be." He scratched his head and turned toward the field. "I's going."

And he was gone through the tall cornstalks. The broad green leaves and stalks barely rustled at his passing.

Not a single soldier outside of the huddled group even reacted to this. Thousands had been dropping out due to illness, exhaustion, or just plain disgust. Many had never wanted to invade the North; they just wanted to defend their homeland. This march to Maryland was an act of aggression that many soldiers could not accept. Others, like Louis, just wanted to go home.

"I'm going, too," Billy suddenly decided. "My Mamma needs me, and I need her." Billy had lost so much weight that Charlie wondered if his mother would recognize him anymore. A belt of rope held his trousers around his waist in big gathered folds of material. Billy ducked into the plants and was swallowed up in an instant.

Ned Hagan snorted in disgust. "What a couple of Nancy boys! Let's go." He looked at Charlie, his hand fondling his long, greasy mustache. "Are you desertin' us too, Charlie?"

For a long moment, Charlie wavered. Maybe this was what she had been waiting for, the time to bring this nightmare to an end and go home. So many were leaving and none of the officers were doing anything to stop them. Soldiers continued to stream around the small group. Ned, Victor, Charlie, and Clarence stood together in the dust.

Clarence frowned. "If y'all is gonna go, Charlie, you might as well go now."

She looked at her friend's grizzled, weary face. The lines around his eyes and mouth were etched more deeply now, and his beard had grown so long and gray that he resembled Father Time.

A new voice, quiet and subdued, broke into her thoughts. "I can't say I would blame any of you for leaving now…but you never heard it from me." Surprised, Charlie whirled around to see Captain Reid standing behind her with his horse in tow. He, too, was exhausted and thinner. While his beard was still neatly trimmed, his cheekbones were more pronounced, and his face and loose-fitting uniform were covered with a layer of dirt. It didn't matter what he looked like. Her heart began to pound again, and the butterflies flitted around inside her empty stomach.

"We have no food," the Captain continued despondently, "and I can't tell you when we expect to have some. The general is hoping the sympathetic Marylanders will provide."

Having said his peace, she watched him slowly walk around the group still leading the plodding horse and disappear into the masses of soldiers. The sparkle was gone from the Captain's blue eyes, and there was no life in his voice when he spoke. It was the first time she had ever seen him this way.

"I'm not leaving, Clarence." Charlie shifted her rifle and turned to join the masses heading toward Maryland. She wasn't sure exactly why she was staying, but it had to do with the change in the surgeon. Why she felt obligated to stay when the man was all but turning a blind eye to the desertions, she couldn't say. She just knew in her gut she had to continue this journey.

* * *

It was a bright, clear September morning. The spot their scouts had chosen for the crossing of the broad Potomac River into Maryland was really quite beautiful. Daniel rode into the cool river, along with close to 50,000 other soldiers, amid lofty trees and colorful wild flowers fringing the edges of the river. He stopped the horse in mid-stream and kept a careful eye on the steady line of soldiers coming across. Even though the river was waist deep to most of the men, some could not swim and feared getting into the water.

Those soldiers who owned shoes, took them off, along with their trousers, and pushed into the water holding rifles and belongings high over their heads. Daniel was able to pick out the men of his regiment. Clarence Stoner was helping the shorter Charlie Garrett splash across, followed by Ned Hagan and the red-haired boy, Victor. Stoner held the rifles out of the water, leaving the boys free to struggle across in the water that was up to Garrett's shoulders. Then, to Daniel's shock, Charlie Garrett gave up wading and decided to swim across the shallow water instead. The men turned in surprise as the small figure, with his slouch hat still firmly on his head, went by swimming like a frog. Cheers and laughter swelled like a wave as Charlie passed soldier after soldier.

A swell of cheers drew Daniel's attention away from little Charlie. Another figure had come into the river that cheered the band of ragged men even more. General Jackson rode out on the opposite side of the column, stood in the stirrups, and doffed his forage cap to them all. The familiar Rebel yell echoed across the river, exciting the soldiers in the water until they pounded flat hands on the surface with resounding slaps. Jackson whooped and splashed across to Maryland.

It was all through the encampment several nights later how thousands of soldiers had dropped out of sight during their march to the north. Daniel walked through the camp hearing the buzz of talk and worry about the loss of their comrades.

By the light of the flickering campfires, the men were happily cooking food that hadn't touched their plates for months. Some kind citizens even offered clothing and shoes to the most scruffy, tattered soldiers. He had seen one woman giving a bundle of her son's clothing to young Charlie Garrett with tears in her eyes.

General Jackson's army was met with mixed reactions from the citizens of Maryland. There was some cheering and waving of Confederate flags, but most of the people appeared to be indifferent or downright hostile.

The unpleasant reception from some of the farmers was, unfortunately, warranted. It had been impossible for the officers to prevent the starving soldiers from helping themselves to the bounty that tempted them every step of the way once they crossed into the fertile state of Maryland from the war-savaged lands of Virginia.

Maryland orchards were ripe with luscious red apples, fuzzy plump peaches, golden pears, and deep purple plums. The mouth-watering scent of apple butter hung in the air as the men passed the farms. Mounds of pumpkins and squash were piled on the porches, and the household gardens were abundant with neat rows of sweet potatoes and onions. It was beyond simple desire for a tempting morsel — the men of the Confederacy were starving. They either begged the citizens for food or…stole it outright.

When the wonderful smell of pork and onions cooking drifted across the compound, Daniel felt his stomach growl hungrily. Saliva filled his mouth. He sure hoped his aide, Joseph, would have some food ready for them when he returned to his tent.

The Union troops were close by, and fighting was sure to begin again soon. There was no way they would let Jackson and Lee march unmolested into Maryland

and take the Federal garrison. He was going to need his strength to do his job once again and try to save as many lives as possible. It was the most frustrating enterprise he had ever undertaken. All of the surgeons tried to save lives as hard as the generals tried to take them.

* * *

Dragging into camp, Charlie was happy to lie down for just a few moments and close her eyes. Clarence was doing the cooking. A kindly woman in Frederick had given them some pork wrapped in newspaper and a dozen eggs she had careful loaded into Charlie's hat. Then the woman, who was about her own mother's age, had pressed a bundle of clothing into both Charlie's and Victor's hands.

"Take these, boys. My boy doesn't need them any more. He went off to fight with your army and got killed at Bull Run." Tears filled her eyes as she addressed Charlie. "He was about your size. I would be very pleased if you would wear these."

What else could she do? Of course she took the clothing. Actually she was very much afraid her own clothing was becoming so threadbare that someone would see her skin. She had a hole in her shirt very close to her right breast and a jagged tear in the knee of her pants.

The swim across the Potomac had down right terrified her. But there was no time to remove her wet clothing as they pressed on to Harper's Ferry. Everyone had to dry as they marched. Once there, the army opened up with nearly fifty Confederate guns, bombarded the Federal garrison, and, with the help of the sharpshooters, eventually obtained the surrender of 12,500 Federal soldiers.

Orders from General Lee arrived soon after the victory. The Twenty-Fifth gathered together and marched immediately on to Sharpsburg. All through the night they walked to join the Confederate line, and now, Charlie was so exhausted that she fell asleep immediately while the others cooked.

Victor woke her from another dream about Josh with a toe poke into her ribs.

"Clarence says come and git it."

"Okay," she mumbled and yawned. She was hit again with the sadness that always accompanied dreams of her husband. As always, Josh had been alive and well in her dream, and they were going about their normal day on the farm. How she longed to be able to turn back time and keep them both from enlisting. Somehow, she should have stopped him rather than join him…

Supper that night was terrific. Charlie, Clarence, Victor, John, and the rest of the sharpshooters feasted on roasted pork seasoned with sage and onions. Clarence was being tight-lipped on where he had gotten the seasonings. They also had boiled green beans with sliced hard-boiled eggs and some fresh-baked bread. Charlie's belly was full for the first time in a long, long time.

The men were all sitting back, rubbing their stomachs, and groaning.

"You did a great job, Clarence," she said with a loud, manly belch, and got unintelligible noises and grunts of agreement all around.

Gathering up the bundle of clothing, her rifle and a

canteen of water, Charlie left the cozy campfire and headed away from the hustle and bustle of the troops. It was not quite dark, and she could see well enough to search out a private place to wash up and put on her new clothes.

Screened behind a thicket of holly and rhododendrons, Charlie removed the ragged shirt she had worn since leaving home so long ago. The corset had long ago fallen apart. Some nearby crickets chirped loudly, and a flock of bats burst out of a pine tree. She gritted her teeth against the sudden prick of fear and kept quiet.

Taking a scrap of cloth, she poured some water onto it and wiped her face first. With no soap she had to scrub hard to remove the dirt. Grime smudged the whole upper part of her chest, and she was sure her neck was in the same condition.

Wetting the cloth again, she began to wipe the back of her neck then ran the cloth down the front to her breasts. The feeling was incredibly wonderful and sensuous. Closing her eyes, she marveled that such a simple thing could awaken the woman in her.

"Hey!" a masculine voice had her scrambling for cover. Crouching down, she reached out for her shirt in a panic. "Hey! You're not a man!" the voice said.

A hand reached out and roughly yanked her erect. A soldier she had never seen before loomed over her. The foul smell of whiskey and tobacco assaulted her nostrils as he spoke.

"I've seen you before. You're that sharpshooter wonder boy…'cept you ain't no boy." Reaching out a grimy hand, he grabbed her breast and squeezed her nipple hard. Charlie went crazy. She bit his hand, she scratched any thing she could reach, and fought back as hard as she could. Where was her rifle? This beast deserved a bullet between the eyes!

But the unknown man was strong, stronger than she could handle. He quickly tied her hands with her own shirt, leaving her naked from the waist up. Opening her mouth, she let out the most ear-splitting scream she could manage. A slap, hard across the mouth, sent her tumbling into the dirt. When he reached for her, she bought her leg up and kicked out, aiming between his legs…and missed.

"You bitch! You'll pay for that!"

Lifting his foot then bringing it down on top of her, he ground his boot heel into her ribs. Pain seared through Charlie's chest as bones gave way with a crack. She screamed again. Through a haze of agony and fear, her panic increased when she saw her attacker unbuckling his belt, as he stood over her with a foot still planted in the middle of her body. *Oh, Dear God!!*

"What's going on over there?" a new male voice boomed out.

"Help—" Her plea was cut short by the pain of drawing a breath and by the foul-smelling hand clamped over her mouth.

Leaves rustled, branches cracked, and another man crashed through the bushes.

"What the—!"

Charlie squeezed her eyes closed and concentrated on drawing a breath. Tears leaked down her cheeks.

Suddenly the pressure on her chest was gone, and she was alone on the ground. Grunts and curses came from her left, and she opened her eyes. In the near darkness, she could see the figures of two men fighting.

Not waiting to see the outcome, she carefully rolled over then crawled on her knees and elbows looking for her rifle. Dirt and pebbles scraped her bare elbows. She finally spied it up against the tree, right where she left it.

Oh, please…oh, please. Trying to breathe in little gasps to keep the pain at bay she reached up with her bound hands and got hold of the gun. Moving quickly, she managed to get the butt between her legs, swing around and sit down with a painful thump.

A dark figure came lurching out of the darkness toward her.

"Hold it right there," she commanded as loudly as she could. It was hard with her hands tied together, but she managed to get the barrel pointed toward the man and position her finger on the trigger.

He stopped. His hands went up in the air. "It's okay, Miss, I won't hurt you, I swear. My name is Captain Reid. I'm the army surgeon here." He paused and took a deep breath. "Are you all right?" His voice was gentle and full of concern.

Oh, my…it's HIM…here…now! It's over.

"C-come here and untie…me." Letting the rifle slip to the ground, she held her hands up imploringly.

* * *

Daniel thought his heart would break right then and there at the sight of the pale young woman with short dark hair tumbling into her eyes, half-naked and obviously hurt as she raised her bound hands to him for help.

He sank to his knees in front of her and started to untie the knots from the cloth. Her arms began to tremble as he worked. "Hold on, Miss, just hold on now, I'll take care of you. You'll be fine."

There, the knot was out, and he unwound the cloth. It was a shirt. Moving closer to her, he held the shirt out, gently took her cold hand, and put it into the sleeve. He could feel the vibrations running up her whole body as he draped the shirt around her bare back and carefully helped her put her other hand into the sleeve. She tensed, and a gasp of pain escaped when she moved.

The woman was hurt! He felt his throat constrict with emotion, followed by an immediate flash of rage that made him want to go back and inflict more damage on the man. How could anyone hurt this small, fragile person?

"Come on, let me help you up." He saw her looking around with jerky movements of her head. "It's okay. The man who attacked you won't hurt you any more. I've tied him up with his own belt."

Standing up, he carefully put a hand under her elbow to help her. "Can you tell me where are you injured?" Moving slowly, the woman got to her feet, swaying just a little. He steadied her.

"H-he stepped on my chest," she whispered. "I-I heard something c-crack."

Good God! The bastard stomped on her chest! It was an internal struggle, but the physician in him won out over the enraged man who once again entertained thoughts of kicking the tar out of her attacker. "You may have some broken ribs. Don't take a deep breath or make any sudden moves."

He shrugged out of his jacket and eased it over her shoulders. Suddenly, he realized she was wearing trousers. *How odd.* "I'm a doctor," he repeated again, "I can help you. Let me take you back to my camp and fix you up before I take you home." He moved around in front of her. "Hold still, and I can button up your shirt for you."

"No," she shook her head slightly, "I'll do that. Will you please help me get my things, sir?"

"Of course," he looked at her for further direction, watching as she slowly worked the buttons.

"Over there, behind those bushes…" she said then added quietly, "…where he attacked me."

Daniel turned to leave then stopped. "Will you be all right for a few minutes alone?"

She glanced around again then slowly bent her knees, keeping her back straight and picked up the Springfield at her feet. With a noticeable familiarity, she positioned the weapon for use and splayed her feet wide for balance.

"Okay," she said.

The rifle looked like a Confederate -issued weapon. As he walked to the group of dark bushes, Daniel wondered how this woman came to have the gun. *Perhaps she took it from her assailant? This woman is obviously comfortable with handling a rifle…that is highly unusual.*

These thoughts ran through his head as he searched

for her personal items. Spying a dark bundle on the ground, he walked over, bent and picked it up. Even in the weak moonlight he could see this was not women's clothing. It was a pair of dark colored pants and a grimy linen shirt, along with a dirty slouch hat and a pair of spectacles. He walked back to where he had left her and couldn't stop thinking of the items he held. Something was niggling at the back of his mind, but he couldn't quite grab hold of the thought.

She was exactly as he left her, standing frozen in position. He could see her physically relax when he came into sight. Daniel held the items out so she could see them.

"Are these your things?"

"Yes, thank you," she said and carefully reached for the bundle without explanation.

"Hold on here, Miss," Daniel pulled the bundle back just a bit. Surprise had her raising her dark eyebrows. The scattered clouds shifted a bit, allowing light to reach the earth's surface. He could see his companion better now. She was indeed a slender, pale young woman with straggled dark hair and a nasty bruise appearing on her swollen cheek.

"Who are you, and why are you out here all alone at night?" Suspicions were beginning to mount in his mind. "Did you come here to meet a soldier? Are you wearing his things? Or maybe that man was the one you came to meet and you had a lover's quarrel?"

He watched her carefully straighten up. "Sir, I never saw him before in my life, I swear it on the Bible."

That remained to be seen, Daniel decided. "Well,

let's go back to camp. I'll send someone back to pick up your attacker. You need to get some medical treatment."

He handed her the glasses and watched her put them in her pocket.

"Don't you need those to see?" he asked and offered his arm.

"No," she said…again without explanation.

This was getting more mysterious by the moment. Stuffing the bundle of clothes under his arm, Daniel took her elbow. Who was this woman? He was determined to get some answers from her as soon as he tended her injuries.

Waiting until they were well on their way back towards the flickering campfires in the distance, he asked one question that could not wait.

"Might I have your name, Miss?" he asked politely.

"I am Mrs. Joshua Garrett," the woman answered in a voice that was barely audible.

They took a few more steps before the name registered with Daniel. He stopped suddenly, forcing her to stop with him. She gave him an annoyed glance.

"Mrs. Joshua Garrett?" he repeated idiotically. He dropped her arm and reached for the uniform jacket she was wearing. "Hold still for a minute." She froze with a guarded look, and he saw her lift the rifle she held just a little higher. There, he found what he was looking for in the front pocket. Opening his palm, he held his hand out to her. The gold ring glinted in the moonlight. "I believe this should go back to you."

"Oh." Her voice wobbled. "Josh's ring." Slowly reaching out, she took the ring and, handing Daniel the rifle, slid the circle of gold onto her thumb. Then, retrieving the rifle, she began to walk again without looking back. "I cannot cry now. It hurts too much. Let's go."

Daniel had not considered that he was hurting her by giving her back the ring. He should have waited. How could he have done this to the young woman without thinking it through? He caught up to her, offered his arm for her to lean on again, and they crunched through the crisp fallen leaves without speaking.

His mind was in turmoil by her revelation. *How did the wife of a fallen soldier come to be here with her dead husband's regiment? Did she know her husband's cousin, Charlie Garrett, was in the same regiment? Perhaps the young man had sent for his cousin's wife?* There were so many questions that needed to be answered.

Chapter Seven

"Ben, can you please send out a couple of soldiers out to bring back a soldier gone bad? About two miles east of camp you'll find a scoundrel tied up under a big maple tree," Daniel told Captain Weaver outside the hospital tent thirty minutes later. "He attacked a young woman out there."

"Man alive! A woman!" Weaver blustered. "What was a woman doing out here in the dark unescorted? Is she from the town? You know how them whores come out, following armies, trying to make some money." He almost sounded hopeful.

"No, it isn't a whore from the town, Weaver." Daniel was disgusted. "Have some respect. It is Joshua Garrett's widow. Do you remember him, one of the Augusta County boys who got killed in the first battle?"

Weaver tipped back his hat and scratched his head thoughtfully. "Well, don't that beat all? I sure remember Josh…nice guy. How'd his wife come to be here?"

"I don't know yet, Ben, she's got some injuries that need tending. After I get them taken care of, I'll get some answers."

"Is she purty, Dan?"

"I guess so…I can't really say…it was too dark out there. I have to go. The bastard stomped on her and broke some ribs."

Weaver clicked his tongue sympathetically. "That ain't no way to treat a woman." He narrowed his eyes at Daniel. "What were you doing walking around late at night?"

"Just needed to get away and clear my head, like I always do before a battle. I heard her screaming."

Ben tipped back his forage cap, scratched his head, and jammed the rumpled cap back on his head. "Come to the rescue, eh, Dan? Better to rescue a purty lady than these sorry boys."

Daniel frowned. "I'd help anyone I could."

"Just playing with y'all. Can't ya take a joke?" Ben slapped him on the back. "You got to relax more, Danny Boy." Captain Weaver turned and walked away, chuckling and mumbling to himself.

"Sorry to take so long, Mrs. Garrett," Daniel apologized as he stepped back into the hospital tent. She was still seated on the cot, exactly where he left her. Setting the lamp on a small table, he moved to his supply trunk and began to rummage through the contents looking for linen strips and carbolic acid.

"If you don't mind, I would like very much to ask how it is that you have come to be here with the Twenty-Fifth Virginia? Did Joshua's cousin, Charlie, send for you?" he asked.

He could hear her moving around behind him, but she didn't answer, making him wonder if the pain of speaking was just too much for her to bear. Straightening up, Daniel turned around to treat his latest patient.

There, sitting right where Mrs. Garrett had been, was a small dark-haired figure with a slouch hat and wire-rimmed glasses glinting in the soft glow of the lamp. Shocked, Daniel jerked back, tripped on a basin and stumbled backwards, falling into the long arms of his wiry assistant, John Dunn, who had just entered the tent.

"Y'all okay, Captain?" John calmly looked up at their patient. "Hi, there, Charlie…what did you say to the doc here to make him do that?" He pushed Daniel back up to a standing position.

Daniel struggled to find his voice, keeping an eye on his patient afraid she…he…she… would change yet again.

"Uh, thanks, John. Say, would you mind terribly giving me and…uh…Charlie…a few minutes alone? He…ummm…well…he…"

John held a hand up and grinned under his bushy brown mustache. "No problem, Captain, I understand," he winked at Charlie, "there are just some things a man doesn't want anybody other than his doctor to see."

A moth fluttered erratically past Daniel's line of vision, drawn to the flame of the lamp. He watched the insect for a moment, grateful for the distraction to allow him to gather his thoughts. Silence seemed to fill the small confines of the stuffy tent. Finally Daniel forced his gaze back to the cot.

Gone were the hat and the spectacles, leaving behind Mrs. Garrett, dressed in man's clothing once more. She was looking at him with fearful green eyes in a heart-shaped pale face. One hand was pressed against her side holding her broken ribs and the other was stretched toward him beseechingly once more.

"Please, Captain Reid, please don't reveal my ruse. I've already lost my husband, my whole reason for being here in the first place," she whispered. "Please help me! Charlie needs to disappear. He does not need to be humiliated in front of his fellows."

"Yes, yes." Daniel moved closer and took her outstretched hand between his, feeling the raw scrapes on her palms. She was very pretty, now that he could actually see her. How could he, of all people, a doctor trained to know the human body, mistake this person for a boy? He was humiliated to think that he had not known.

Slowly he studied the very feminine bone structure of her face. A woman's face...there was no mistaking her sex now. The purple bruise on her cheek made his grind his teeth. Such a brave, brave woman to do what she had done, to fight just like a man, and witness the horrors of battle! Well, no more. He was determined she should suffer no more.

"Just answer me two questions, and I will not make you speak anymore tonight."

She nodded, her short dark curls bobbing.

"Did the army give you an examination before you mustered in?"

She shook her head.

"What is your first name?"

"Charlotte."

Slowly he raised her unresisting hand, wondering what drove him to do it, and pressed his lips to the back of her hand. "Nice to meet you, Charlotte Garrett."

* * *

Each breath hurt, but she knew it wouldn't last much longer. The odd, swirling sensation that laudanum induced was beginning to make her feel strangely disconnected from her body. For the first time in months, despite the recent horror of the attack and the fear of revealing herself to Captain Reid, Charlotte felt at peace. There was something about the surgeon that was very reassuring and familiar. He was a kind man, with a wonderful twinkle in his blue eyes…and he was very handsome.

She lay on the cot with her ribs wrapped securely in strips of cloth and her hands cleaned and treated. His warm hands had been so gentle as he examined her, feeling down her chest carefully, searching for the broken bones. Even the pain of her injuries could not stop the tingling that shot through her abdomen when he touched her. Her traitorous body had no right to respond to a man's touch…a man who was not Josh.

Soft rustling sounds reached her ears and, though she could not open her heavy eyelids even if she wanted to, she knew it was the surgeon. Soft footfalls told her that he was moving about the tent. A warm, soft blanket settled gently over her chilled body, and she sighed gratefully.

Beside her, the chair creaked under his weight as he settled into it. Captain Reid turned down the lamp wick and was apparently planning to sit beside her in the darkness. She should tell him that he didn't have to stay, he could go back to his own tent, but she just couldn't do it. The laudanum was dragging her down, down, down.

* * *

It seemed as though only a few minutes had passed, and someone was gently shaking her shoulder. She opened her eyes to the gray pre-dawn light.

"Mrs. Garrett…Mrs. Garrett…I need you to wake up

for me now."

A booming sound echoed in the distance, broken by the distinctive rattle of gunfire.

"Has the fighting started, Captain Reid?" she asked sleepily.

"Yes, I've sent for Clarence Stoner. I'm going to ask him to take you into town for your own safety."

That bit of news had her sitting bolt upright, despite her broken ribs. Concern was obvious on his handsome face.

"Are there very many of them?" Charlie turned to sit on the edge of the cot, putting on her old brogans.

"Yes." He spoke as he moved around the tent, gathering things and stuffing them into haversacks, "McClellan's army is amassing by the thousands. Unfortunately, they outnumber us by quite a bit. Most of the townspeople have left, but I want Clarence to escort you there. It will be safer."

Charlie had had enough of this war. Something had happened since the attack the night before. Her confidence and energy were gone. No longer did she have the will to continue pretending to be a man or to keep on fighting. All she wanted right now was to go home, crawl under the bed covers, and stay there.

On the other hand, Charlie, the sharpshooter, had friends here, and those soldiers didn't have the opportunity to become female and go home. They were here now, and they were going to fight, whether they liked it or not.

She watched Captain Reid walking back and forth inside the small hospital tent. He was getting supplies and instruments ready for the battle to come. His tension was palpable. It was going to be bad. His face was tight, and his body rigid as he bustled around.

"What should I tell Clarence about Charlie?"

"I'm sorry, Mrs. Garrett, but you are on your own there. I have a suggestion, and then you will just have to excuse me. Things are going to very busy here in a few minutes, and I don't expect it to let up."

Slowly, she stood and straightened, feeling aches where she had never had them before. The worry on the surgeon's face had her very concerned. This was going to be a very bad battle.

"I'm listening."

He faced her, but it was obvious his mind was elsewhere. Immediately she was drawn to those beautiful, clear blue eyes that looked right through her. Perhaps he saw in his mind's eye the horror that was already starting.

Another artillery blast shook the air and shadows moved in his eyes.

"If I were you, I would tell Clarence the truth about Charlie."

Charlie's heart pounded. "But how can I tell my best friend I have been lying to him for months?"

Spying an errant roll of bandages, he turned away and bent to retrieve it, carefully adding it to the growing pile. "How can you continue the lie?" he asked quietly, reaching for his uniform jacket. "These next few days will see many men die, Mrs. Garrett. Do you really want Mr. Stoner to take your lie with him to the grave? Would you be able to live with that knowledge?"

He shrugged into the jacket. Charlie could not tear her eyes away from the man. What in the world was wrong with her? A huge battle was about to start, she had to think of what she was going to tell Clarence in just a few minutes, and here she was, thinking of Daniel Reid.

"Excuse me." It was Clarence Stoner, ducking into the tent, rifle in hand and a look similar to the Captain's on his weathered face. "You sent for me, sir?" He removed his tattered cap still looking at the surgeon, and inclined his head toward Charlie. "Ma'am."

"Hello, Clarence."

With an almost audible snap, his head whipped around toward her, and his eyes widened in confusion.

"Uh, sorry, Ma'am, but you sound and look just like my friend, Charlie. I'm kinda worried about Charlie, Captain Reid," he cut his eyes toward the officer briefly then looked back to Charlie. "He didn't come back last night."

"Clarence, you're going to have to excuse me, I've got work to do. This is Mrs. Joshua Garrett. I would like you to please escort her to a safe house in town. She will tell you all about Charlie Garrett."

With that the captain was gone, and Charlie was left alone with Clarence. The time of reckoning had arrived.

* * *

September 17, 1862

The Confederate guns began pounding away, the sound fraying everyone's nerves. Daniel had seen the position Jackson's divisions held behind ridges, limestone ledges and piles of fence rails. Trying to retrieve the wounded men from this widespread line was going to be a serious challenge. These thoughts occupied his mind to the exclusion of almost all else. He had sat beside the woman, the widow of one of his own regiment, all night long, planning his strategy for the next day and trying to keep his mind off the feisty lady who had fought so bravely.

Sending her away was the only option for any woman, even one who was a great shooter. Now that her secret was out, he could not keep it to himself and was very grateful she had been so ready to give it up and become a woman once more. The fear in her eyes at having to confess her secret to Clarence was more fear than he had seen in "Charlie" during battle. The calm that the boy solider had shown was impressive then and was even more impressive now that Daniel knew the boy was not a boy.

The Union guns, high on a ridge on Joseph Poffenberger's farm opened up, firing up to sixty ear-shattering rounds a minute. Though Daniel heard the big guns, he had no time to reflect on their impact—he was dealing with it right now. He and John Dunn had raised the yellow flag with its green letter H over an empty barn for the regimental hospital. Several other barns and houses in the beleaguered town of Sharpsburg had been commandeered as hospitals for both sides.

The wounded did not trickle into the barn. They poured in non-stop from the moment the guns had sounded.

Already covered with blood, which was not his own, Daniel stood at a table with John Dunn assisting and Joseph Hill doing anesthesia duty at the head of the table. Neither of his colleagues was in any better state. The surgeon wiped the perspiration from his forehead, quickly poured carbolic acid over his instruments, and waited for the next patient. No one spoke.

Orderlies carried in a litter, transferred the bloody writhing man to the table, and left.

"I tell ya, Cap'n, them Yankees are using bayonets against us in them cornfields!" the wounded soldier said, gritting his teeth as John cut away the soldier's pants leg and poured water over the wounded knee.

Daniel probed the wound to determine the extent of the damage. He sighed and shook his head. Nothing remained of a kneecap; the long bone of the lower leg was mangled on the end and, from all appearances, split down the middle. There was no chance he could save this leg. Flies hovered and darted around the wound, drawn by the smell of blood and sweat to fulfill the role nature had allotted them.

"That corn is done trampled flat, and the dyin' goin' on is powerful bad. Me and other soldiers were droppin' on both sides. It were lucky for me that my friend dragged me outa there…"

Joseph, taking his cue, lowered the chloroform-soaked cloth over the man's mouth and nose.

"Sorry, son," Daniel said, "the leg has to come off, or you'll die."

The man began to protest but was cut short as the chloroform took effect.

Swiftly, John applied the tourniquet above the knee and pulled it tight. Daniel cut away the remaining skin and muscle until a flap was created and the bone was exposed. Scraping the bone clean with a long instrument with a flat, spoon-like end, called a raspator, he cut off the bone with three strokes of the surgical saw, allowing John to dispose of the leg. Grasping the exposed ends of the blood vessels with the hooked tenaculum, Daniel tied them off with silk thread. He smoothed the stump of the bone, then pulled the skin and muscle flap over the stump, and sutured the wound closed.

Joseph removed the chloroform from the soldier's face. Then Daniel put a finger to the man's neck. His heart still beat strongly.

"Okay, John, get him bandaged up." His assistant was already in motion, tightly binding the wound with strips of linen. It had taken less than fifteen minutes to perform the surgery...and in such a short time, a man's life was forever altered...but it would most likely be saved.

Taking a moment, Daniel washed his hands in the basin of soapy water and moved on to the next patient, lying on the table a few feet away. All around him the screams, cries, and moans of the injured and dying threatened to steal away his composure. He looked down into the face of a man who had no more left ear, closed his eyes briefly for strength and continued.

"Relax, my friend, you can be sure I will do the best I can for you," he nodded to Joseph who was ready with the chloroform cloth.

* * *

Charlie and Clarence walked together weaving around soldiers, dodging mounted officers and cavalrymen, and avoiding teams of horses pulling cannons into position. In the distance they could see tiny blue figures, too numerous to count.

Clarence began to head toward the small town of Sharpsburg, whose buildings could be seen across the planted fields.

"I'm not sorry I joined…I want you to know that. If I had not followed my husband into the army, I would not have been with him when he d-died." She swallowed the lump in her throat. "I-I don't regret it for a minute…you see…I also met the best friend I ever had next to Josh…you."

His faded blue eyes flicked over to her face for a second before turning away. They stepped between two rows of tall green cornstalks and followed the natural path. One step to the left or to the right and either one of them would disappear immediately. Clarence shifted his rifle to his shoulder so it would not get tangled in the broad stiff leaves.

"I sure wish I could have my weapon back." She spread her empty hands. "I feel so lost without it."

"You're a woman. Women cain't have rifles," he growled grumpily.

"And why not, may I ask? I am just as good with it as you are." Charlie stopped and folded her arms across her chest. "…Maybe even better."

That got his attention. She watched his gray head whip around to look at her. His gaze moved up and down her body as if he were looking for something.

"You still look like Charlie and talk like Charlie, but you ain't him. You are a lying, scheming woman, and it don't matter a hoot that you can shoot good. Were you lying about bein' an orphan, too?"

A hot rush of shame swept over her. It was wrong to lie about that, too. But she didn't need to answer. Clarence saw her reaction to his question.

"Thought so." He reached out and grabbed her arm, yanking her along with him. "Let's git going, I gotta follow my orders and take you to a safer place and git back to doing my job…as a real soldier!"

"Please don't be mad at me, Clarence. You kept telling me I had to follow my gut and then I would know what to do. Well, I followed my gut. You can't tell me that I didn't fight as hard as any man. Now, let go. I'm not going to turn around and go back."

He released her arm. "War ain't no place for no woman."

"I know it now. It just took me a long time to figure it out, that's all. I just want to go home as soon as I can."

"Good." They continued to make their way across the field, pushing the ribbed leaves out of the way. "What happened to you last night, Ch—I guess I should call you Mrs. Garrett now."

"You can call me Charlie. It's short for Charlotte." A lock of hair fell across her face, and she brushed it away impatiently.

"Okay, Charlie, what happened to you last night? Why didn't you come back to camp? And why did you spend the night in the hospital tent?"

"I-I just had a little problem and hurt myself."

Again the familiar pair of eyes looked her up and down. "You okay?"

She nodded. "Yes, fine."

The two had emerged from the cornfield and approached a white clapboard farmhouse with colorful flowers planted on either side of the back step. Drab shirts and skirts hung on the clothesline along with startlingly white sheets that flapped in the breeze. A well-worn path led from the clothesline to the back door. The yard was deserted.

When Charlie stopped and turned around, she was horrified to see thousands upon thousands of men in the distance. From the elevated rise, she could see tiny blue and gray specks moving around. Wagons, horses, and cannons were scattered in among the men. Smoke belched from the guns, followed by the sounds of the explosions.

Suddenly she was grabbed by the arm and pulled up to the door of the farmhouse by a very tense Clarence.

"Stop right there, Rebs!" a voice boomed from behind the weathered green door.

They froze.

"I got you both in my sights!" The door creaked open just a crack and a rifle barrel poked out. "What do you want?"

Clarence pulled off his forage cap and gave a polite bow. "Ma'am, I ain't here to do no harm. This here woman needs a place to stay away from the battle."

The door swung open slowly on creaky hinges. The stout, gray-haired woman, coming out of the house with her shotgun still trained unwaveringly on them, did not flinch at the sound of the cannon fire.

"My name is Clarence Stoner, Ma'am, and this here is Mrs. Joshua Garrett."

"I can't say it is nice to meet you at all, Mr. Stoner. I'm Mrs. Helen Treager, and I got a basement full of women and children who ain't got no man to protect them. She can come with us. You got a first name, Mrs. Garrett?" The woman turned her bespectacled gaze on Charlie.

"Call me Charlotte, Mrs. Treager." Out of habit, Charlie offered her hand to the older lady.

Down went the gray head to stare at the offered hand then up again without touching it.

"Ladies do not shake hands, Charlotte. They curtsy. Didn't you mother teach you that?"

A hot flush crept up Charlie's neck and spread to her face. She was humiliated. For so long she had been forced to concentrate on acting like a man that she had forgotten how to act like a woman.

"No matter." Helen Treager had apparently had enough small talk. "You," she pointed to Clarence. "Are you staying here? If not, you'd best git going."

Charlie turned to Clarence and threw her arms around his thin shoulders. The warm smell of tobacco, coffee, and body odor filled her nostrils. He smelled like…Clarence.

"I'll be fine, Clarence," she told him, planting a kiss

on his bearded cheek. "You stay alive, and I will find you after the battle is over. Y-you should go now."

She heard his rifle clatter to the ground. His arms went around her tentatively. "Take care of yourself, boy...I mean, young lady."

"You too, Clarence. I love you."

"Y-yes, well...me too, even if you did lie to me."

Charlie saw the curiosity light up Helen's face. Her eagerness to get to the bottom of that statement was clearly visible, but it would have to wait.

A series of explosions echoed across the fields, reminding the old soldier of his duty. Grunting, he bent down, retrieved his Whitworth and, without a backward look, headed back to the Confederate line. Making no attempt to fight back the tears, Charlie watched the ragged figure until the cornfield swallowed him up.

Chapter Eight

The wounded poured into the barn at a rate that quickly overwhelmed the army physicians. Daniel had to give up trying to save badly damaged limbs. Saving as many lives as possible was the only thing he could do. Trying to repair an arm or a leg took too much precious time when other men were bleeding to death outside on the ground.

Daniel, John, and Joseph worked together as quickly as humanly possible to remove an arm or a leg and stem the bleeding. With each leg or arm he was forced to remove, a little piece of Daniel died along with it.

His eyes burned with the sweat trickling down his face. The team had been working at a feverish rate since dawn, and the number of casualties was climbing.

"There's got to be thousands of dead men out in them cornfields," a filthy soldier reported as he and his comrade rushed in to put yet another patient on the table. "And they say our dead are lying so thick in the Sunken Road that you cain't even see the dirt!" The din of the battle nearly drowned out his words as the cannon pounded, and the clatter of gunfire kept up a steady staccato of mind-numbing noise.

"Jeeesus!" John exclaimed, "He said thousands, didn't he?"

"Yes, John, but just concentrate on the man we have here. We can't help the poor fellows out there until this man is cared for. Only one man at a time, John...one at a time."

Joseph nodded in agreement, trickled the liquid onto the well-used rag, and kept his gaze on the patient's powder-blackened face. But a single tear streaked down his dirty cheeks, leaving a silvery trail on the young man's olive complexion.

"I know, I know," John grumbled and wiped away some of the blood that had pooled in the open wound so Daniel could see inside.

Don't think about it. Just do it, he commanded himself. *Keep it going, keep it going…a bad shoulder wound here…find the bullet…no time…more men dying…* Abandoning the use of the instruments, he stuck his fingers directly into the open wound. Using his sense of touch alone, the surgeon closed his eyes to ease their burning for a moment and searched for the bullet. *There!* He extracted the metal and quickly sewed up the wound.

"Joseph, time to move to the next one. John, bandage him up."

"Captain, we're running low on bandages."

Daniel cursed. "Find someone to go and get whatever they can—blankets, extra shirts, whatever. You!" He shouted over the artillery to a private who was just placing another injured soldier on a table. "Go out and find something for bandages…don't come back without any!"

"Yes, sir!"

Grabbing a canteen left lying on the floor, Daniel opened it, tipped it back, and was thankful for the water that gushed out and cooled his parched throat. He splashed a little on his hands and face then passed the water to Joseph.

The next man lay still as death on the table with blood pouring from a single hole in his chest. There was good reason for his lack of movement. Outside the barn the artillery continued to boom.

"Get this man off this table," Daniel shouted to an attendant, "he's dead. Please check before you bring them in here. We can't help the ones who are already gone. Get the chaplain for him."

Another bloody form took the dead man's place and he took up his surgical instruments once more, cursing the war, cursing the cannons, cursing the damned Yankees, and cursing the inventor of the rifle.

Joseph let out a nervous giggle. "I hain't never heared you curse so much at one time, Captain Reid."

Daniel looked at the anxious, tired face of his best anesthesia man and tried to force a reassuring smile on his face. It wouldn't do to upset the others any more than the situation had already upset everyone. "Well, there's just some times when a good streak of cursing helps clear a body's mind, Joseph."

"Well, if that's the case—" John let out a string of curses the likes of which Daniel had never heard before in his life. If the air weren't so smoky, he would have sworn it turned blue. He laughed.

"John, I do believe you are the champion of swear words! Don't you agree, Joseph?"

The young man's brown eyes were about as wide with surprise as he had ever seen. He just nodded, tongue-tied with shock.

Across the barn, a soldier screamed in terror and began to sob uncontrollably, begging the surgeon not to remove his leg. The moment of levity passed as if it had never happened. Daniel saw Joseph's hands begin to shake.

"John, why don't you take over for Joseph for a while? Go on and take a break, son. Get something to eat, if you can find it. See if you can rest for a bit."

Without a word, Joseph handed the cloth and chloroform bottle to John, turned on his heel, and ran from the barn. John shook the bottle.

"Almost out, Daniel. After this man, we won't have any more chloroform."

The blood drained from Daniel's face in a rush, and he had to breathe deeply to clear the dizziness. *Dear God! Operate with no chloroform?* The sounds of battle showed no signs of waning, and the wounded were still pouring in.

"Hey, William, Henry!" he called out to the other surgeons. "Have either of you any more chloroform?"

"Sorry, Daniel."

"None here, either."

"Jeeesus!" John exclaimed once more. "Dear Lord, have pity on us all!"

* * *

The battle, named after the Antietam Creek running through the middle of the battlefield, raged all day. By the time night crept in, Charlie thought she would go mad waiting in Mrs. Treager's dank basement with the women and children. Her fingers itched for the trigger of her Springfield, but she had no gun, no powder, and no way to help her friends. She was back to being a woman—an impotent, helpless woman.

There was little choice but to wait until the fighting was over. However, sitting around was not Charlie's forte. In no time, she had convinced the women and children to begin preparing rolls of bandages for the wounded. Helen gathered up every spare piece of cloth and blanket she could find and set them all to work.

They didn't have to look far to find the first of the wounded when dawn broke over the town of Sharpsburg. Leaving the others behind, Helen and Charlie stepped out onto the front porch just as three ambulance wagons rattled past. Down the dusty street they clattered, leaving a grisly river of bright red blood in their wake.

"Oh, my Lord!" Helen exclaimed and clapped a hand over her mouth as she watched the wagon disappear around the bend.

"We'll have a lot of work to do, Helen," Charlie said quietly and turned to her new friend. "Are you sure you still want to come with me?"

The older woman's face was ghastly pale. Her wide-eyed gaze was drawn to the trail of red that stretched along the road as far as they could see. One hand was still covering her mouth and the other held tightly to the cloth bag filled with rolled bandages.

"I can do this, honey. They need us, poor fellows." She shot a quick glance in the direction of the battlefield. "Are you sure the fighting is over?"

Charlie listened carefully. No cannon fire or gunshots could be heard. "I think so, but we can always turn around if it starts again."

The two women made their way into the center of

the small town. The houses along the way looked deserted and sad. Doors and windows were closed and shuttered. No children played in the yards. No ladies tended their colorful gardens. No townspeople's horses or carriages came down the street. Only wagons, from both the Confederate and the Union armies, passed them, each one filled with bandaged and bleeding men. The battle that drove the citizens of Sharpsburg away was over. It had been very bad…for both sides.

"Do you have a dry goods store in town, Helen?"

"Yes, Kennedy's Dry Goods, why?"

"I need to make a purchase."

"I don't know if Mr. Kennedy's store is open. Besides, we have work to do." Helen's displeasure at her request was written all over her pale face.

"I'll just have to get him to open up for me," Charlie said.

An hour later, she pulled a borrowed child's wagon along behind her, loaded heavily with reams of muslin and cotton cloth along with several pairs of scissors.

Unsettled by the force of her emotions, Charlie didn't speak as they walked. Breathing slowly, she took time to get herself under control. She had no idea this would be so hard, but she knew Josh would have approved. She could feel his presence slowly and steadily cloaking her with a feeling of peace that gradually drove away the tears.

"Are you all right, Charlotte?" Helen finally broke the silence.

Watching the dust swirl around her badly scuffed brogans and feeling the unaccustomed pull of the skirt wrapping around her ankles, Charlie thought about that. "Yes, I think I am."

"You didn't have to do that, you know. Mr. Kennedy would have given us the cloth for free."

A riderless horse clattered past them, zig-zagging through the street in its fright. Charlie looked around at the streets littered with debris. So many things had either been discarded or had fallen off wagons driven by citizens anxious to get away. Baskets, shoes, books, haversacks, and even pieces of assorted furniture were strewn from one side to the other. She watched the lone horse spook and rear at the sight of a dressmaker's form that had somehow ended up in the middle of the road.

"I know, but the Garretts always pay for what they need," Charlotte finally responded.

"But the price was too high," Helen protested, not for the first time.

"No, the price was exactly right." This time she turned and looked steadily at her companion and smiled. "It is time for me to move on with my life. My husband is gone, but he would have said to me, 'If you feel it in your heart, Charlie, you know it is right.'" Helen looked doubtful so she continued.

"I would like to think that someday soon a young couple will buy those golden wedding rings...and, in a beautiful ceremony, they will put those rings on each other's fingers. They will look into each other's eyes, pledge their love and their lives each to the other, and the love Josh and I shared can live on in them."

Helen pulled out a hankie, removed her glasses, and wiped her eyes.

Stopping for a moment, Charlie turned to the older woman and wrapped her arms around her. Helen smelled of the freshly baked bread they had loaded into the wagon along with the cloth and jugs of water. *Mama…she smells just like Mama did after her baking day.* A fresh flood of tears filled her eyes, but she sniffed them back.

Dear Lord, she would like to see Mama right now. How she would like to be home right now, rather than facing what she and Helen were about to face. Knowing what to expect made it so much worse.

Helen studied her closely. "My girl, you have done a wonderful thing today. There are men out there who need our help. May God have mercy on both sides today."

* * *

All day Charlie participated in the morbid harvest, gathering up shattered human beings. She and Helen walked up to the first soldier they encountered, sitting propped up against a tree on the outskirts of town. The Union soldier was already dead, so there was nothing that the women could do for him, but they didn't know what to do about the body.

"We cannot just leave the poor lad just sitting here dead," Helen said with a look of profound sadness on her wrinkled face. The soldier was indeed a pitiful sight, despite his hated blue uniform. The man had died with the picture of a woman clutched tight in one hand and the other pressed futilely against the gaping wound in his side.

Biting her lip, Charlie tried hard not to cry at the

sight. "But we can't take the time to dig a grave, Helen. There are so many out there, and we have to help them."

A painted buckboard wagon rattled to a stop beside them. A tall man with graying hair jumped down from the seat, accompanied by several other men. Down the road more wagons were coming, bearing women and supplies, along with the men.

"Hello, Mr. Atwell, " Helen greeted the man.

In no time Helen had made the introductions all around, and the townspeople of Sharpsburg set out to do whatever they could for the soldiers. The plan was simple but the undertaking enormous. The women would walk ahead and bandage any wounded they could help. They would get the men to carry any injured soldiers to the wagon and take them to the army surgeons. Later the men would come back for the dead.

As the morning progressed and they made their way further onto the devastated battlefield, they quickly lost their optimism. None of them had anticipated the magnitude of the task. Everywhere they looked there were soldiers lying on the ground. Most were dead. Singly or in groups of two or three or, in case of the sunken road, piled so deep on each other no one could count them. Stiffened arms were raised beseechingly, and legs were tangled among the now useless rifles. The sight had been Helen's undoing and had nearly sent Charlie screaming into the trees. They were Confederates who had been mowed down where they had fought so bravely. The Federals had not escaped easily. Blue-coated bodies lay everywhere just beyond the bloody lane…earlier victims of the Rebels who were now dead.

Mr. Atwell took a shaken and sobbing Helen back home. The elderly woman had been out for hours and had finally given in to the emotional turmoil they were all feeling. Charlie turned away from the sight and searched for anyone living among the macabre spectacle of death. The air was putrid with the smell of already decaying bodies of horses and men. And so it was throughout the day of September 19th. Charlie and the other civilians were doing the best they could for the 17,000 injured soldiers scattered far and wide from the Antietam Creek. She and the others pressed bandages onto wounds and wound cloth around damaged limbs and heads. They gave water and whiskey to men crying desperately for help and loaded as many as they could into the wagons for transport to the makeshift hospitals.

Charlie searched for her friends among the bodies clad in the gray uniforms. It was late afternoon when she encountered a familiar soldier among a group that had apparently been gunned down beside a wooden fence. She stared down into his sightless cold eyes and frozen grimace. It was her attacker, the angry man who had tried to have his way with her only…when was it? Only two days ago? It seemed like a lifetime had passed.

Dismissing the corpse, she looked carefully at the group and didn't recognize another man. Then, her duty done, she turned away. Her mission was to find men who were still alive and leave the dead for the burial detail.

Dusk was beginning to cast purple shadows over the decimated cornfield. She couldn't take anymore that day. Tears leaked from her eyes as Charlie climbed up on the seat next to Mr. Atwell.

"Will you being coming back to camp with me and the injured boys in my wagon, Mrs. Garrett?" he asked. "You can't do much good out here without any light."

"Yes, Perhaps I can help further at the hospital. There are just so many…"

He nodded. "This carnage is a sight no woman should see."

Neither of them spoke as they rode away into the gathering gloom.

* * *

Daniel was bone weary, but he just couldn't take a break. Too many soldiers were bleeding to death before they even made it to his table. It was making him crazy. With his heart pounding from the fast pace and the demands of standing on his feet for forty-two hours straight, he operated as quickly as humanly possible. Darkness had fallen, and the surgeons were operating by torchlight. It was next to impossible. The endless amount of blood was sickening—pools of it had gathered on the dirt floor.

"Somebody get some hay over here to soak up some of this blood!" he shouted hoarsely.

Moments later, a private came in with an armload and spread it around. It was a relief to feel the dry material under his boots.

John Dunn and Joseph Hill had left to get some rest a few hours ago. Daniel had to rely on inexperienced men to help out, and it was fraying his nerves. Add to that the fact that the chloroform had run out a long time ago and that he was operating on men who were awake and aware of the agony he was inflicting on them…and Daniel Reid was seriously on edge.

"No! No! Please, Captain, please just take the bullet out!" the soldier cried, reaching up to grab hold of his blood-encrusted sleeve. "Dear God, I'm beggin' y'all…don't cut m' leg off!"

"All right, son." The soldier was young. With his round face he looked to be barely eighteen years old with a sprinkling of freckles among the black powder smudges on his face. "I won't take your leg. You just have to do something for me."

Daniel looked down into the young man's blue eyes, so filled with pain and terror. The soldier had faced a horrific battle with hoards of Yankees and now…it was the surgeon the man feared. So much pain and suffering had already been inflicted on so many people. Outside the barn it was chaos. Men lay in the yard bleeding, screaming, moaning, and…dying. It was impossible to stem the tide of wounded. No matter how quickly he treated one soldier, another took his place.

"What! What do I have to do?"

His attention was jerked back to the bleeding man in front of him. He hadn't even realized his mind had wandered. His two assistants stared at him.

"Oh, yes…you have to try not to scream and hold as still as you can, son. I'm sorry, but I don't have anything to give you for the pain."

The soldier nodded tersely.

"Hold him down, please."

Daniel wiped his perspiring face on a grimy rag, and with a silent apology for the lack of sanitation, dug the forceps into the entrance of the wound searching for the minie ball. The man's leg trembled, and his body stiffened, but, true to his promise, he did not scream or cry. In no time the metal was removed, and the torn leg was stitched up.

As soon as the freckled soldier was being bandaged by one of the assistants, Daniel staggered back from the table and sank to the ground as his legs just gave out. He dropped his head into his still-bloody hands. It didn't matter that he got blood on his face and in his sweaty hair. Nothing much mattered…he was just so damned tired. Just as he was about to fall asleep right there, he felt himself being pulled to his feet. Blearily he forced his eyes open, saw Captain Weaver's unsmiling face on one side of him, and turned to see an unknown private on the other.

"Ben…I just needed a minute to rest my eyes…"

"Oh, no, you need more than a minute, Dan, my boy," he said. "Let's get him outside."

The two of them took him under each arm and steered him out of the door, past the many injured soldiers waiting. Most of them were quiet. Once in a while someone would let out a moan or a desperate prayer. Even when Daniel closed his eyes, all he could see was blood.

"Has the captain been hurt?"

It was a female voice, but when he managed to lift his eyelids, he couldn't get his eyes to focus enough to see who was speaking, so he let them slam closed again.

"No, Ma'am. He's just dead on his feet, so plumb tired he can't do anymore cuttin' today. We're just trying to find a tent for him to lie down in."

"It's okay," he mumbled. "Just let me lie down right here."

"Just a minute. Hold him right there," the woman's voice said. He heard a rustling of skirts. Moments later the men lowered him onto a blanket, and he went boneless with relief. For a moment, he heard the low murmuring of conversation before all of his senses shut down.

* * *

When she saw the two men practically dragging Captain Reid who was covered in blood, fear had washed over her with unexpected force. There had been no sign of anyone she knew the entire horrific day, until she had seen the captain's very recognizable figure. Charlie had asked Mr. Atwell to take her to the Confederate's hospital camp area. She was able to help the Federals she found out on the fields — they were helpless and hurt human beings. But she could not stomach being among the healthy Bluecoats who had done so much damage to her army.

As the wagon lurched into camp, she had searched every soldier's face in the vanishing light for the ones she held dear. Two men, almost carrying a third, had caught her attention. At first she had not recognized Captain Reid with his head down and his hair dark and matted with filth. But the wide shoulders, narrow waist, and long legs of this man made her take a second look.

After dumping their burden on the blanket, Captain Weaver and the other soldier nodded at her and disappeared into the shadows.

The night was alive with flickering torches, whispered conversations, and cries and moans carried by a restless autumn wind. The remnants of the Confederate army bustled around her. Charlie was sensitive to the pulse of the army and knew the mass retreat back to Virginia would commence in the morning. She could only pray they would be allowed to leave unmolested.

Staring down at the sleeping, blood-encrusted man at her feet, she wondered what it was that drew her to him. The cool breeze found its way down her neck, and she shivered. She had never felt so alone in her entire life as she felt now. Although he was her regimental surgeon, and he had saved her from her attacker, she really didn't know this man…and he didn't know her.

Perhaps because Daniel Reid had been kind to her…perhaps that was why she stood staring at him now. Maybe it was why she wanted to lie down beside him and curl up against his warmth.

The sleeping captain mumbled something incoherent and flung an arm out wide. The action roused her from her selfish thoughts. *This was no time to be feeling sorry for yourself, Charlotte Garrett. There is work to be done yet. Here is one more man who could use your help.*

Moving to his feet, she pulled off his boots one by one, shuddering at their sticky feel. Taking the boots, she went off in search of a rag, jug, and basin. This was one small thing she could do for him as well as for herself. She could not bear to touch one more injured or dying man just now. True, Daniel was covered in blood, but it was not his own. At this hour, after this day, she could deal with that. Washing him would do him a service, and she could touch a warm, healthy human being. It was something she needed.

The soldiers were surprised to see a woman among them, but they gave her what she sought. She explained, with yet another partial lie, that she had come from the town to help nurse the wounded. They assumed she lived in Sharpsburg, and she did not correct them.

Charlie headed toward the sound of gurgling water with a sense of rising fear. Antietam Creek was close by, but her footsteps dragged reluctantly. *You pretended to be a man just a short time ago, silly girl! You can do this. You can do it for Captain Reid.* But the idea that she could encounter Yankees, dead or alive, left her hands perspiring with terror. Ghostly sycamores and weeping willows fringed the sloping banks of the creek. Tangles of hazel and elder thickets pulled at her skirts, but she finally reached the water.

Nervously glancing around as she scrubbed the boots, she nearly swallowed her tongue when an owl swooped low, scaring up a wild rabbit from the brush. She worked quickly.

Returning to where Daniel lay, she sat beside him with a sigh of relief, poured the water into the basin, picked up his hand and began to wash it, watching his face in the murky lamplight. There was no reaction. Gently she traced his hand with her finger. After washing his hand, she dried it then bent down and pressed his fingers to her cheek. Oh, how tempting it was to just put this warm masculine palm to her breast.

Where had that thought come from? Oh, Dear Lord, multitudes of men are dead and dying all around me, and here

I sit…thinking about putting this man's hand on me!

But she didn't. Turning his hand over, she pressed it to her face. Sometimes she would take Josh's hand and hold it to her face this way. The roughness of his calloused hand had been so different from Daniel's smooth skin — the difference between a farmer's and a surgeon's hands. Still, it felt so good to hold…even though this man was a virtual stranger.

His shirt was stiff with dried blood, and the metallic smell of it clung to him. She couldn't bear it a moment longer and began to slowly, carefully unbutton the cotton shirt. One by one the buttons came begrudgingly free, yet the captain did not stir. Charlie peeled the shirt away from him inch-by-inch, using the wet rag to free the material from his skin until the shirt gave way, and his glorious chest muscles gleamed in the lamplight.

Even knowing the cool air might wake him, she sat and stared. Here was a vital, healthy man and she was having traitorous thoughts about someone who was not her husband. *For shame, Charlotte…* And yet she made no move to cover him. It had been so long since she had last made love with Joshua…so very long since she felt his touch. She missed Josh with a pain that ran deep in her heart. But as she looked down on the sleeping surgeon, she could not deny the pull Captain Reid had on her.

Somewhere, a horse let out a panicked shriek, startling Charlie to her senses. She glanced around. Seconds or hours could have passed while she was engrossed with this man. Shadowy figures still moved helter-skelter in the darkness. Low murmuring of conversations amid the cries and moans of the wounded seemed disembodied from the owners of these voices.

Just get a grip on yourself. She reached out once more to gingerly touch the shirt with two fingers, wondering how to get it off him.

Suddenly, Daniel sat up and, without opening his eyes, pulled his arm out of the sleeve. She gasped aloud. He responded to her unspoken request just like a sleepy child being put to bed! He sat with his head bowed and one arm bared until, realizing he was waiting for her, she hurried to pull the shirt off his other arm. Immediately, he sank back onto the blanket, curled up into a ball on his side, and began to snore softly.

Smiling for the first time in what seemed like years, she pulled the blanket around the sleeping man, stood, and headed for the barn. She would see what she could do to help before taking her own rest. It seemed proper that she would tend to others after taking such pleasure in helping this one.

* * *

Daniel was surprised to wake up bare-chested under the blankets. After groping around in the dark he found a clean shirt lying beside him, along with his de-encrusted boots. Pulling the clean articles on, he made his way quickly back to the hospital rubbing the sleep from his eyes. He had no idea who had brought him the shirt or cleaned his boots, but he was grateful.

Torches dotted the black night, and the smell of gunpowder still hung heavy in the air. Soldiers were still moving about despite the lateness of the hour. Stretchers bearing injured men continued to come in from the far reaches of the battlefield.

Daniel walked briskly into the barn, anxious to banish the guilt that assaulted him for having left. She was in the barn, leaning over a man propped against the wall when he saw her again.

The light inside the hospital was poor, but somehow she must have sensed his presence. Mrs. Garrett looked up when he entered, their eyes meeting from across the room. Those beautiful eyes were directed at him! His heart skipped a beat. Instantly, every cell in his body came to attention. Now that she was wearing a skirt and dark colored blouse, her femininity was obvious. How could he have ever mistaken this lovely dark-haired woman for a boy?

She smiled at him, a tired smile of welcome.

Hesitantly, he returned the smile with a nod. Why did he feel as though Charlotte had been with him recently? He had sent her away several days ago, but he was not surprised at all to see her here. For some reason he expected her to be here…but why?

* * *

Tucking in the end of the bandage, she patted her patient's arm in a comforting gesture. "There you are. Try your best to keep it clean and put on a new one tomorrow, if you can."

The dazed soldier nodded, rose, and walked away silently.

Charlie yawned. Exhaustion was setting in, and she needed to lie down. She looked around, reluctant to leave this place. Spying a relatively clean spot in the corner of the barn, she curled up on a small pile of hay and fell asleep. It seemed someone was shaking her awake only minutes later.

"Go away," she grumbled without opening her eyes.

"Charlie...uh...I mean Mrs. Garrett. I wanted to come and say goodbye."

Her eyes snapped open. "Clarence!"

Jumping up, she threw her arms around the thin shoulders and nearly knocked the older man off his feet. He stumbled back a few feet, reflexively putting his arms around her.

"Oh, I am so glad you are alive!" She nearly yelled, causing heads to turn in their direction. A few people even smiled at them, glad to see a glimmer of hope.

"Missus Garrett!" Clarence shook himself free of her grasp. "This here is bad behavior for a widow lady!"

Charlie laughed. "Oh, Clarence, I am still the same person who marched beside you for months now...the same person you taught to load and shoot. And the same person who you taught to spit."

A reluctant smile spread across his face. "If'n I hadn't taught you better, you'd still be spittin' on a body's shoes like y'all did the first time I laid eyes on you!"

"I can still do it."

But he only scowled at her. "I can see y'all is wearing a skirt, and y'all has decided to be a woman again as is well and proper like. So you gotta go back acting like one too."

She knew he meant to correct her much like a father corrects his child, but she could see the hint of a smile through the scraggly gray beard.

"Have you seen Ned Hagan or Victor Marshall?"

They were the last two Augusta Country, Virginia soldiers unaccounted for. The rest were already gone.

He shook his head sadly. "Poor Ned went down right beside me. Me and a few others buried him ourselves." Then he glanced around the barn as if he were looking for someone.

"I ain't found the boy, Vic, yet."

Charlie's hand flew to her mouth in horror. "Do you think…?"

The grizzled head shook slowly. "Nah, I bet he's safe and sound around somewhere. We'll be forming up, and he's bound to show up." He met her gaze and put a gentle hand on her shoulder. "I'm leaving now, Charlie…I feel better callin' you that…and I wanted to make sure you is gonna be okay without me."

How could she say goodbye to this man who had been so good to her for all this time? This was something she had not anticipated when she decided to take back her identity.

"I'll be fine, Clarence. I think I will stay here in Sharpsburg for a while and help before I go home."

"But you will go home?"

"Yes," she assured him, "I'll go home to Mamma and Papa…and our farm." A bolt of sadness ripped through her at the thought of going home without Josh. But if she could survive the war, she could walk into her bedroom and see the spot where he had slept, where they had made love…

"That's good." Clarence gave her an awkward pat on the arm. "You take care of yourself now."

"You, too," she forced the words past her tight

throat. Standing on her toes, she kissed him on his dirty cheek. "Write to me and let me know how you're doing, okay?"

He nodded. "I cain't promise too much writin'—I ain't good at it—but I will try."

All she could do was nod in return and watch him turn away. His scarecrow-like form headed for the open barn doors. She watched him until he was gone from view, then she threw herself onto the pile of straw and wept.

* * *

Daniel turned to see what was causing the excited woman's silvery laughter. He witnessed her happiness and then her sadness as Clarence Stoner said his farewells. His awareness of this woman was so damned bothersome. All during the night and early morning, despite the challenging injuries he treated on his table, he knew where she was and what she was doing. When she finally lay down to cry herself to sleep, he inwardly sighed with relief. Thank heavens she was finally going to stay in one place for a while, and he didn't have to keep looking for her.

Exactly why he felt as though he needed to keep track of Charlotte Garrett, he couldn't say. Time and time again he found his head turning in her direction just to catch another glimpse of the small, dark-haired beauty, whether she was asleep or awake.

Not that he was the only one who watched her, not by a long shot. He could see the eyes of the other soldiers on this woman and, for some reason he couldn't understand, he didn't like it. *Forget her*, he chastised himself and continued to stitch up the belly of the patient on the table, *you have more important things to deal with.*

Chapter Nine

As the hours ticked by and the pile of amputated arms and legs grew, the magnitude of this horror began to seep into Daniel's consciousness. But he pushed it deeper into his mind so it would not interfere with his ability to keep working. He dared not step outside to view the multitudes of dead and dying soldiers outside the barn doors, or he would never come back in again.

"Next!" he yelled.

Never looking at the face of his patient and shutting his ears to their screams and pleas, he continued to work at a fever-pitched pace. Sometime during this period someone came and plucked at his arm saying something about "leaving" and "orders to pull out." Shrugging the man off, Daniel merely said, "Not leaving," and continued to work on the latest leg amputation.

That was all they were to him now, all they could be—a leg wound, belly wound, shattered jaw, multiple bullet wounds. No more Billies, Georges, or Johnnies, just a medical case to be dealt with. He didn't know where they went when they left or how they arrived on the table in front of him. They just did.

On and on they came. Day turned into night. Sweat poured from his body, ran down into his eyes, and someone wiped it away.

"Wash the table," he barked, and a bucket of water was splashed over the murky surface. He picked his bone saw out of the bucket and shook the water off. "Next!" he shouted.

A soldier was put on the table. He went back to work. The man screamed and writhed, and Daniel's head pounded.

"Hold him still!"

"Wait, please sir," a quiet voice broke into the chaos. "I can help his pain."

"Chloroform?" he asked hopefully as he turned to look into the round bespectacled face of an older gentleman…a civilian by his dress.

The white-haired man shook his head, "Sorry, no…but wait a moment, and I will demonstrate."

Daniel shook his head, "There is no time to waste—"

The man stuck his hand out as if to shake Daniel's then withdrew it after noting the blood. "I am Doctor Oliver Riley from Frederick."

"Happy to have you here to help out, Doctor…now, if I can continue… Hold him still, please." A hand was placed gently on his arm, stilling the rise of the instrument.

Moving to the other side of the table, his shoes making a sucking sound as he lifted them from the grisly floor, Doctor Riley spoke to the injured patient.

"Please listen carefully to the sound of my voice, son, and fix your eyes on the watch. Concentrate, if you want to ease your pain."

The new doctor's voice now had a sing-song type of quality to it. Daniel found it soothing, and his tensed shoulders relaxed.

Light from the lanterns gave the gold watch a warm glow as it swung rhythmically in front of the eyes of the patient. Within moments those eyes, which had been so filled with pain, began to soften, and the eyelids became heavy as the doctor continued to speak.

The Frederick doctor picked up the young man's good arm. It was limp and relaxed in his grasp.

"Your patient is ready, Doctor."

Daniel studied the soldier's face. His eyes were open, but glassy and unfocused.

"Hold him down all the same," he ordered his helpers.

They obediently held down both legs and the uninjured arm of the young man. Moving quickly, Daniel set to work removing the badly shattered arm below the elbow and sewing up the wound. Most of the bone in the forearm was gone and little was left to salvage. The young patient merely twitched a foot from time to time during the procedure. But the most wondrous thing of all was the absence of spine-tingling screams.

Amazed, he looked up at the civilian doctor, who was still speaking to the boy. There was nothing unusual about his words...they were just any words used to soothe an anxious child.

"This will all be over soon, Adam," Doctor Riley said. How did he know the soldier's name? "Just relax and let all your pain flow out of your body..."

There was also nothing unusual that Daniel could see about the gold watch. It looked just like one his grandfather had used for many years.

Wrapping the end of the wound securely with clean bandages, he watched his patient closely. He appeared to be in a sort of mesmerized state.

"How long will he remain like that, Doctor Riley?"

The man chuckled slightly. "Until I release him from the trance or it wears off."

"Let's get the next patient in here," Daniel ordered. The boy was removed and another took his place. "Doctor Riley, can you put all people into this trance of yours?"

"It is called hypnosis, son, and…to answer your question. No. Not everyone will allow themselves to be put into this state of subdued consciousness."

The eyes of the older man had a quality Daniel could not define. They were large, kindly brown eyes that held depths of knowledge and wisdom.

"If you don't mind, could you try with this man here? We have no chloroform to help with the pain…I would be extremely grateful if you would attempt your procedure. Perhaps later, when there is more time, you could show me how to do that."

"Of course, sir. It is a practice that has been around for almost eighty years. I learned it on a trip to Europe several years ago…"

"Uh, sir, I would love to hear all about it later, but now, I could really use your help." He was already cutting away the man's bloody clothing.

"Oh, yes, yes, of course." Doctor Riley swallowed hard and took his watch out of his pocket. His voice trembled just a little, but Daniel noted with satisfaction that the good doctor kept his eyes on the patient's agonized face as he reapplied his magical skills. It took a few more minutes to get this one to relax, but it was accomplished.

Over and over again, the physician from Frederick

mesmerized man after man. A few could not be helped, but many were relieved, albeit temporarily, from their agony while he removed shattered limbs and stitched up torn bodies.

As the work continued, Daniel had to reach deep inside for strength. He shifted from foot to foot. His head and back ached, and the blood that liberally covered his clothing was beginning to dry into stiff, irritating patches. In addition, he was starving. His belly had been grindingly hollow for so long now he could scarcely remember how it felt to have a full meal.

Suddenly, Charlotte Garrett was standing at his side quietly assisting him. She held a cup of coffee up inquiringly. He opened his mouth, and she tipped the wonderful brown liquid into it.

"Thank you."

Merely nodding, she put a bite-sized piece of bread into his mouth next. Her small hands moved quickly and efficiently. She hand fed him and sponged away blood so he could clearly see the wound. Then she passed him instruments and…wonder of wonders…cleaned them with soap and water.

* * *

How long had the man been on his feet working like this? She had taken two breaks to eat and sleep, and he had been at this table each time she came back. She studied Daniel Reid closely. His handsome face was blank and expressionless. Exhaustion was taking its toll. Dark circles shadowed his blue eyes. Before this battle, they had been full of warmth and humor and…life.

Her admiration for the surgeon grew with each

patient he tended. Charlie wiped his perspiring brow with the cleanest cloth she could find. He gave her the briefest of grateful smiles before returning his attention to the patient.

This hypnosis thing was helping tremendously. Many of the men stopped their thrashing and moaning almost as soon as the little round Frederick doctor spoke to them.

But it was the Confederate surgeon who fascinated her. She watched his hands move with a sure grace that gave flight to her imagination. *How would those hands feel touching her? It had been so long since someone had touched her willingly. She wondered how much longer it would be before it happened again, if ever, now that Josh was gone.* Inadvertently, she sighed.

He turned his head, a dark blond eyebrow raised, and his scissors halted in the process of cutting away the bloody trouser cloth. "Are you tired, Mrs. Garrett?" he asked gently. "Why don't you go lie down and get some sleep? The hour is late."

"Please, call me Charlotte…or Charlie, Captain Reid. No, I can work a while longer. But I am concerned about you. Perhaps you should stop to eat and rest?"

He nodded, keeping his eyes on the patient. "Soon, soon. I appreciate your help…Charlie. Now that we have known each other for a while, you can call me Daniel…unless you decide to come back into the army…in which case you will have to call me Captain Reid."

"Back into the army?" Doctor Riley asked incredulously. "Whatever does he mean, Mrs. Garrett?"

She had forgotten the Frederick physician was there. "Ummm, Captain Reid just meant that I might decide to come back and help the army again."

The round head nodded, and he turned his soothing voice back to the man lying on the table. Charlie watched the glittering watch as it swung back and forth, back and forth rhythmically.

"Relax. Let your mind and body drift…" the doctor's liquid voice intoned.

Oh, my, suddenly she was so very tired…tired and sleepy. "I think I had better…"

The last thing she knew, a strong arm slipped around her waist as her knees buckled, and her eyes slid shut.

* * *

Daniel was stunned at what he found when he finally made his way into town. He had operated on every soldier the civilians had gathered up to bring to him. After checking on a peacefully sleeping Charlie, he lay down on the ground beside her cot and slept for a few hours. She had not known he was there, but being next to her was the only place in this hellhole he wanted to be. Later, Doctor Riley asked Daniel to accompany him to town.

People hurried about the streets of Sharpsburg with grim faces. Everywhere he looked, the civilians who had not left town were helping injured soldiers. The wounded sat or lay on the sidewalks, were carried on makeshift litters from one place to a more suitable spot, or hobbled along on their own. Women bustled between shops and homes with blankets, linens, buckets, and boxes full of bottles and jars. A whole group of children moved past, their little faces a picture of serious resolve as they carried armfuls of golden hay into a general store.

It was more than obvious to Daniel that the small town of Sharpsburg was overwhelmed by the amount of casualties the Confederate army left behind when they retreated back over the Potomac River into Virginia. Yellow bits of cloth fluttered from every window, roof, and chimney, marking the town hall, schoolhouse, shops, and houses as hospitals.

He followed the children into the store. All of the goods normally stacked on shelves and tables were pushed to the side. The children dropped their burdens onto recently swept floorboards. The piles of straw were quickly covered with blankets and two men deposited an injured soldier gently on the bed. Soldiers crowded every available place on the floor.

"Are you injured, sir?"

Turning, he regarded the grandmotherly woman who addressed him. He swept off his hat. "No, Ma'am, I am not, but I appreciate what you have been doing here."

In her sturdy, work-reddened hands she held rolls of cloth. Her apron was liberally smeared with the dark stains of unidentifiable human fluids.

"Are you hungry, then?" she asked. Not waiting for an answer, she beckoned to a young girl across the room. "I'm sure you are, darlin', you're a Rebel, and you are all hungry."

At the sight of sandwiches in the girl's basket, Daniel's mouth began to water, and his stomach gave a loud growl. Reaching into the basket, the grandma pulled one out and handed it to him. It was with effort that he managed to refrain from stuffing the food into his mouth. Even with restraint, the sandwich was gone in seconds.

Licking his fingers, he sought out the woman, who had not gone far.

"If you have some water I might use to wash my hands, Ma'am, I'd be glad to help out here."

She looked at him skeptically.

"Why haven't you moved out with the rest of the Rebs, if you aren't injured? You are some kind of officer, aren't you?"

"Yes'm, Captain Daniel Reid, Surgeon for the Twenty-Fifth Virginia, at your service." He grinned at her, knowing a smile often helped him to soften up a rigid lady.

"Hummph, if your title was supposed to impress me, you can forget it. So many of your men are sorely suffering for lack of medical attention, you should be ashamed. They are starving, filthy, and deserve better than what you have provided, sir."

She turned her back on him and walked away. He was stunned at the quick turn of attitude—one second friendly and the next sour.

A light touch on his arm caught his attention.

"Don't worry about Mrs. Treager, sir, she is just so upset at how many soldiers have been dying that she just wants to be mad at somebody." The young girl with the basket stood beside him, giving him a shy look from under her thick lashes. "She told Mrs. Atwell she found dead soldiers in her corncrib." A hand fluttered to her throat, "Poor Mrs. Treager was very upset. Mr. Atwell said he would go take care of it."

"I can imagine," he said. "Thank you…"

"Becky. Becky Franklin."

"Nice to meet you, Becky Franklin, and I thank you kindly for the sandwich." Bowing slightly, he tried hard to pry his eyes off the remaining food in her basket. His stomach was still asking for more, and he had already wolfed down one sandwich. Daniel swallowed.

Becky giggled and handed him another sandwich. "You sure do talk funny…all of you do. Momma says Southerners have the best manners, too, and you just did something I've never seen a boy in this town do!" She tittered again and smoothed her dress with her free hand. "Too bad you smell so bad, but you are very handsome…in a skinny kind of way."

"Uh…thank you, I think."

"I like that…you said it again, you said 'ahh think.' You really do speak differently, sir."

He was getting a little annoyed with this young lady. Men were suffering all around them, and she was flirting! A headache and barely dampened hunger added to his bad mood.

"I thank you for the food, but if you will please excuse me, Miss Franklin, I need to get to work."

"Doctor Reid!" a voice called from across the room. He looked around. It was Doctor Riley. He nodded to the girl and hurried away.

Kneeling on the floor, Daniel concentrated on picking small pieces of canister metal out of a soldier's back. Performing the medical task helped take his mind off his empty stomach. He looked up to see Helen Treager approaching, this time with a less hostile look on her face.

"Sir, there is someone here to see you who has been looking all over town for you, although I am sure I don't know why."

"Who would that be, Ma'am?" he asked politely in a voice that felt hoarse and dry. Perhaps he could get a few of the children, or even Becky, to fetch some water.

"Ma'am?" asked a muffled voice. The soldier lying with his raw back exposed to Daniel's forceps turned and lifted his head. "Is there any chance y'all could spare a drop o' water?"

The older woman's face softened further and as she turned to leave, the visitor stepped out from behind her.

Daniel could not believe his eyes! He stood up so fast that his vision darkened momentarily. There, in the midst of all this chaos and human disaster, was a very nervous, very agitated Lucy Masterson. His fiancée had come to find him in the middle of a war!

Chapter Ten

"Lucy! Whatever are you doing here?"

"Oh, Daniel, I am so glad to see you. I have been so afraid you were dead!" With that she began to cry in hysterical gulping sobs. Her perfect blond curls bobbed up and down. She held a lace-edged handkerchief to her face.

"I…uh…dear Lucy, don't cry."

"It took us so long to get here…and there are horrors at…at every turn. It is just beyond any sense of propriety that so many sightseers and soldiers are clogging the roads!"

"Us? Who else is here?" He spread his bloodied hands open, palm up and looked at them and at Lucy helplessly. Mrs. Treager took a cloth and began to wipe his hands off for him.

"M-my f-father brought me here," Lucy sobbed and reached down with gloved hands to pull the skirts of her mint green gown away from the soldier lying at their feet. The man was looking up with a pained but interested expression. "O-oh, look at what they have done to you, Daniel!" she wailed.

By now a crowd had gathered around them. Both injured soldiers and their civilian rescuers were drawn to the mounting drama. A perfectly coiffed and expensively dressed lady was a rare sight in this region. No one wanted to miss a single word!

There was a stirring in the crowd around them. A stout, balding man pushed his way to the front. He was attired in a manner meant for the wealthy as well, in a fine suit that fit his rotund figure quite well.

"Daniel, my boy, how glad I am to see you have not suffered the same fate as so many of these poor souls," Mr. Masterson puffed. "I insisted Lucy come to see you."

Daniel put a hand up. "Wait just a minute, please, sir." He squatted down to the soldier he had been treating and began to bandage the man's back

Lucy gasped, and Mr. Masterson huffed loudly. "Now, see here, son, we have come a long way to see you…"

Looking up, Daniel saw the revulsion on the faces of both father and daughter. Anger burned his insides. He finished the bandaging job and patted the soldier on his filthy bare shoulder. Then he stood and faced the pair. "I have a few things to take care of here then we can talk. I think it would be best if you waited outside."

"But there are…soldiers everywhere…outside also," his fiancee complained, "and they are all as dirty and uh…unsavory as this one."

"Lucy, I stand in front of you as your intended husband, and I am every bit as filthy as these men. Would you show your contempt so boldly for me as well?" he asked softly.

"Daniel!" she gasped. "How can you speak to me that way?"

Charlie had come into the store. Daniel sensed her presence even before he saw her standing at the edge of the growing crowd. She had brushed her short, dark hair and washed her face. The clothes she wore were the same stained clothing from the day before, but he thought she was beautiful...even more beautiful than the perfect woman standing before him in the shimmering green gown.

"Have a care with your words, my dear. These men have suffered enough already without having to tolerate your cruel barbs as well," he continued quietly.

"It's okay, Cap'n," the soldier spoke up from the floor, "lookin' at her is like looking at an angel come down ta earth."

"Thank you, kind s—"

Lucy looked down at the man. Daniel followed her gaze. Blood oozed from several damaged areas of the man's back. When Lucy saw the bandaged stump where the soldier's hand had been, she gasped and slumped right into his arms.

Scooping her up, he carried her outside. As everyone stepped aside to allow him passage, he wondered again why had Lucy come. *This isn't like her. She stays as far away from unpleasantness as possible.* Mr. Masterson followed behind, making little anxious twittering sounds.

* * *

Daniel strode past Charlie without even glancing her way as he carried his beautiful wife-to-be out of the store. Charlie was horrified. How could she have feelings for a man who was already betrothed? The woman he was going to marry was in a class so far above Charlie that she wanted to cry.

I am just a farmer's widow with simple ways and simple clothing. A tear trickled down her cheek. She wiped it away angrily.

She tried to deny her feelings for Daniel, but every

time she saw him, a jolt of heat and yearning spread out through her body. Like a fool she followed as the crowd of onlookers poured onto the street outside the store.

Everyone, including Charlie, had been so focused on the tender love scene unfolding that they failed to notice the Federal cavalrymen riding up the road. Jerking the horses to a stop, the dust boiled around them. Ten Yankees leveled rifles at the group. Almost in unison the guns were cocked.

"You, captain…and all you Johnny Rebs! You are now our prisoners. Move it out. Now!" the officer in front of Daniel shouted.

Once more Charlie wished she had her Springfield. Captain Reid stood in the middle of the street holding his sweetheart. The woman was starting to stir, raising her golden head from his broad shoulder. It was then she noticed the town was crawling with Bluebellies. They were rounding up any and all Confederates who could walk, which, unfortunately, meant they wanted the captain, too.

There was nothing she could do, nothing anyone could do, but watch as he set the beautiful lady gently on her feet and passed her over to her father. Lucy broke from her father and clutched at Daniel desperately, saying something to him that Charlie could not hear. Then the woman pressed something into his hand. She watched Daniel's face. Whatever Lucy had said surprised him at first. Then a shadow of sadness passed over him, and he nodded, his face locking into an unreadable mask. His gaze passed over Charlie briefly, but his expression didn't change.

One of the mounted soldiers nudged Daniel in the shoulder with his rifle. "Get moving, you filthy Reb."

"He's a surgeon!" Charlie cried, stepping forward. "These injured men need his help!"

Helen reached out and pulled at her arm hissing, "No, Charlotte, don't interfere."

"Yes, Charlotte, don't interfere," the Union officer mocked with a sneer. "You might get your pretty little self thrown in prison as well."

"I'm so sorry, Daniel," Lucy said through her tears and turned her face into her father's shoulder. "Papa, can you get me out of here? I just can't abide this a moment longer."

Daniel didn't say a word. He just turned away from everyone and began to walk away.

With sorrow thickening her throat and tightening her chest so she could barely breathe, Charlie watched the tattered soldiers limp and hobble away with their bandaged wounds and bare feet. But the pride and honor of the men who had not retreated with their army could not be denied—their spines were straight and their heads were held high. Captain Reid did not look back to see the Mastersons get into their fine black carriage and drive in the opposite direction as if the devil himself was on their heels.

* * *

Charlie lay abed in Helen Treager's guest bedroom again. It was very late, and she was exhausted, but couldn't fall asleep. The little calico cat snuggled against her side, purring contentedly, oblivious to the agitated state of its companion.

Downstairs, one of the injured soldiers crowding Helen's house groaned loudly. Another man hushed him. Trying to block out the sounds, Charlie put the pillow over her head. Her tears soaked into the clean pillowcase. It smelled of lavender…she had lavender flowers when she married Joshua. She sobbed harder.

It seemed as though things could not get much worse. The work to bathe, treat, feed, and house the injured soldiers, from both North and South, was non-ending. The entire town was in a frenzy to come up with enough food, clothing, bandages, blankets, and supplies needed for thousands of uninvited visitors who were helpless to do much of anything for themselves.

She stroked the cat and sniffed. At least the little cat was happy. Meanwhile, Charlie was dying inside.

The scene she had witnessed this day had rattled her to her soul. The realization she was hopelessly, helplessly in love with a man who was promised to another left her mortified with shame.

But her love for Daniel gradually changed humiliation into a deep sadness that seeped into her soul. Long into the night she cried for her loss of her husband and now the loss of a man she hadn't even known she cared for, until today.

Charlie was with Helen the next day in her cozy kitchen, trying to make the chicken soup stretch into enough to feed fourteen men, when the Yankees came.

Helen, stepping over the prostrate men, went to answer the knock. She peered through the lace curtains on the windows.

"There are Union soldiers out there, boys," she

called. "Don't any of you make trouble now. There has been enough bloodshed."

The Confederate soldier on her sofa, Corporal Alan Smith, who had been wounded in the chest, answered for them all in his hoarse whisper. "Go ahead…let them in…we want…no more trouble."

"Hush, Alan, the doctor told you not to speak," Charlie said, as she came in holding a tray of soup bowls. Everyone will control themselves, right?"

Assorted grunts and "Yes'ms," were heard around the room. She began to distribute the food to those who could feed themselves.

Helen opened the door with a slow creak of its hinges. The pitter-patter on the roof of a newborn rain shower was the only noise accompanying the appearance of three Federal soldiers.

"Mrs. Treager?" At her curt affirmation, he continued, taking off his hat respectfully. "My name is Captain Falkrod. I am with the Twenty-First Connecticut. I am told you are housing wounded Confederates. Is this true?"

Helen stepped aside to open the door wider. "Yes, as you can see, I am. Would you care to come in?"

"Thank you, Ma'am." All three stepped inside, wiping their feet and removing their hats.

The contrast between the well-clothed, well-fed Yankees, and the starving, ragtag Confederates, was startling.

Charlie's stomach rolled over as she thought about the long-term consequences of this one factor. It could spell disaster for the South.

"We need to get your names, and you must surrender any weapons, immediately," the officer said. "You are now prisoners of war." He continued in a firm tone. "I trust you will all honor the goodwill of Mrs. Treager and not use the first opportunity to run."

There was a rumble of unhappiness among the bandaged men lying on the floor and gathered in the doorway. All three Yankees put their hands on their guns.

"The U.S. government would not look kindly upon any citizen who helps a prisoner escape. If it were me, I would not want to bite the hand of the angel who saved my hide."

The barely veiled threat was not lost on the angel in question. Helen's surprise was reflected on her kindly face.

"What will happen to the men, sir?" Charlie managed to ask. Her hands trembled as she passed a bowl of soup to another of the wounded men.

"We will be sending our soldiers out here to check on their progress. As soon as anyone is able to walk, they will be taken to our camp first and then held at St. John's Catholic Church until arrangements can be made for transfer to a permanent Federal prison."

Charlie nodded. She couldn't speak for fear of bursting into tears. At least she knew now where Daniel was being held…and what lay in store for him and all the Confederates left here in Sharpsburg…herself included, if her role as a soldier was revealed.

* * *

Daniel had always been able to roll with the

punches, but this final blow, coming on the heels of the worst kind of hell, was his undoing.

When the Yankees had arrived, just as Lucy was breaking her news, he had been all too willing to be led away from her, her twittering father, all the injured crying out for help, the shell-shocked and hollow-eyed townspeople, and the burden of dealing with them all.

He sat in the dirt with his back against the post of the paddock fence, folded his arms on his raised knees, and allowed his head to fall forward. There, with his face hidden from the other soldiers, he allowed himself silent tears of misery.

Never before, in his twenty-six years of life, had he felt so much pain. It really did seem as though God had left them all to be ruled by the hand of Satan. Wagon after wagon had rolled past, loaded with either dead or injured soldiers from both sides. The noise and the smell alone were enough to send any sane man over the brink. And now his Lucy, gentle-hearted, beautiful Lucy, had piled on the agony, too.

Slowly he clenched his hand into a fist, crumpling the letter he had already read a dozen times. He closed his burning eyes, his face still shielded from view. His betrothed had broken their engagement. The few letters he had received from her before had not held a hint of what she had told him now. The diamond ring felt heavy in his trouser pocket. The damned letter, which still held the scent of her damned perfume, said it all. While Daniel was working so hard to save lives, darling Lucy had grown bored and tired of waiting for him. She had fallen in love with a young banker from Baltimore whom she had met at a summer ball. The banker had won her heart and now she realized she had never really been in love with Daniel after all.

...and so, my dearest Daniel, I came to the heart-wrenching conclusion that I had mistaken the fondness of friends for a love of the heart. Now that I have found true love for Mr. Horatio Appleby, I have no recourse but to dissolve our engagement forthwith. There is still a place in my heart for dear friends such as you, Daniel, so it is my fondest wish we remain so.

Yours,

Lucy

Weary and hungry, as always, Daniel was filthy with human effluents, which had been deposited on him, and heartsick with the magnitude of loss. So he sat wallowing like a pig in self-pity. What else was left anyway? He was a prisoner of war with nothing to do and nowhere to go.

Chapter Eleven

Helen made Charlie eat a large bowl of chicken soup with thick slices of bread after she had finished passing out the food to the men.

"You are just as skinny as these Southern boys, Charlotte. I don't know how any of you managed to march here from Virginia in the first place," Helen said as she fussed around the kitchen. "It amazes me you were able to make them all believe you were a boy." She turned and gave Charlie a long, searching look then clicked her tongue, shaking her gray head. "Men are such foolish things," she muttered, "all this war nonsense...and they can't tell a woman from a boy..." Turning back to the bread she was kneading, the older woman continued to grumble to herself.

"Helen," Charlie interrupted after placing the empty bowl in the sink. She rolled up her sleeves and began to mix the ingredients for another batch of dough. "How long has your husband been gone?"

"Oh, honey, my Peter has been buried for over five years now."

"J-Josh has only been gone for about eight months. How is it I can miss him so badly and yet..." Her voice trailed off to a sigh. She felt guilty, sad, and confused all at once.

"...And yet your find yourself attracted to another man?" Helen asked softly.

"Y-yes." Charlie stopped mixing and stared miserably out the window. From here she could still see the debris and dead horses on the field of battle. Figures in blue, along with the civilian-clothed souvenir hunters scuttled to and fro.

A floured but sturdy hand covered hers. "Because, honey, you are still alive."

Tears that Charlie thought she had run out of long ago began to flow once more.

"Charlotte, I saw the way you looked at that nice young Confederate doctor…and the way he looked at you. It was obvious to me he has feelings for you and you for him."

"But—" Charlie sputtered.

Helen put her hand on Charlie's shoulder and turned the younger woman to face her. Taking the end of her apron, she wiped the tears from the younger woman's cheeks. Leaning into her solid warmth, Charlie wrapped her arms around Helen's waist.

"You are allowed to love again, my dear," Helen soothed, patting Charlie's back and raising little puffs of white flour. "God's greatest gift is our ability to overcome adversity and learn to love once more. God would want it…and your Joshua would want it, too."

"Excuse me, ladies."

They both turned to see Private Rufus Johnson leaning against the door jam, holding his bandaged arm close to his side.

"Corporal Smith is having a right bad time gettin' his breath. Kin y'all come see if'n y'all kin help."

* * *

Charlie ran for the Yankee encampment as fast as her legs would carry her. Frantically looking in the larger makeshift hospitals, she had already tried to find Doctor Riley or any doctor to help Corporal Smith, but to no avail. No one could be found. Rather than waste more time looking around town, she headed off to the place where she knew a doctor could be found — the prisoner-holding area in the middle of the enemy camp.

Down the dirt road, past the place that was now known as the "Bloody Lane," she ran.

None of the U.S. soldiers paid her any mind as they went about their duties or sat around their campfires. Huffing and puffing, she had to stop to ask several times where she might find the Confederate prisoners. It came as no surprise they were being held in an animal paddock on a confiscated farm.

Nearing the corral, she saw him immediately. Daniel sat on the far side of the fenced-in area in the dung-infested dirt with his back against a wooden post. His dark blonde head was cradled in his arms. He didn't move.

"Sir, would I be able to have a word with Captain Reid, please?" she asked the Yankee guard as politely as she could.

The guard, a middle-aged soldier with a pot belly, turned and looked at the twenty or more C.S.A. soldiers scattered around the small paddock.

"Which one of you Rebs is Reid?" he bellowed.

Daniel raised his head. She could see him blink sleepily, trying to focus. He raised a hand.

"Get over here, Reb! This lady wants to talk to you!"

Watching him get slowly to his feet, Charlie could see the change in him immediately. His whole countenance spoke of someone who had lost hope, someone who was suffering. Gone were the proud bearing and the energetic step as he walked slowly to the gate where she waited. When he saw her, a brief smile touched his lips then faded away.

"Hello, Mrs. Garrett." There was no life in his voice…and he was back to calling her Missus Garrett. Her heart plummeted.

"We need you at Helen Treager's house, Doctor Reid." Her words came out in a rush. "There is a man with a chest wound, and he is having a hard time breathing…I am afraid he may die if he doesn't get some help immediately!"

Hearing this, the guard immediately thrust the rifle barrel between them. "This here Reb isn't going any where, Ma'am. This man is a prisoner of war."

"There has been enough bloodshed. If I can help save one man, I intend to try," Daniel declared and started to push past the Yankee.

"Oh, no, you ain't! You're staying right here!" The bigger man gave Daniel a hard shove with the rifle.

Charlie gasped as the surgeon staggered backwards from the blow to his midsection. When he raised his head, the sorrow had been replaced with sheer determination and anger. The guard lowered the rifle to Daniel's chest. With a cry of outrage, Charlie grabbed the man's arm. The shot went wide, narrowly missing another soldier.

Shouts brought more Yankees who ran into the paddock as Daniel put his fists up and began to move through the gate, his eyes fixed on Charlie.

"Daniel! No!" she screamed. "Don't give them a reason to shoot you!"

"Is he bleeding from his mouth?"

"What?"

The Bluecoats advanced but he didn't back away.

"Is the man bleeding from his mouth?"

"No!" Charlie shrieked. Two of the Federals grabbed the captain by his arms and dragged him backwards.

"Here's what you need to do, Charlotte…ugh!" A hard blow hit him in the stomach. "Y-you…have to…" Another blow stole the air from his lungs. Dust boiled around the scuffling soldiers.

"Shut up, Reb!"

With a cry of anger Charlie started to run toward Daniel, only to be jerked off her feet by a beefy arm clamped around her waist, lifting and dragging her back toward the gate. She tried to fight back, hitting the man on solid arms. Getting to the entrance, he dropped her unceremoniously on her rear in the dirt, closed the wooden gate, and faced her down with his gun at the ready.

"You'd best not try it again, Miss, if you want to keep that man in there alive. Won't be no one missin' any Rebs, if he were to disappear tonight," the guard growled.

Fear jolted through her. It was true! Who would even notice or care if Daniel or any of the prisoners didn't survive the night?

Untangling her skirts and scrambling to her feet, she ran to the fence. Daniel lay curled up on his side in the dirt. His face was already swollen and bruised. Blood trickled from a split lip. Landing a last kick to his kidneys, the Yankees turned to leave the paddock.

"You'd best be remembering this…all you Rebs…" the soldier looked around at the other prisoners, "…don't be causing no trouble or this will happen to you!"

"Oh, Daniel!" Charlie sobbed. She watched him raise his head. Spying her, he crawled over the where she stood. Dropping to her knees, she reached through the fence, stretching out her fingers, desperate to touch him.

"Y-you said," he huffed, "the m-man is not bleeding from the mouth?"

Oh, God! She couldn't stand the pain, both physical and emotional, she saw in his blue eyes.

"N-no," she tried to control her sobs. "He is not." Their fingers touched, and he pulled himself closer until he was sitting up, leaning against the fence railing.

"Is h-he bleeding from the wound?"

"Not much." Now she could reach his face and touched her fingers gently to his bruised cheek.

"L-listen to me, Charlotte." He spit blood into the dirt and wiped his mouth on his sleeve.

"I-I'm listening." His fingers closed around her outstretched arm, sending a warm, liquid sensation flowing through her abdomen.

She concentrated on listening to his instructions.

He shook her arm when he finished telling her what she needed to do, still trying to catch his breath. "Go now, quickly. You can do it. You can help him!"

Reluctant to leave him, she got to her feet and looked down at his face, so hopeful and battered as he sat with one hand pressed against his side and the other holding the fence for support.

"Go on," he urged again. "I'll be fine."

"All right. I'll be back when I can." With one last look over her shoulder at the man she now knew she loved, she began to run away from him.

* * *

For the rest of the day, Daniel sat and watched the movement of the Yankees as he nursed his bruised body. He watched a parade of wagons, laden to the bursting point with foodstuffs and medical supplies, come rattling into camp. His belly growled its protest at being empty, while he watched sacks of cornmeal and wheat flour, barrels of pickles, bags of potatoes, and heaps of smoked hams roll past.

The Confederate army was starving and so were the majority of the Southern civilian population of Virginia, thanks largely to the needs of the army ravaging the farmlands. The injustice of it all burned deep inside him. There must be something that could be done to remedy the situation…but what?

Lurching to his feet, he staggered over to the water barrel, dipped his tin cup in and poured the water over his hands. He scrubbed his face with his wet hands, feeling each bruise and swelling. This was just more than he could bear. Not only was he useless as a physician, he could not even act as an officer should.

None of the other prisoners came near him. Not that he could blame them. He was an officer who was supposed to be in charge, but he had not been able to defend himself against the six Yankees when they decided to beat him. It was not the mark of a leader of men. He couldn't get food or water for them, and, unlike the soldiers around him, he was not injured...at least he had not been injured until he was attacked. What must they think about his presence in Sharpsburg, when every other able Confederate had already retreated across the Potomac River?

Going back to the fence, he held his bruised ribs and slowly slid down to sit heavily on the ground. The shadows were lengthening, and a cool autumn breeze blew across his face, bringing the smell of cooking meat with it. His mouth watered, and he shivered. It would be cold tonight.

Two soldiers appeared, bearing a large black pot of pork and beans, a dipper, and several bowls and spoons. The prisoners, gathered in an anxious knot, had to share the eating utensils, but it was a small price to pay for having something solid in your stomach. He waited until the other prisoners, who were all injured in some way, had eaten before he ate a few spoonfuls scraped from the bottom of the pot.

Licking his fingers without shame, he moved back to his previous position. Darkness was complete now, and the temperature was dropping. The greatcoat was long gone, but Daniel still had his uniform jacket. One young man with a bandaged foot, clad in a thin shirt, shivered and shrank into himself as he sat with the others.

Shrugging off his jacket, he removed the captain's bars and slipped them into his trouser pocket. Stiffly getting to his feet, he walked over to the group, holding the jacket over his arm.

"Hello, I am Captain Reid, Daniel Reid, surgeon for

the Twenty-Fifth Virginia."

The men began to slowly get to their feet…apparently to salute him, but he held a hand out to stop them. "No, don't get up. I came to see if anyone has need of a doctor." Hesitantly, each one returned to their positions.

"Uh, not me."

"No, suh, thankee."

They all answered negatively. He nodded and held the jacket out to the shivering young man. "Here, take this, you need it more than I do, Private."

"N-no, sir, I couldn't do that."

Daniel smiled at him, though he knew it was difficult to see anyone's face in the darkness. "Yes, you can. Put this on, and that's an order, son."

"Yes, sir. Thank you, sir," he said, in a voice that sounded suspiciously ragged as he shrugged into the garment.

"You're most welcome."

With a nod to the rest of the men, he turned and went back to his position, knowing they would not appreciate his company for much longer. No self-respecting private in the infantry could relax in the presence of an officer. They would obey him, if he gave an order, but they would not befriend him.

So he had managed to assuage just a little bit of the guilt he felt for sitting around while others suffered with injuries he was powerless to treat.

He wondered how Charlotte had fared treating her soldier with the chest injury. She was such a pretty little thing to be mistaken for a boy—he supposed he should be ashamed of himself for not picking up on that fact months ago. But he wasn't ashamed. The entire Twenty-Fifth had been taken in by her charade.

Memory of the night he had stumbled upon her being abused by another soldier was enough to make him ashamed of the male population in general. Daniel thanked the Lord he had come upon the pair when he did…in time to save Charlotte from a worse fate. With a pang, he realized he had not thought to ask her how she felt when he saw her again. He had been so occupied with trying to save the lives of the soldiers that he never asked her about her injuries. But she had not appeared to be in any pain as she helped him in the barn…of that he was certain. Then she had run all the way from town to get his help for yet another injured man…how amazing Mrs. Garrett was. No, she wanted to be called "Charlie" he reminded himself.

Lucy would have never done half of what that woman had done. His fiancée had fainted dead away at the first sign of blood. Fainted right into his arms, in fact. Why was it he had not felt the appropriate feelings when she was in his arms? Why was annoyance his number one emotion at the time?

Daniel sighed, an action that hurt his bruised ribs. Sadness was reasserting itself. Sorrow at his loss of the perfect future he thought he had with Lucy, sorrow at the loss of so many fellow soldiers' lives and limbs, sorrow that Charlie had lost her own husband, and sorrow at his present situation. Once again he lay down in the dirt, curled up into a ball, and fell asleep dreaming of food, blood, and death.

Chapter Twelve

It started to rain, a cold steady rain, which changed to a downpour. Charlie and Helen went about their morning duties feeding their charges, helping them bathe, changing bandages, and soothing fevered brows. A few of the men were led away at gunpoint to the makeshift prison. The Federals were taking no chances that anyone would escape and visited regularly to count heads and check names.

Corporal Smith was steadily improving, thanks to the treatment Daniel had recommended. It had been very unnerving for Charlie to cut into the man's side and insert the boiled pipe stem into his chest. But it had done what the surgeon said it would do. The blood that had built up inside Alan's chest came out through the pipe, and he was able to breathe easier. Charlie planned to visit Captain Reid today to give him an update on how their patient was doing.

According to the Bluecoats, many of prisoners had been moved into the local church with its solid stone walls. But the Rebel captain was to stay in the horse corral as punishment for his actions.

Hearing the rain on the roof made Charlie anxious to be on her way. The weather had turned colder, and she knew from her last visit that he had given away his jacket. When she had told Helen this, the kind-hearted woman had immediately gone to her attic and come back with a warm woolen coat that had belonged to her late husband.

"Oh, Helen, this is just so kind of you to loan your cloak to me and your husband's coat for Daniel. I don't know how to thank you."

The rain blew against the windowpanes. One of the soldiers hobbled over and put another log on the fire. It was warm and cozy, albeit crowded, in Helen's parlor. The eight soldiers who now remained watched the two women with interest from their positions on the sofa and floor. Charlie sat on a chair, stroked the coarse woolen coat, and stared into the fire. The blanket covering the sleeping Corporal Smith had slipped down, and Helen gently pulled it up over his shoulders.

"We all have a lot to thank you fer, Mrs. Treager," Private Finley piped up. He was lying on the floor with his injured leg propped up on a red velvet sofa pillow.

All of the men, save Corporal Smith, added their thanks. They were grateful to be fed and warm on a day like this…and so was Charlie…but all she could think of was how cold and wet Daniel must be. The thought of him soaking wet, shivering, and being held in an animal paddock drove her crazy.

"I think things are quite in order here, Charlotte, if you would like to go out for a bit. The boys and I can handle things well enough." Helen wrapped an arm around her shoulders and gave her a squeeze. "Doctor Reid could really use the coat in this rotten weather, honey."

"Yes, he really could."

"There are sandwiches and turnovers in the kitchen you can take to him."

"You are so good to me, Helen." She wiped a tear

away. "How will I ever repay you?"

"Oh, honey, you don't have to worry about repaying me. God put us on this earth for a reason, perhaps mine is to help out where I can."

Charlie jumped up, planted a quick kiss on Helen's cheek. "Thank you!" Helen's words echoed in her mind as she ran to get her things, and she wondered what her own purpose on earth was to be.

* * *

Water continually ran down the back of his neck in a cold stream, wetting his already soaked shirt. He couldn't possibly feel much more miserable, but tonight was the night he was going to escape. The time for wallowing in self-pity was done. His engagement to Lucy was a thing of the past.

It was time to go forward with his life and rejoin the army, but there was one problem. Daniel didn't know how he was going to get free of the chains. Lightning flashed across the sky in jagged streaks. He hoped with all his heart the storm would continue into the night and cover his escape.

So he sat with his legs straight out in front of him in the mud, leaning back against the post that was chained to his ankle and tried to form a plan.

"Hey!" he called, trying to make his voice heard over the pounding rain. "Yankee! Can I get something to eat today?"

The guard raised his head momentarily, shouted, "Later!" and went back to ignoring Daniel.

A hunger cramp welled up painfully inside his empty stomach. He sighed and hugged his knees to his chest, trying to ease the cramp. At least the injured men were dry inside the church. Still, he didn't regret his attempt to leave with Charlotte, despite being punished for it now. Being here alone and forgotten would be to his advantage later tonight.

* * *

Ignoring her discomfort, Charlie struggled through rain, making her way to the Yankee encampment at the Pry family's farm. *So slippery and messy!* Watching her footing as she went, she began to notice something strange about the puddles the storm was producing. For many long minutes as she crossed the battered fields where so many men had died, picking her way through broken wheels, abandoned rifles, and assorted debris of battle, she did not realize what the difference was. Then, about to step over yet another puddle, it struck her. It was dark red in color! *Dear Lord! That looks like blood! Could it be the blood of the fallen soldiers leeching up out of the soil?*

With a gasp of horror, she looked around at the flattened corn and trampled terrain. The human bodies had been removed, but the stench from the dead horses still filled the air, despite the rain. So much broken military equipment lay scattered around that it was staggering to think of how the folks of Sharpsburg would be dealing with the aftermath of this battle for a long time to come.

She began to move a little faster now, anxious to reach Daniel and get away from the scene of so much bloodshed. Her boots were covered with the dark red mud, and the hem of the blasted skirt dipped repeatedly in the muck. Trousers would have stayed clear of the mess, but she had promised Clarence she would not go back to her male disguise and intended to keep that promise.

Ahead she could see the big white farmhouse with Yankees coming and going like blue rats scurrying about. Shaking the water from her hooded cloak, she skirted the main house to reach the livestock pen. Charlie could see the lone figure inside sitting slumped against the fence post, and her heart skipped a beat.

Shifting her bundles to one arm, she pushed back her hood and ran her fingers through her dark hair, which hung in a wet mass about her head.

"Hello, sir," she greeted the sentry politely. "Would you like a fresh-baked apple turnover?" Turning back the cloth, she revealed the baked goodies in the basket.

"Why, yes...thank you, Ma'am," the wary soldier replied with surprise.

Reaching into the basket, Charlie put one into the man's outstretched hand. His face lit up like an eager little boy.

"I'll give you two more, if you will let me see your prisoner, sir. I vow I am not going to cause any trouble. He helped with the injured, and I wish to speak to him." She smiled at the man with what she hoped was a flirtatious manner.

The soldier rubbed his whiskered chin with his free hand. His rifle was tucked under one arm, and his other hand was full of the apple turnover. "Ain't nobody told me not to let visitors in." He paused, took a bite of the pastry and chewed thoughtfully. He glanced down at the basket and up at Charlie's smiling face. He broke into a mischievous grin, put the rifle on the campstool and reached into her offered basket. The delicious smell of the baked goodies wafted up faintly in the damp air.

"Sure, honey, you can see him. Can't do no harm, him being chained and all."

She looked sharply at the captain, who was still in the same position. A heavy chain ran from his ankle to the upright post. *Just like animals, that's the way these Yankees treat us.* Although anger surged through her, she smiled at the guard.

The rain had eased to a light mist, but the mud in the paddock was deep and sticky. Charlie had to pull each foot from the muck and place it carefully. Poor Daniel was thoroughly soaked and covered with mud. She was glad for the dry shirt and woolen coat, both wrapped securely in oilcloth and offered the generous Helen silent thanks.

He looked up at her slow approach, surprise registering on his handsome face. The bruises were only slightly faded on his cheek and under his eye. A beard, darker blond than his hair, had grown fuller, easing the gaunt look of him. Slowly, using the fence for support, he got to his feet—manners not forgotten, no matter the circumstances.

"Charlie! What are you doing out in this weather?" He stopped and cleared the hoarseness of his voice.

"I have some food and dry clothing for you."

He smiled at that bit of news. "How wonderful, though I am afraid," he glanced at the sky, "I shall soon be wet all over again."

"Well, Doctor, as you should know, it is bad for your health to be in wet clothing on such a cold day. Here…" She looped the basket over the fence post and pulled out the shirt. "…Put this on."

She watched him fumble, stiff-fingered with the buttons on his own soggy shirt. Those hands had never once been clumsy during surgery, as they appeared to be now. Peeling off the sodden garment, he turned to spread it out on the fence. Her eyes widened when she saw the large purple and blue bruises staining his side—the aftermath of the beating a few days before—but she didn't say a word.

"You'll be pleased to know that Corporal Smith, the man with the chest wound, is much improved thanks to you." Charlie tried to take her eyes off his half-naked torso and failed. Though thinner, he was still as attractive as the day she saw him at the river.

He didn't appear to notice her gaze; he seemed preoccupied as he put on the dry shirt then accepted the coat, fastening it as well. Then he looked at her, smiling just before an odd light came into his clear blue eyes.

Suddenly, all of his stiffness seemed to be gone. He reached out and roughly pulled her to him, spinning her around so her back was against his chest, and clamping his arm roughly around her neck.

Startled, Charlie let out an involuntary scream. He said something in her ear that she didn't comprehend.

"Hey!" The guard was coming toward them. "What are you doing, Reb?"

"Hold it right there," Daniel bellowed, "or I'll break this pretty little lady's neck!"

Break her neck! Now she was angry. To think she had fallen in love with Captain Reid! He had her in a tight vise-like grip, or she would have kicked him so hard he would not be able to straighten up for a week!

"Drop your gun!" he commanded the guard, giving Charlie a pinch in her side where he had slid his arm tightly around her. She squeaked and jumped. "I've got nothing to lose, Yankee. I will not be going to a Federal prison!" he shouted.

"Okay, okay! Don't hurt the lady!" The soldier dropped the rifle and held his hands up in the air.

"Get over here and take off these chains! Now!" Daniel yelled and she jumped again. His hand, concealed under her cloak, had moved up to gently cup her breast. She shot a look at him. His mouth was set in a grim line, and his face was fierce. The captain seemed a stranger now.

"Stop—"she started to say, but he pinched her again, this time on the end of her sensitive nipple. She jerked against him. His rock hard arm didn't move from around her neck.

"Move, Yankee…get these irons off!"

The Bluecoat pulled out the keys and unlocked the padlock holding the chain around Daniel's leg. No other soldiers had arrived, but Charlie knew they would be there soon. A wave of thunder cascaded across the sky.

"Now wrap that around your ankle and lock yourself up," he demanded.

Charlie's heart was pounding so hard she thought it would fly out of her chest. Daniel's unseen left hand softly caressed her right breast again as he watched the guard obey. Was he using this opportunity to fondle her?

"What are you going to do?" she asked shakily.

With his arm around her neck, he slid his hand out of her cloak and took the basket down from the post. Slowly backing away, pulling her with him, they moved away from the anxious guard. "Don't make a noise, soldier, I can snap her neck like a twig!"

"But—" she protested. He cut her words short again, this time by thrusting the basket into her belly.

"Carry this!"

Continuing to pull her by the neck, he backed away. Reaching the rifle, he bent and picked it up, then released her.

"Let's go!" He pushed her toward the gate.

A Union soldier chose that moment to ride up. Spying the gun in Daniel's hand and his comrade chained to the post, he reached for his pistol. The guard in the paddock began to yell.

Charlie, stumbling ahead, saw the Yankee go for his gun. With all her might she swung the basket, hitting the man's arm. The shot went wide.

Oddly, when she turned, Daniel flashed her a brief, but dazzling grin before using the rifle to motion the soldier to dismount. "Off!" he commanded. "Give me your gun!" Hands raised, the man complied.

"Get on, Charlie!" Daniel took his free hand and pushed her rump as she mounted the horse. He leaped up behind her, putting the rifle in the holder and both arms around her to grab the reins all in one fluid motion.

"Go, boy!" he dug his heels into the horse's side. The

animal snorted and took off.

* * *

The next few hours became a blur of weaving and dodging soldiers, obstacles, and bullets. They headed directly away from Antietam Creek toward the Potomac River.

Yankee cavalry pursued them for a while, but Daniel and the horse worked as one to elude the riders. Charlie did the only thing she could do…she held on. The rain made everything slippery, including her hold on the horse's neck. The basket jostled on her arm, and a few of the apple turnovers bounced out despite her best efforts.

They finally reached the river at the same spot where they had come across only a few weeks ago. The Confederates had such high hopes for ending the war with a decisive victory. Everything had changed now.

There had been no time to talk yet, but she planned to give Captain Reid a piece of her mind when she got the chance. How dare he treat her that way? He could have told her he was escaping. She could have helped, been prepared, brought more food and supplies…after all she had been a soldier, too…

They started across, feet dragging in the water as it crept up the horse's belly. Her mind was churning with annoyance at Daniel's actions when they heard a shout from behind them.

"Faster!" she heard him urge the horse.

Zing! Zing!

They were shooting at them! She turned back to see a group of Bluecoats standing on the riverbank with rifles spitting fire, framed by colorful autumn trees behind them.

Daniel pushed her head in front of his shielding body.

"Don't look back!"

Then she heard the sickeningly familiar sound of a bullet striking flesh and heard Daniel grunt. He had been hit!

Chapter Thirteen

The white-hot pain punched into Daniel's left arm, nearly unseating him. With effort, he managed to tighten his legs around the horse and hang on as his arm fell away uselessly.

"Take...the...reins," he gasped to Charlie and was thankful when she complied.

He wrapped his good arm around her, pressing up against her back, trying to make himself as large as possible to shield her. He had dragged her into this for his own selfish reasons and was determined to make sure she got home safely. The bullets continued to whistle past them and land in the water with little explosive fountains all around them.

"Are you all right?" she shouted back to him. They were almost out of range. The shoreline of Virginia... beautiful Virginia...loomed closer.

"No! Keep going...we're almost there!"

They splashed onto shore. Breathing heavily, he turned around and looked back. The Union soldiers were still standing on the riverbank taking shots but making no attempt to pursue them. When he twisted back to urge the horse forward, he found Charlie looking at him anxiously. He shook his head and gritted his teeth, feeling the warm flow of blood down his hand as his arm dangled at his side. The arm would not respond to his attempt to move it...that was not good.

"Keep going. We...need...to put distance between us."

They continued to ride away from the river as fast as the animal could carry them. His arm was on fire, he broke out in a sweat, and his stomach began to roll with nausea. It took everything he had to concentrate on riding as they made their way deeper into the trees.

He listened carefully for any riders behind them and heard nothing but the hard breathing of the horse and himself. Gulping air, it was getting harder and harder not to give into the need to vomit. The bile rose in his throat time and time again, and he swallowed it down.

God, he was tired! The initial rush of energy had passed, and the pain was threatening to take over. Daniel knew he was losing blood at a rate that could not continue. The coat was soaked with it. Time to stop and take care of it while he was still conscious. His head spun and tiny lights kept dancing across his vision.

"Stop…Charlie."

She brought the horse to a stop in a clearing surrounded by sheltering oaks and maples dressed in brilliant yellows and oranges. Carefully, he swung his leg off the horse. A feminine hand gripped his good arm tightly as she attempted to help him dismount. The jostling motion sent new bolts of pain shooting up his arm. As he slid down, his knees buckled, and the ground rose up to meet him. The world turned gray then black.

* * *

Charlie watched in horror as Daniel crumbled to the ground. Dropping the basket and quickly jumping down from the horse, she knelt at his side. His forearm was bent at a strange angle, and blood soaked the sleeve of his coat.

"Daniel! Wake up, Daniel! You have to tell me what to do!" she cried, slapping his cheeks lightly. His eyelids fluttered open. Struggling to sit up, he began to shrug out of the coat.

"Help me."

She could barely hear his words. Quickly she stripped off the coat and helped brace him upright. He looked down at his arm. The sleeve was dark red.

"Tell me what to do!"

"Stop the bleeding," he whispered then leaned to the right and proceeded to be sick.

Holding him tightly with one hand, she reached under her skirt to pull off her petticoat with the other.

"I have this!" She showed him the garment. "What do I do with it?"

Haltingly, he instructed her how to make a tourniquet with a strip of the cloth. Easing him onto his back, she knelt by his left arm and carefully did as requested. The cloth was in place high on his upper arm. His eyes closed briefly, pain tightening his lips into a grim line.

"My arm is broken." Leaning close, she had to put her face right up to his to hear what he was saying. "You are going to have help me to see if the bullet is still in it and then set the bone."

Charlie took a deep breath. She could do this…she could…she had to.

"Rip off the sleeve."

It took some effort, but she managed to rip off the shirtsleeve, jarring his arm in the process. He gritted his teeth, and his face glistened with sweat.

"I'm so sorry," she sniffed. Tears were running down her face. How she hated to hurt him.

"Help me sit up again, Charlie."

Moving to his good side, she assisted him to an upright position.

"I want you to lift up my arm so I can see it."

"But it will hurt you!"

"I have to see how bad it is, and I can't move it myself."

Nodding, she braced him against her shoulder, reached over and grasped his left elbow and forearm. Slowly she raised his arm, watching his hand flop limply while feeling his entire body tense and shudder. He drew in his breath sharply and, leaning against her, explored the bloody wound on his left forearm with his right hand. His shirt was soaked with perspiration, and he was breathing in small gasps.

"I...need to lie down again."

Gently she lowered him to the ground again.

"What do you want me to do?" Charlie wiped her nose on her sleeve and sniffed.

When his breathing regulated again, he answered in a strained voice. "The bullet hit the bone, breaking it, and ricocheted back out again. I need you to help me set the bone." Closing his eyes, he continued, "Charlie, I...need you to find two straight pieces of wood for splints."

Scrambling up from the ground, she began to cast around, looking at the trees. She spied the horse a few yards away contentedly chewing on grass. The basket lay on the ground. Quickly she went to the animal and searched the saddlebags. To her surprise she found some supplies Daniel could use.

It took a few more minutes, but she was able to find two straight branches and quickly stripped the leaves and twigs from the main branches. Picking up the basket, she returned with the items she had gathered.

"How are you feeling?" He looked bad. His face was a ghostly gray and glistened with sweat, but he opened his eyes and managed a brief smile.

"Better, now that you're back."

"I have the two pieces of wood, and look." She held up the rolls of bandages, a tiny bit of soap, a needle, and thread, "this was in the saddlebags."

"Great." He smiled wanly. "Get the rope from the horse."

"What do you need the rope for?"

"To set my arm."

Oh, she did not like the sound of this, but got the rope and knelt beside him once more. His eyes were closed as if he were gathering his strength for what lay ahead. She brushed a lock of dark blond hair from his forehead and put her hand on his cheek. Heavy-lidded blue eyes slowly opened and focused on her. He smiled again, making the corners of his eyes crinkle in a way she knew well. But the smile faded quickly.

With Daniel instructing her, she looped the rope around a tree standing a few feet in front of them. Then she tied to one end to his left wrist and helped him to sit with his feet braced against the tree.

"Give me the other end of the rope," he said, gasping with effort. "Get ready with the splints and the bandages."

Charlie crouched beside him anxiously with the items at the ready. She watched as he began to pull the rope with his good hand. Slowly, gradually, the rope went taut around the tree and his injured arm rose from his lap with the pull of the rope around his wrist. Daniel was panting loudly. The muscles in his neck and shoulder bunched.

His crooked forearm began to slowly, slowly straighten. Daniel screamed. "Now! P-put the splints on now!" His face was twisted with pain, sweat and tears streamed down his face.

Ignoring the sounds of agony, she quickly placed the splints on either side of his forearm. She wrapped it tightly with the bandages, tying his hand and wrist at one end and the crook of his arm at the other end. According to Daniel's instructions, the wound was to be left exposed. They would sew it up after the bone ends had been pulled back into position.. As soon as she nodded that she was finished, he let go of the rope and fell back with his eyes closed, breathing heavily. The bones were in place.

* * *

Daniel was exhausted. Charlie had done a wonderful job helping him set his arm and acting as his other hand while he stitched up the wound with the thread and needle. Then she had carefully cleaned the wound. With any luck, he would not have to lose his arm, thanks to the Union soldier who had been interested in both mending his clothes and getting clean.

Beside him, the campfire his companion had built danced and crackled. His left arm was swathed in bandages and lying on his chest in a sling. The arm throbbed incessantly, but the white-hot searing pain had subsided...that is if he didn't move.

"Daniel," a sweet voice called. He forced his eyes open.

"Charlie, what an angel you are to help me. I think I love you." He had said it to get the anxious look off her face...and it worked, but he wanted her to smile...not look surprised and suspicious.

She knelt and handed him a sandwich. In her other hand she had a cup and placed it beside him.

"Coffee, too," she said, but made no response to his declaration of love. Instead she looked troubled once more.

Neither spoke as they ate. Daniel was fading fast and wanted to eat before he passed out completely. He stole a look at Charlie. She looked pensive and worried. What a cad he was to tell the woman he loved her...she was a widow...she wasn't ready to hear something like that. But was it really just a teasing comment? He wasn't sure; he was just too tired to think.

With effort, he swallowed the last bite, carefully lay back down, and closed his eyes. The events of the past few days caught up to him in a rush, and the world faded away.

* * *

Charlie unsaddled the horse, gathered the rifle, and returned to the campfire to place the things near Daniel, then returned to the animal. The horse turned his head to look at her with big brown eyes and tossed his head, getting the dark forelock out of the way. He pushed his nose into her arm, asking for a scratch. So she complied—rubbing the sleek neck and down his bare back with her hands, having no brush to groom him.

"Good horse. Sorry, I don't have a brush for your coat. You did a good job getting us here." The creature blew the breath between his lips, making them flap loudly. "Why do you horses do that with your lips? Hah, why is the crazy woman talking to a horse?"

Giving him a pat, she tied him securely to a tree then went back to the campsite, reluctant to leave Daniel alone too long.

He groaned in his sleep. Shaking out the horse blanket, she covered him with it gently, making sure she didn't touch the bandaged arm. Then she put more logs on the fire and sat next to him with the rifle and a bit of cloth. She cleaned and oiled the rifle, and then loaded it. It was up to her to be ready for whatever came their way—good or bad.

With a glance around the clearing, she rose and dragged the saddle and rifle near the sleeping man. Settling down, she leaned against the saddle and gently lifted his head into her lap. He didn't awake. Dark circles shadowed his eyes. The past few days had been especially hard on him. What she didn't know was what happened between him and the beautiful woman in the fancy gown. Something had upset him that day, something his fiancée had said to him.

Are they still to be married? If so, what was he doing touching my breast and telling me he loves me…and why did I like it? She pulled her cloak tighter around her against the cold and closed her eyes, keeping one hand on the rifle and the other buried in Daniel's thick hair.

Am I being unfaithful to Josh's memory? How can I still feel as though I am a married woman and have these feelings for this man? Confusion muddled her thoughts, but what could she do? Events had unfolded that were beyond her control and here she was…with Captain Daniel Reid, the regimental surgeon. Part of her still felt like a soldier, part of her still felt like a farmer's wife…and, in actuality, she was neither. Who was she now? Was she still the same Charlotte Garrett she had been for twenty-two years? No…the war had changed her. Its horrors and brutality still jangled in her brain.

Somewhere an owl called, and a breeze rustled the treetops. The fire crackled and popped, giving off the smell of burnt sap.

Images of people danced through her mind—her Mama and Papa, brothers Eric and Scott, Clarence Stoner, the other Augusta country Confederates, and finally, Josh. Josh was so proud and handsome in his new butternut and gray uniform, standing in their bedroom before leaving to join the regiment. He had looked at her then with so much love that a lump rose in her throat even now.

But it didn't take long for the pleasant images to be crowded out by unbidden images of the dead and dying soldiers of the recent battle. The sounds of battle and cries of the wounded resounded in her mind, and she put her hands over her ears to block them out. But they could not be blocked out because they were not real…they were in her mind. She opened her eyes to banish the ghostly sights and sounds.

Nervously trying to peer into the dark night, she saw no one and heard nothing unusual. Daniel, with his head still cradled in her lap, slept on. Charlie was scared…but of what, exactly, she had no idea. She felt so alone and, what was worse, uncharacteristically vulnerable and helpless. Desperately seeking reassurance, she put her hand on the rifle, pulling it closer.

Get hold of yourself, Charlie! You have fought battles and faced cannon fire! How can sitting in the woods of your own home state be frightening? But she knew what the difference was. In battle she had Clarence with her and now… All right, Daniel was there, but only in body. She couldn't wake him up just to talk to her and reassure her…that would be plain foolish. Still…maybe if she moved her legs just a little to prevent cramping…

With a weary sigh, he rolled over. "Oh, my God!" he cried, sitting up and clutching his left arm.

A rush of guilt flooded Charlie's face with hot shame. She did this to him for her own selfish reasons. "I am so sorry, are you all right?"

Obviously in pain, he rocked back and forth, breathing hard and cradling his arm before turning to face her.

"Charlie, I'm sorry for falling asleep in your lap," he murmured. "Lie down. Sleep." Slowly he scooted around until he was next to her. "Come lay beside me…for warmth."

Carefully, Daniel lay down with his injured arm on his belly and the other arm spread wide. He waggled his fingers invitingly, so Charlie snuggled up at his right side, pulling the blanket over them both. Wrapping his good arm around her, he hugged her tightly against him.

The guilt faded quickly in the face of the wonderful feeling of warmth and security that enveloped her. With her head on his shoulder and the rifle within easy reach, she was able to relax for the first time in a long, long time. How right it felt to be here with Daniel...it felt almost too right for a widow who had loved her husband dearly.

* * *

The smell of roasting venison greeted Daniel when he awoke from a fitful sleep. Riding southwest to follow the trail of Lee's army had been extremely hard. Several times he had to stop and get off the horse to give his arm a break from the painful jostling the riding caused. Meaning to lie down under the big oak tree for just a few minutes during one break, he ended up falling asleep.

Squatting by the fire a short distance away, turning the meat on a stick held over the fire, and crying quietly, was his travel companion. Her green eyes were brimming with tears. He watched her sniff then wipe her nose with the hem of her soiled skirt. Charlotte Garrett's face was streaked with travel dirt, her short sable-colored hair was tangled, and her blouse had stains from the butchering of the deer she had killed...in short, she was breathtakingly beautiful. But something wasn't right. Why was she upset?

"What is the matter, Charlie?" he asked quietly as he struggled to his feet and went to her. "Why are you crying?" He crouched down and put a gentle hand on her shoulder.

The meat sizzled in the heat of the flames. The

bravest woman he had ever known looked up at him with liquid eyes. "I think it is done. Do you want s-some?"

"Yes, I'm famished."

Picking up the knife lying beside her in the dirt, she pushed the venison onto a nearby rock, wiped the knife on her skirt, sliced off a chunk, speared it, and offered it to him. "Careful, it is hot."

Leaning over, Daniel blew on the meat before removing it from the knife with his fingers. "You didn't answer me. Why are you crying?"

To his surprise, Charlie plopped backwards onto her bottom, dropped the knife, covered her face with her hands, and began to sob harder.

"Oh, Daniel," she wailed, "I-I killed this beautiful animal!"

He looked down at the piece of meat in his hand and swallowed the saliva filling his mouth. "But…we need to eat." He was confused. Then a thought occurred to him. "I should have been the one to shoot the deer…I am sorry, Charlie. I'm letting you down."

Without raising her face from her hands, she shook her head violently. "N-no, that's not it," she sobbed again. "I-I told myself I would never take another life when I gave up being a soldier." She raised her tear-streaked face now. The sorrow he saw there just about tore his heart out. "And now I-I had to k-kill again."

He put down the meat and moved directly in front of Charlie. Leaning down, he put out his good hand and pulled her to her feet. He wrapped her in a hug, pulling her close against him. She didn't resist or pull away as he thought she might…after all, she barely knew him, and he had taken her away by force. Even through the pain, hunger, and exhaustion, this woman felt so right nestled here in his embrace…better, he realized, than Lucy had ever felt. She melted against his body, and he could feel the warmth of her, despite their winter garments. Lucy had always been as unyielding, perfectly pretty and painted as his sister Nora's dolls had been.

"It is all my fault, I shouldn't have left you to hunt alone. I should have been the one to get us food not you. I am truly sorry, Charlie."

She shook her head again. "N-no, that is only p-part of it." She hesitated then said, "I-it's you."

He started and looked down at her. "Me?"

"Y-yes, you. I shouldn't be with you like this."

"Like what? With me holding you like this?"

"Y-yes," she shuddered but didn't pull out of his embrace.

"Do you want me to stop?"

"N-no."

Now, he was really confused. "Let me get this right. I am the problem. You shouldn't be here with me holding you…but you don't want me to stop?"

He felt her nod against his chest.

"Explain this to me."

She grabbed him by the waist and steered him over to the fire. "Sit," she commanded, pointing at a log. "Eat," she ordered and handed him the piece of meat. "I'll talk."

Then she gracefully moved beside him, daintily spread her skirts, and sat down. "There are two main reasons why you should not be hugging me... One, you are engaged to be married and, two I am...was...a married woman."

He chewed, thought for a moment, and then swallowed, feeling the food pass all the way down to his stomach. His arm was throbbing again, and he had to change the bandages. Then they needed shelter for tonight, and he needed to find the Confederate army. But Charlie was hurting...

"Charlie," he said quietly, "Lucy and I are no longer engaged to be married. She came to tell me she never loved me. She is marrying a banker whom she met at a ball." He bowed his head into his good hand, covering his face for a moment then raised his gaze to meet hers. " —I also know how much you loved your husband," he said. She nodded jerkily but didn't speak. "Joshua died a hero for the Cause. You should be proud of him. You should never forget him and your life with him. It was a time that was precious to you both."

He stopped and shifted uncomfortably. A cold wind blew across his face and scattered sparks from the cook fire. She looked at him expectantly. "But life goes on. If there is anything I have learned from the horrible waste of human life this war has brought, it is that. The sun comes up, the grass will grow, and life goes on. You have your whole life ahead of you. Do you think Josh would expect you to never be touched or comforted...or hugged again?"

"I suppose he would not...no...Josh would not have wanted that." Her voice was stronger now, more confident, more like the woman he had come to know.

His stomach rumbled loudly. "Are you ready to eat now?"

Rising, she cut off two more pieces of meat and returned, handing one to him as she sat next to him again with her hip against his. Even though they both wore heavy over garments, the idea that her body was in contact with his, made him long for more. Even now he could still feel the way her breast fit into his palm.

"Daniel, why did you take me with you?" she asked and bit into the roasted meat. He watched her pink tongue come out and lick a bit of juice from her lips. Involuntarily, he licked his own lips.

He turned to meet her eyes...her beautiful green eyes with those thick dark lashes. They were filled with anxiety as if she were afraid of his answer. How much could he tell her? Could he tell her he had strong feelings for her? Were his feelings real or just a reaction to Lucy's rejection? He looked down at his left hand and tried to move it again. Nothing happened. Not even a twitch.

"What is it? Are you in a lot of pain?"

Her concern for him made his chest feel tight. "I took you with me because I needed a hostage to get out of there."

The anxiety on her face was replaced by disappointment. What did she expect him to say — the truth? That he was attracted to her? That he couldn't bear to leave her there surrounded by the enemy? If he said that, she would expect more from him and deserve more, but he couldn't give it. The future was so uncertain, and now... He looked down at his limp hand. His future was as uncertain as the country's.

* * *

Charlie tightened her arms around his waist and laid her head against Daniel's broad back. She wondered what Helen Treager would think when she didn't return from the Union camp. Would the woman go looking for her? She really hoped Helen would realize that with Daniel Reid she would be safe...not loved perhaps...but safe. After all, she thought bitterly, to him she was just a convenient hostage who happened to be a fellow Confederate.

The dusky purple shadows of late afternoon were lengthening all around them as they traveled. Even with the horse walking, the bouncing was causing Daniel pain. Charlie sat behind him to keep from bumping up against the broken arm, but she knew from the rigid set of his shoulders he was not doing well. He hadn't spoken for almost an hour now.

"There's a light ahead," he said, pointing with his right hand. "Do you see it?"

She looked in the direction he indicated. A small, single light glowed in the distance between the trees. "Yes, shall we see if they will take us in for the night?"

A shudder ran through him. Reaching up, she put a hand on the side of his neck. He was burning up with fever.

"Yes, I don't think we have much choice."

Cold wind blew through the dry leaves overhead, ruffling Charlie's hair. She shivered and pulled the hood of her cloak over her head. The horse snorted his impatience, so Daniel clicked his tongue, and they moved toward the light.

A large white farmhouse loomed ahead, appearing ghostly in the moonlight filtering through the trees. As Charlie peered around his shoulder, she could see the house with its scattered outbuildings and barn. Several shadowy figures could be seen moving furtively around the corner of the barn before they disappeared in the inky blackness.

"Did you see that?"

"Sorry, what?" His voice seemed thick, almost slurred.

"Did you see those people sneaking around and going into the barn?"

"No, I didn't see anyone." She felt him stiffen his spine then roll his head.

As they approached the house, the golden glow of a lantern hanging from the hitching post caught her attention. Perhaps the people who lived here were expecting visitors? Try as she might, she couldn't see anyone moving about. All was still near the barn and the outlying structures.

Stopping the horse by the hitching post, he gave her a hand and helped her down to the ground. Smoothing her cloak and running her fingers through her hair, she tried to make herself presentable. Swinging a leg off the horse, Daniel made it down but staggered away from the horse clutching his broken arm, breathing heavily. She put her arms around his waist to steady him. Together they made their way up the front porch steps and knocked on the door.

"Who's there?" a voice asked from behind the wooden door.

"My name is Captain Daniel Reid from the Twenty-Fifth Virginia Infantry, sir. I wonder if my companion and I might impose upon you for a night's lodging."

"You say you're from the army…our army?"

"That's right," Daniel replied and glanced down at Charlie. She could see his face shining with perspiration in the shadowy light. There was no doubt now, he was ill.

"What are you doing way out here?" The door opened a crack, and the narrow, white-bearded face of a man peeked out. Charlie saw his gaze travel the length of Daniel with his long woolen coat, sling made out of her petticoat, and uniform trousers. Then he looked over at her. She smiled.

"We escaped from the Yankees, sir, and are trying to locate our army. My husband was shot, and we are in need of some help."

Daniel's head snapped down to look at her then suddenly his eyes rolled back, and he started to fall.

"Oh!" The older man gasped. He flung open the door and grabbed Daniel as his legs buckled. "Jacob, come help me. Mother, we have visitors!"

The floorboards creaked loudly, a tall slender man appeared, put Daniel's arm around his shoulder, and the two men half carried him into the house. She followed.

Inside, the house was aglow with soft candlelight in the front room. The transition from cold, dark night to this picture of homey coziness made it feel surreal as she looked around. A fire burned brightly in the grate, and the wonderful scent of coffee filled the air. Colorful rag rugs adorned the highly polished floors. The furniture was simple but adorned with bright blue, purple, and green embroidered pillows. A brass clock ticked loudly on the mantel next to a vase filled with yellow, orange, and red leaves. The room was a cheerful riot of color.

"Father, who do we have out on this cold night?" Charlie turned to greet the speaker, a thin white-haired woman, who bustled into the room. She clucked her tongue at the sight of Daniel as they eased him onto the sofa. "Oh, my!" She turned to Charlie. "What happened to your poor husband, dear? Is he a soldier?"

Holding her hand out, Charlie said, "Hello, I'm Charlotte…Reid, and yes, my husband is a captain in the Confederate army. He was shot while we were escaping from the enemy two days ago."

"I'm Rebecca Gimble, and this is my husband, Thomas, and my son, Jacob."

Charlie hurried to Daniel's side, just as his eyes fluttered open. "I'm so sorry to intrude on you this way, but my husband is ill and in need of shelter for the night."

Thomas turned to his wife. "Mother, we could give them Jacob's room. He can sleep on the sofa."

"Sure, Pa, I can do that," the younger Gimble spoke up, "I would be happy to help a soldier. I wanted to join the army, too, but Mother wouldn't let me." His black eyes shone with excitement as he looked at Daniel with something akin to hero worship.

Daniel struggled to sit up. "No, I wouldn't think of putting anyone out. The sofa would be fine for me."

"Nonsense," Rebecca countered sternly. "Jacob, help the young man to the room. Young lady, you follow me, and I will get you the things you need to see to your husband." She turned to Thomas. "Would you please get these folks some coffee and something to eat? There is some food still left out in the cookhouse. While you are out there, Thomas, you can make sure everything is all right."

"Certainly, my dear." With that, Thomas grabbed his coat from its peg by the door and was gone.

Ten minutes later, Daniel had been helped out of his coat and was already asleep on the large bed in Jacob Gimble's spacious room. On the table stood two steaming cups of coffee, a small loaf of bread and two apples, along with a basin of hot water, several towels, and a roll of cloth for fresh bandages.

Rebeeca, with her hand on the doorknob, watched Charlie shed her cloak. "Tomorrow, when you have both had a chance to rest, we can get you cleaned up as well, Charlotte. Go ahead and take care of your husband tonight. Would you like me to send Jacob to assist you? I imagine you would like to undress the young man to bring his fever down."

Charlie nodded. She felt her throat close and tears gather. "I-I don't know how I can ever thank you for taking us in, Mrs. Gimble." She glanced at the bed. "I know Daniel thanks you, too."

"Don't you worry about a thing, my dear. Taking care of folks is something we Gimbles do very well. I'll send Jacob in. Oh, and if you hear someone walking around later tonight, don't worry…it is just my son. Jacob often has difficulty sleeping and wanders the house during the night." A gentle smile touched her lips. "Good night now."

Yawning widely, Charlie sat on the edge of the bed with the coffee in her hand. It was black, but it was delicious and warmed her all the way down. She was tired of being cold and hungry and tired of sleeping outdoors. Spending time in Helen Treager's house and now this one made her yearn to go home.

She glanced at Daniel. Going home to an empty house, with no Joshua, was going to be hard, but she had had enough of war…except…she was going to lose this man…perhaps forever.

Picking up the bread, she tore off a chunk and ate it slowly. Then she ate another piece and the apple. Oh, it felt so good to have food in her stomach. The venison steaks were long gone, and hunger had returned hours ago.

The gentle knock on the door had her opening it in a flash. Jacob stood outside the door smiling. "Mother sent me to help you take the clothes off the soldier man."

"Yes, yes, he is burning up with fever."

With Jacob's assistance the two of them had Daniel undressed quickly. When they had to move his injured arm, he moaned and opened his eyes. "Charlie," he whispered hoarsely, "Are you all right?"

"Yes, hold still now."

"All done, Missus, your man is naked as the day he were born." The youngest Gimble was grinning widely, a long thatch of brown hair falling in his eyes. He looked at Daniel's belt buckle with the letters, raised letters C.S.A., with reverence as he reluctantly handed the belt to Charlie. "That be a right nice buckle."

She nodded, "Perhaps I can send you one of your own when I get home. Thank you for your help, Jacob." She looked over at the long-limbed form lying on the bed. "I can handle it now." Raising her head, she met the young man's gaze. "I do appreciate the use of your bedroom."

"Shucks, it ain't nothin'. I'd do anythin' to help the soldiers."

The door shut behind Jacob with a gentle click.

Charlie went to the basin and dipped the cloth in the tepid water and began to wash Daniel with slow strokes over his hot skin. His eyes were closed, his body bathed in sweat. She washed his face, smoothing the golden hair from his forehead. The darker blond, week-old beard hid much of his face, but she bent and kissed his warm lips.

It was easy to kiss him with his eyes closed. She wouldn't have to see that he didn't want her to love him. Hurt began to gather around her heart, but she fought it hard. *This is no time for injured feelings…not when he is sick and needs me.*

Slowly the wet cloth moved over his broad shoulders then down to his muscular chest with its sprinkling of golden hair. The hair tapered down to a thin line that disappeared into another golden thatch further down his body. For a long moment, Charlie stared at him, her mind going blank. Finally, she pulled herself back to reality. The man was an officer and a gentleman…she didn't wash him there.

Dipping the cloth back into the basin, she swished it around and squeezed out the excess water. Then she turned her attention to his long, leanly muscled legs, which were flung wide at the moment. Unconsciously she licked her lips, and tiny beads of perspiration broke out on her forehead.

For shame, Charlie! You are enjoying this all together too much! Guilt...that oh, so familiar feeling hit her in the gut, and she stopped washing to step back and stare at the naked man. She had felt guilt in association with Daniel Reid for some time now...guilt, affection, desire, and more guilt. And, how she longed to touch him with her hands not just the wet cloth.

With a sigh of frustration, she moved to the little table and rinsed out the cloth again.

Suddenly, he gripped her arm with his right hand as she was bending over him. She jerked up in surprise. "Charlie, be careful of these people!"

"What? But...why?"

His blue eyes glittered with fever, and he pulled her down closer to him, pressing his fingers deeply into the flesh of her arm. "Something is going on here. I just feel it! Promise me!"

"Okay, I promise, I'll be careful. But these are good people, you don't have to worry."

"I c-can't protect you now. Get the rifle from the horse."

"All right, as soon as I've changed your bandage."

Releasing her, he heaved himself to a sitting position and sat on the side of the bed. "Get the gun now! You have to do this, or I will!"

"No, no, lie down again before you fall. I'll get the gun."

Taking his bare shoulders with both hands, she

gently eased him onto his back again and put a hand on his forehead. She thought he felt a little cooler, but his wild imaginings told a different story. Heavy lids dropped over his eyes again.

Sighing, Charlie pulled the sheet over his nakedness, picked up her cloak and left the bedroom. The idea that these people would hurt them was ludicrous. She clenched her teeth in annoyance at his strange ideas.

No one was about as she stepped into the dark hallway. Keeping her steps as light as possible, she made her way quietly through the house. The lights had all been extinguished, save the fire still burning in the front room. A blanket-wrapped figure lay on the sofa snoring loudly. It had to be young Jacob.

Opening the front door, she was hit with a blast of cold air. She shivered and pulled her cloak closer around her body. The idea of spending this night outdoors was enough to make her cringe.

The horse was not tied to the hitching post, so she assumed he must have been put into the barn. Once again a wave of thankfulness for the kindness of these strangers filled her with warmth.

Remembering the direction to the barn, Charlie moved toward it. The barn was large, but luckily boasted of a few high windows that let in some moonlight—enough to see the outline of the objects inside. As her eyes adjusted she was able to make out the stalls. She went to the first one. It held a small donkey, not the horse. Moving onto the next stall, she peered in...it was a cow. In the third stall, the animal turned around and came over to greet her.

"Hi, there. Glad to see you are keeping warm tonight. I came for the rifle, and I might as well get the saddlebags. Do you know where they are?"

The horse snorted and moved his head up and down as if he were saying, yes, he knew. But she didn't see the items, so she would have to continue searching. It was difficult, groping around in the dark, but she finally located the rifle, saddle, and saddlebags in an empty stall. Throwing the saddlebags over her shoulder, she picked up the rifle and headed for the barn door. A tiny sound caught her attention. She stopped. It might be a cat or, she shuddered, a rat. There…the sound came again.

A small dark shape was slowly creeping down the ladder from the hayloft. As she watched, the shape resolved itself into a tiny dark girl with braids sticking straight out from the sides of her little head. Reaching the bottom rung, the little one hopped down to the ground. The sound she heard was a barely detectable humming coming from the girl.

"Oh, hello, lady," the girl said. She didn't seem surprised or scared to encounter an adult in the wee hours of the night.

Charlie moved closer and crouched down in front of the small black girl. She was dressed in the well-worn garb of a slave. "Hello. Where are you going in the middle of the night?"

Big brown eyes met hers. "I's gotta go piddle. Mamma says I cain't piddle in mah pants no mo' since I's a big girl now."

"Where is your Mama, honey?"

A little finger pointed up the ladder.

175

"Is there anyone else up there?"

She nodded vigorously and held a finger in front of her lips. "Shhh, Mama says I's not supposed ta tell anybody me and her and Papa and brudder are runnin' away." A white smile flashed in her dark face. "Mama says we'uns gonna be free so no massa gonna hit me no mo'." Suddenly she squirmed and crossed her legs. "I gotsta go, pretty lady. Bye." She was gone, out of the door in a flash, disappearing into the inky blackness, leaving the door swinging open on its creaky hinges behind her.

Charlie stood, gathered up her things and followed the tiny girl into the cold night air. No one was there. Slowly, she closed the barn door and searched the dark shadows, trying to catch sight of a fleeting movement or hear a whisper of sound. But all was still; the earth was slumbering deeply on this chilly autumn night. Not even a breeze stirred as she began to walk cautiously toward the house.

So this was what Daniel had picked up on somehow. There was an undercurrent of secrecy in the air at the Gimble house. Smuggling slaves to freedom was illegal. If the Gimbles or the runaway slaves were discovered, there would be hell to pay.

Her family didn't own any slaves, but she knew many wealthier Virginia families did. Some slave owners were cruel to their people, and some were kind. For a long time, slavery had been a hot topic in many area households, but Charlie had paid it little mind. It just didn't affect her everyday life.

Now she was forced once more to consider the issue.

What had the little pixy girl said? "…so no massa gonna hit me no more?" Did slave owners beat tiny, harmless children like her? The idea was a shock. In her world, people were kind to each other… Except… No… That wasn't true. Weren't people killing each other right now in this hideous war?

Her thoughts were in such a jumble. She did believe in states rights for the South and for any state. *But what about slavery? Are the Gimbles doing the right thing by helping these hidden slaves flee their masters? Yes, the master was beating the child. No, the South needs the slaves to survive.*

Charlie nearly groaned aloud at her own indecisiveness. She shook her head. This was no time to be thinking about such issues in the middle of a cold night with an injured, nervous man waiting for her return. What was going on here was none of her business. She just hoped nothing would happen to either family, and everyone would be safe.

Quietly easing the front door open, she stepped back into the house. No one was on the sofa now, and she wondered where Jacob had gone. Tiptoeing down the hall, a board squeaked under her foot, and she froze. Then she heard it, another squeak then another! She turned around and almost screamed aloud. Behind her was the lanky form of the youngest Gimble.

"Shhh, y'all don wanna wake anybody up," he put his finger in front of his lips.

"Right," she whispered. "Well, good night, Jacob."

"Night, Mrs. Reid."

Charlie shivered, shifted the rifle to her other hand

and took a steadying breath. It was time to get back to Daniel.

Chapter Fourteen

As it turned out, Charlie didn't have time to give the runaway slaves another thought that night. She opened the door to see Daniel sitting on the edge of the bed, rocking back and forth holding his injured arm. He looked up as she entered, pain etched on his handsome face. Firelight cast his naked body in a warm, golden light.

"What is it?" She rushed in and dumped her burdens on the brightly colored rag rug.

"Thank goodness you're back," he whispered hoarsely. Taking his hand away, he revealed the bandage on his arm. It was thoroughly soaked with his blood. "I need you to help me stop the bleeding."

An hour later the bleeding was once again under control. His arm was tightly bandaged and stiff in its splint. With a weary sigh, Charlie blew out the lamp. Lord, she was tired. Bending over, she unlaced her boots and pulled them off.

"Are you all right now?" He lay under every blanket she could find. The fever had given way to teeth-chattering chills.

"I h-hate to be a b-bother, but could you lie d-down with me, C-Charlie? I n-need you."

Need me? Just like you needed me to be your hostage? But the feelings of annoyance vanished quickly in the face of her love for the man and his obvious illness. She could no more deny his request than she could stop breathing.

Hmmm, she couldn't get between those clean sheets

with the mud and filth on the bottom of her skirt. So she took it off. The blouse might as well come off too, so she stripped it off and crawled between the blankets in her shift.

He shivered and shook so hard the bed vibrated. So Charlie scooted beside him, pressed the length of her body along his, and wrapped her arms around his shuddering form. She closed her eyes. It felt right, so wonderfully right. *Please forgive me, Josh, I love you and always will…but I love this man, too. God help me, but I do.*

"Shhhh, Daniel. Relax now. Go to sleep," she whispered in his ear as she hugged him tightly, feeling the wonderful textures of the smooth bare skin of his back and the rough coarseness of the hair on his chest. He was harder with more lean muscles than she expected. Josh had been all hard muscle as well, but he was a farmer. This man was a surgeon, he didn't work at heavy labor…and yet…

* * *

Daniel was exhausted. He wondered if a person's heart would stop beating from plain weariness, not to mention the fever, chills, and pain. A severe chill held him fast in its grasp now, causing his teeth to chatter and his body to quiver out of control, sending white-hot pain shooting through his arm. Several times he had tried to move his hand, but nothing happened. The thought that he might be crippled like this for the rest of his life…or even lose his arm…was enough to send additional chills down his spine.

Thank God for Charlotte Garrett! What a remarkable woman she was! He could see the doubt in her face when he insisted she go for the rifle, and yet she did it anyway. She did it for him. The rifle leaned against the side of the bed within easy reach for either one of them.

What she had gone through for him was incredible…and it wasn't over yet.

He tried to relax and let the chills subside, but they wouldn't leave him alone. Charlie tightened her hold on him as if she could stop the draining vibrations running through him from head to toe. She was still dressed in her shift and he wished so much she were naked like he was. Her breasts were pressed up against his bare back, but the illness stole away his body's normal reaction to a situation like this. He had wanted this moment, dreamed of having Charlie in his bed, and now his body wouldn't allow him to be anything but a gentleman. Part of his fevered mind had stored away the fact that Charlie had passed herself off as his wife…that SHE wanted to be in his room. They could be in separate rooms right now as befit an unmarried couple, but they were here together and for that he was grateful.

Finally exhaustion overwhelmed him, and he slept in her arms.

* * *

The fever left him sometime during the night, and the chills finally abated. A more restful slumber took him deeper and deeper. He opened his eyes once to see it was daytime outside the window, but the weariness dragged him back under, with Charlie sleeping peacefully beside him.

Several times the bedroom door opened. Daniel lifted his eyelids to see Mr. Gimble come in, stoke the fire, peer at them huddled under the blankets together, and then leave, closing the door again. He was not able to force a word past his lips to thank Thomas Gimble, then Rebecca Gimble who came in bearing food. He heard her whisper to her husband, "Poor things are just done in. Just let them sleep. It is what they need."

Daniel slept on. Gradually the gray mists of his mind parted and opened the path to horror. Screams and cannon blasts filled the air. Bloody men were everywhere! He had to stop their bleeding, but they kept coming and coming until streams of red ran in torrents over his feet. No matter how hard he tried to stem the tide of blood and ease their pain, nothing he did would help.

"Help me! Stop the bleeding!" he cried, "Dear Jesus, they are dying, so many dying, dying!"

"Hush, Daniel, it's okay now…shhhh," Charlie's voice whispered in his ear, waking him and breaking the dream of misery. Her gentle hands moved up and down his spine massaging. Then she was kneading the muscles in his neck and shoulders. Her hands were soft and strong and very, very soothing. He did relax again and fell into a deep slumber once more.

The sound of trickling water and an occasional slash penetrated his consciousness little by little until he cracked his eyes open, curious to see what was causing it. Darkness had come once more. There, backlight by a roaring fireplace, in a large hip tub, was the woman who was calling herself Mrs. Reid…and she was gloriously naked. His eyes popped open, but he forced himself to stay still and quiet. There was no way on God's green earth he was going to ruin the view he had directly in front of him.

Charlie was bending over, washing her short hair with her eyes closed, humming softly. Her long fingers scrubbed and kneaded through the dark strands, working the soap into lather. She was far too thin, Daniel decided, but still gorgeous. Pale wet skin glistened on her lithe form. He feasted his eyes on the beautiful slope of her back and the curve of her breasts visible above the edge of the battered tub. By now, he was fiercely aroused. He had awakened without any sheets or blankets covering him, probably due to the warmth coming from the fireplace. Unless he moved to cover himself, all she had to do was turn around, and it would be very easy to see the reaction he had to her.

Then she pushed her hair back and tipped her face up to the ceiling. With a cup she dipped water out and poured it slowly over her head. He watched her, fascinated by the way her back arched, causing the slick mounds of her breasts to thrust forward tantalizingly. She opened her eyes and turned in his direction.

The deep emerald green of the eyes meeting his was bewitching…Daniel was instantly under her spell. Slowly, stiffly, he rose from the bed and walked to the tub without taking his eyes off the water nymph before him. She blinked, surprise flashed in her eyes, then her eyelids fell once, and her gaze rose to meet his once more. Peace and serenity filled her face. Gracefully, wordlessly, she rose, with water cascading down every subtle curve and swell. She held a hand out to welcome him, so he stepped into the hot water.

They stood face to face. He touched the softness of her cheeks, running his fingers over her lush, full lips. Her moist pink tongue came out to meet his sensitive fingertips, sending a thrill through his body. His need for her swelled even further.

Briefly, reaching for strength within, he closed his eyes. He felt her kiss his eyelids and cheeks so gently and tenderly, as a wife would do to a husband. But they were not married, he reminded himself. Being in the same room and then the same bed was bad enough…but this…

Shame inflamed his face with a rush. He opened his eyes, ready to step away from her and put an end to this madness. But before he could move, Charlie put both hands around his waist, resting them on his naked hips and held his gaze.

"It does not make any difference if you do not love me in return," she said huskily. "I love you…and…for me…that is enough."

She was telling him the truth. He could see it in her eyes…love was there. Now that he had seen it, he knew he had never seen love in Lucy's eyes…not for him. But did he love this woman standing here so boldly in front of him? She was brave and strong and definitely beautiful. They shared so many of the same values…for home and family. This he had learned in the past few days they had spent together.

He was strongly attracted to Charlie, but was it love? If he said he loved her, would she see it in his eyes? Would it be the truth? How could it be the truth when he was not certain he was even ready to love again?

She waited for his answer. But he knew he didn't

deserve this…he didn't deserve her love. So many men had depended on him, and he let them down…he could not save them. Bowing his head, he let his hands drop to his sides, causing his broken arm to throb. This woman should be married to a man who had two good hands, one who didn't walk around burdened by his failures.

"I-I can't…do this…to you."

Pain flashed across her face, and it speared him in the gut to have been the one to cause it.

"I'm sorry. I lost my head to be here with you like this…for that I am ashamed." He began to turn away. *Leave now before you cause further heartache.*

"A gentleman as always, Daniel," she said quietly. "But that makes me desire you all the more. I lost my husband. I have seen many men die, and our world is falling apart around our ears. What will it matter if we seek a few moments of pleasure in each other's company?"

"But at what price, Charlie? You would be the one to pay…and you already have given so much."

He put his good hand on the edge of the tub, ready to step out.

"No. Don't go." He turned to look at her, and she smiled suddenly, surprising him once more with her resilience. "You stink, Reb. You need a bath. You…need…me."

Putting her hands on his shoulders, she urged him down into the water and he went, propping the splinted arm on the edge of the tub. Moving behind him, she slid down into the water holding him in her arms.

Never before had Daniel had such a wonderful bath

as this! She didn't speak. With agonizing slowness she sponged his skin, lathering it with the homemade soap, then rinsing his shoulders, his chest, abdomen and legs. Closing his eyes, he leaned back against her softness and loved every blessed minute of it.

When she was finished, they sat for a long time in the tub without saying a word. Daniel didn't dare turn around and look at her for fear he would lose his resolve to do no more than this. Her slender arms wound around him from behind. Her left arm rested around his waist and the other draped over his shoulder.

Gently taking her hand in his good one, he raised it to his lips and kissed her water-wrinkled fingertips. Then he moved to her palm and heard her sigh softly in his ear. It was a sound full of longing, sorrow, and despair. Daniel's chest tightened. This woman, who had suffered so much loss already…would he be the cause of more pain for her? The answer whispered itself to him through his own sorrow…yes.

He felt her stirring behind him and leaned forward, allowing her room to stand. But instead of leaving the tub as he expected, she moved around in front of him and lowered herself onto him. Charlie had taken the matter into her own hands, and he was torn between gratitude and guilt. But then she started to move. All thoughts of guilt fled. Faster and faster, up and down she moved. Water splashed and sloshed, hitting the floor. Daniel's hips moved with a rhythm that matched hers until the world disappeared and only the two of them existed.

Chapter Fifteen

The voice came floating out of a dense fog. "Y'all be careful now. I done tol' y'all where to go, right?" Though Thomas Gimble stood on his front porch only a few feet away, Charlie could only see the trio of Gimbles as dark, indistinct shadows.

"Thank you for your generous hospitality, Mr. and Mrs. Gimble," Daniel replied in a voice stronger than it had been in days. "We will be heading to Winchester, you can be sure of that. God bless you all...and you too, Jacob, I thank you again for the use of your room."

"Shoot some Yankees fer me, Captain Reid!" Jacob shouted.

"Hush now, Jacob," Rebecca Gimble admonished. "Goodbye now, Mrs. Reid. May your family be safe and this war over soon."

Daniel reached behind him and patted Charlie on the rump then, picking up the reins, turned the horse away from the barely seen farmhouse.

"May we all find peace soon, Rebecca! Goodbye, goodbye!" She waved but realized they could probably not see her. "Daniel, shouldn't we have stayed until this fog lifted?"

The horse moved through the mists, the sound of its hoofbeats muffled in the thick moist air as it walked at an easy pace, setting up a rhythm for the long trip ahead.

"No, Charlie, I did not want to stay any longer and impose on the family. They had so little food as it was." His voice sounded bitter and angry. "All of Virginia is starving, including the army and us, damn it!"

He was right. Since leaving bountiful Maryland, they had both seen how devastated the farmer's fields and how empty the pig pens and chicken coops seemed. How were her parents doing, Charlie wondered anxiously. Were they going hungry, too? …And her two brothers…were they even alive? She heaved a sigh and settled her arms around his waist, laying her head against his back.

"I don't know what we can do about it…steal food from the Yankees? It is just impossible."

He grunted with a noise that sounded like agreement. They rode on in silence. The trees were ghostly images in the fog swirling around and between each one. A bird called mournfully in the distance. There was no sign the sun was going to come out and burn off the thick stuff any time soon.

The gloom of the day, coupled with Daniel's silence, was beginning to grate on her nerves. So she gathered up her courage to ask, "What will you do when we get to Winchester?"

He was quiet so long she was beginning to think he would simply ignore the question. Then he finally spoke. "Go back to work. I gave my oath to help heal people, and I am not going to stop now. I will recover, and I'll be able to perform surgery again."

Charlie wished she could see his face, but he didn't turn around as he spoke. Apparently there was no thought for her in his plans. What had she expected? That he would marry her as soon as they could and take her to live with him happily ever after? It was the stuff of fairy tales not real life. In this life, cannon balls rained down on soldier's heads and bullets took a woman's dreams away forever in the blink of an eye.

"What about me? What am I going to do?"

"Whatever you want, I imagine. Go home like you promised. That would be best."

Hurt and disappointment flooded her entire body, drowning her with emotion. Not once had Daniel mentioned last evening. When they awoke in the morning, he had acted as if there was nothing between them…as if they were no more than acquaintances. He had avoided her eyes and had not even touched her again until he put his hand out to help her mount.

Squeezing her eyes shut, she willed herself not to cry. Tears were useless things, and she had already cried a river since losing Josh. She would not cry over the impending loss of Daniel Reid, she would not, would not…

* * *

Daniel sat in the tiny room and waited. He eased his arm out of the sling and laid it gingerly on the rickety wooden table. The wounded bones throbbed relentlessly. They had found the Confederate army in Winchester with no problem.

The fog had finally lifted about mid-afternoon, but the tension between them had not eased. They had spoken very little to each other. It had taken all of his energy just to handle the horse with one hand and keep riding.

Upon arrival at the camp, Charlie had tersely informed him she was going to find Clarence Stoner. She left him in the street without a backward glance as she headed toward the masses of tents. He had warned her to be careful and reminded her how men could be. But she only tossed him a withering look and strode away.

Immediately he sought out fellow army surgeon, William Mattingly. He was told his friend was working here, in Lovington Hospital. Daniel trusted William and, more importantly, he knew Will would not cut off his arm before exhausting every possible treatment.

Concentrating as hard as he could on his fingers, Daniel struggled to make them move…even a twitch would be welcome. Nothing happened. His stomach rolled with nausea. It was all he could think about as they rode toward Winchester today. He was doomed to have a crippled hand the rest of his life. His career as a surgeon was over.

Fully realizing he was not being fair to Charlie, he had wanted to make conversation with her, wanted to tell her he cared for her. But, selfish bastard that he was, all he could think about was this damn lifeless hand. Even if he wanted to make her his wife, it was a laughable idea now. Suppose he never regained the use of his hand?

The door opened with a rusty creak, and Doctor Mattingly came in. He wore a long white coat and dark strands of hair stuck out of his head in all directions.

Will's boyish face broke out into a grin at seeing his old friend. He put his hand out and took Daniel's, pumping it heartily, his big brown eyes twinkling happily behind the spectacles.

"So good to see you again, Daniel! So good. Yes, sir,

it is good! I was told you were waiting for me." Will spoke almost as fast as he moved. "Managed to escape them Yankees, huh? I see you paid a price. What's the story? What can I do to help you?"

Quickly moving to the glass-fronted cabinet behind him, Will took out some scissors and a towel then picked up a basin of water. Placing these things on the table, he sat down and began to carefully cut away the stained bandages.

"It's a compound fracture, Will, radius and ulna. Bullet plowed a path, broke both bones, and exited on the same side. They were fairly clean breaks. The shooter was too far away for anything worse."

Daniel stopped talking and clenched his teeth, sweating profusely as Will began to press on the swollen, bruised flesh around the wound.

"Hurts?" Will asked casually.

All he could do was nod and concentrate on not vomiting. Will picked up his limp hand. "Squeeze my hand."

Shaking his head, Daniel managed, "Can't, Will."

Will squeezed his fingertips, watching them pale then pink up again. "Can you feel that?"

"Some."

He squeezed harder. "Now?"

"Yes, barely. All feeling dulls past the break point."

Peering down at the wound, Will examined it closely then turned his head and looked at Daniel over the rim of his glasses. "Good sewing job. One-handed?"

"I had some help."

Nodding, Will washed the wound, poured carbolic

acid on it, placed clean army-issue splints on the forearm, and wrapped it all tightly, speaking as he worked. "You're right. It feels like a clean break that should mend well. The bone ends seem to be aligned fairly well. Good job setting it. The bruising and swelling may be causing some nerve damage. Might be you will regain use of your hand again, but I wouldn't count on it coming back any time soon. No, my friend, you will have to be very patient, I'm afraid. Keep trying to move those fingers, and you might want to try taking some of your own advice…" Will finished and gave Daniel a pat on the shoulder.

"What advice is that?"

"The advice I heard you give to a patient we saw together in Philadelphia."

Daniel shook his head, he could barely focus on what Will was saying, the words "nerve damage" kept ringing in his head.

"Come now, don't you remember telling that boy who lost the ability to walk from a bad fall that he should never give up? You told his mother to keep moving his legs, even though he couldn't move them himself, and maybe someday his legs would remember how to work?"

"Humph, I remember how all the senior physicians laughed when I told her that."

Will put a hand out and shook his good arm. "The boy's mother didn't laugh. You gave her hope. You gave her a way to feel as though she could help her boy. Besides, I think you might just have something there. Why not work the muscles? It makes sense to me. As soon as you can handle the pain, take your other hand and keep moving your left hand and fingers. It will curl into a claw if you don't."

With that, Will took Daniel's hand once more and slowly bent it at the wrist. It was all he could do to keep from screaming as the action pulled at injured muscles and skin. He might not have feeling in his fingertips, but he sure had it at the wound site.

"Painful?" Will asked and allowed the hand to relax once more.

"Yes," he croaked and wiped his sleeve across his perspiring forehead.

"It's your only hope. "

Daniel prayed, with every fiber of his being, that Will was correct.

* * *

Charlie's feet dragged as she walked toward Lovington Hospital. While it had been wonderful to see Clarence, her visit had not gone well. Young Victor Marshall was there when she found the Twenty-Fifth Virginia and Clarence Stoner's tent. It seemed Victor had suffered some kind of mental breakdown after the battle of Sharpsburg. He had taken one good look at Charlie and began to rock back and forth, clutching his arms and shouting, "Charlie Garrett's ghost! Charlie's dead! His ghost is a woman! Charlie's ghost! I'm gonna die now jus' like Oliver. I seen Charlie's ghost!"

She was horrified and tried to tell Victor she was Charlie's sister—what difference did the lie make now—but he clapped his hands over his ears and rocked harder.

"I'm gettin' Vic sent home to his Mama just as soon as I can get somebody to come git him," Clarence said, his eyes filled with sorrow. "Glad as I am to see you is okay, Charlie, you have got to leave now." He looked back at the red-haired boy sitting in the dirt. "I guess there's some that jus' ain't cut out fer fighting."

Once again she had hugged the older man and bid him goodbye, promising to write. Would this be the last time she saw him? What was she to do now…go home? There was no money for food or lodging along the way and she had no horse to ride. If only she could get paid for her soldiering time.

Smoothing her skirts and adjusting her cloak, Charlie lifted her chin and moved determinedly toward the hospital. It was then she saw Daniel coming toward her. He wore a clean gray and butternut uniform, complete with captain's bars under the open wool coat. Oh, how handsome he was with his thick blond hair, broad shoulders, and narrow waist! Though his arm was in a sling, he carried himself with a powerful grace and moved toward her with long-legged strides. His face was an odd combination of relief and concern.

To her surprise, he held his good arm wide and swept her up in a big one-armed hug that lifted her clear off her feet. Suddenly Daniel was showing affection again?

"I'm so glad to see you are all right, Charlie!"

She slipped her arms around his neck and held him tight. Setting her on her feet again, he bent his head and they stood together, foreheads resting against each other's. Whatever the reason for this change, she was not fighting it...just as she no longer fought her feelings for Daniel. She loved him now with an ache that lodged deep in her chest.

Massaging his neck, she could feel the tension in him. "Of course, I am fine. What about you? What did Doctor Mattingly say?"

"I have long road to recovery ahead of me. I will be leaving tomorrow. I am being sent home on medical leave, effective today."

* * *

Anxiety leaped onto her pretty face, and her green eyes clouded with sorrow.

"Will I ever see you again, Daniel?"

Those full rosy lips drew him before he could answer her. He had to taste them. Gently he pressed his lips to hers. She parted her mouth and allowed him in to stroke the silky lining with the tip of his tongue.

"Oh, Charlie," he whispered, "How can I answer what I don't know?"

A horse whinnied and snorted nearby. Soldiers, anxious to reach warmer quarters, bustled all around as they stood in the middle of a cold street in Winchester, Virginia with nothing but the clothing on their backs and a little bit of pay in their pockets.

Daniel reached for her hand. "Come on, sweetheart, let me buy you a decent dinner, or as nice as we can find, and we can talk."

After asking around, they managed to find a tavern that would serve a full meal in these times of deprivation. Darkness was beginning to creep in with purple shadows when they entered the cozy warmth of the eating establishment. Despite the hard times hitting the people of Virginia, every effort was made to make it seem as though nothing had changed. White tablecloths and glowing candles graced every table, and they were greeted at the door by a pleasant, smiling staff.

Helping Charlie off with her cloak, he handed it to the serving girl. Then she had to help him take off his coat when he had trouble doing it with one hand. His embarrassment at being disabled grew when she also had to help him cut his ham into bite-sized pieces.

"I'm sorry, I did not think you would have to do this for me as if I were a child."

She simply grinned at him and slid the plate back in front of him.

"Don't worry about it, I am so thankful to get a nice meal like this I would do a lot more than cut up your meat!" Then she winked at him. *What did she mean by that?* "I would stand on my head and whistle Yankee Doodle, if I had to," she continued.

"Oh." Daniel was disappointed, which disgusted him. Hoping she meant something else was just plain wrong. He was letting his imagination run away with him.

It was wonderful, both to dine like a normal person again and to watch her eat with such enjoyment. Every bite she put in her mouth was carefully chewed with such a look of bliss on her face that he wished he had put it there.

"Charlie, I bought you passage on the stagecoach leaving tomorrow for Staunton with a connecting stage that should take you close to your farm." Her face, so full of hope a second ago, fell. "I'm going home to Maryland."

"You could come home with me to recuperate. I would love to take care of you."

Daniel shook his head. "You mean a lot to me, but I have to go. I have things to take care of at home that I can't do here. Wouldn't you like to see your parents again?" He had to take away the sad look on her face.

"Yes. I would very much. I assume you will be happy to see your own parents as well as your brother and sister."

He smiled at the thought of Nora and Bradford. Both were younger, and he had loved being their big brother. "Mother will be most upset when she sees this." He lifted the broken arm. "I'll get enough coddling to last a lifetime you can be sure of that."

Suddenly Daniel remembered, sweet little Charlie had actually done the job of a soldier for months. "What about your family? Do they know where you are and what you were doing?"

The smile that had brightened her face faded. "No. They think I went to visit my aunt in Florida. They had enough to worry about with Scott and Eric going off to war, not to mention their son-in-law." She stared mournfully into her now-empty plate and spoke without looking at him.

"I don't know if they have learned about Josh. My brothers might be dead as well." Tears shimmered in her eyes, and Daniel's chest tightened painfully. "I suppose it would be a good thing for me to go home." Her voice dropped to almost a whisper.

Standing, he held his hand out to her. "Now, I think it is time to retire."

"But I have no place to go, Daniel…and no money either." Charlie looked up at him with such a look of despair that he wanted to gather her into his arms and kiss it off her face. He grinned at her, delighted he could give her something unexpected.

"Yes, you do. I got a room for you right here."

"You did? How nice." Pushing back her chair, she came to stand beside him, and he could feel her relief. With an expectant smile, she asked, "Will you be staying here also?"

Just then a woman came with their coats and collected the money for the meal. With one hand, Daniel held Charlie's cloak for her while she put it on. Then she helped him get into his coat and pull it carefully over the sling.

How he hated to tell her. He didn't want to be the one with the high morals. He wanted to go to bed with this wonderful woman, make sweet love to her, and tell the world it didn't matter that they were not married. *I have to be strong enough for both of us.* "No. Will has a bed for me at the hospital. I'll be fine." *Damn, my foolish sense of honor.*

* * *

Charlie lay staring at the ceiling. She mentally thanked Daniel for insisting that freshly washed linens were used to make up the bed. Then she cursed him for making her feel the fool for wanting him in her bed.

He is right. I should not even wish to do such an immoral thing…but Lord, help me…I do.

Taking the extra pillow, she hugged it close and closed her eyes. Behind closed eyelids lurked the image of Daniel's naked body next to hers in that tub. *It was torture.* Why couldn't she push out thoughts of the surgeon and remember her own beloved Josh instead? Guilt lay heavy on her chest.

She sighed and tried to concentrate on Josh's memory. What right did she have to love another man...a flesh-and-blood living man? She had no claim on Daniel and would never see him again after he put her on the stagecoach tomorrow. Why wouldn't he stay here with her for one last night? They had already been staying together as husband and wife...and Charlie didn't regret one moment any more than she regretted her time in the army with Josh. Both men held a place in her heart...but one was living, and the other was gone, never to return.

The sorrow and loneliness made her throat ache with unshed tears. She started to whimper just a little, and the next thing she knew, sobs were coming hard and fast. In only a day she would be going home to Mama and Papa and her own little house. That was something to be thankful for, right? But so many brave soldiers, including her husband, were not coming home. That thought made her cry even harder. It was no use. She cried until exhaustion overtook her deep in the night.

A soft, but persistent knocking brought Charlie awake with a start of fear. *Where am I?* She looked around wildly trying to peer through the darkness with a pounding heart. The gentle knocking continued. Oh, yes, now she remembered. She was in a room at the inn.

Pulling the blanket around her and lighting a candle, she made her way to the door.

"Who's there?"

"Daniel."

Joy surged through her. He had come back. She fumbled with the lock and opened the door wide. Her happiness was short lived. The man who stood there in the dark hall was so different from the soldier who left only a few hours ago, that she thought he might be ill. His face, by the dim candlelight, looked haunted, his eyes dark and troubled, and his mouth drawn into a tight, grim line. Gone was the sparkle in those blue eyes that had only recently been rekindled. She reached out for his hand and pulled him into the room.

"What is it, Daniel? Are you all right?"

He walked in and sank into the nearest chair as if he could stand no longer. His head dropped back against the chair and put his good arm over his eyes.

"I am such a coward." His voice was low and filled with despair.

Putting the candle on a table, she knelt beside him, placing a hand on his knee. "No. You are not a coward. You are one of the bravest men I have ever known. What has happened to make you feel this way?"

"Nothing happened to me. That's the problem. I went to the hospital to the bed Will had for me, in the middle of the ward with the most grievously injured soldiers. I tried to sleep, but the moans and cries of the men tore through me in a way I c-cannot explain. I had to help them. So I tried to see if there was anything I could do." Raising his head, he looked at her with eyes full of anguish, the likes of which she had never seen in him before.

"T-the soldier only had half a face, Charlie! He was struggling to b-breathe and could not talk. I have never seen someone alive with such an injury!" He fell silent, struggling to regain control.

Her heart was breaking. She hugged his knees and put her head in his lap, feeling the cold buttons of the coat and rough wool against her face.

"The nursing staff came running in and pulled me away. Will was there and did what he could, but they wouldn't let me stay. I knew that soldier was in serious trouble." A shudder ran through his body, and she held on tighter.

"I-I couldn't stay there and listen to him die! He fought it so hard...I-I could hear him! Like a coward I left."

"There is nothing you or anyone else could have done. You know Doctor Mattingly did everything there was to do," she shook his leg, "you know that!"

He looked at her now, his face full of raw pain. "I have seen men die before, and it has not done that to me. They have died right on my table, and it has never been as bad as what I felt tonight! Something is wrong with me."

"Oh, my darling, there is nothing wrong with you that some rest and time away won't cure." Getting to her feet, she held out her hands to him. "That's all you need. Decent food and rest and you will be yourself again. The war has done this to you. You are a kind, caring man, Daniel Reid. There is only so much suffering a man like you can witness before it affects him."

He rose and she took his cold hand in hers, pulled him to her, and wrapped her arms around him. He laid his head on top of hers.

"I'm so tired," he whispered into her hair.

"I know."

With her help they removed his coat, boots, and uniform. He sat on the side of the bed gloriously naked, and she wanted so much to make him hers. But this was not the time. Gently, she helped him lie down, pulled the blanket over him, and slid in beside him. She wrapped her arms around him as she had done the night before.

The future seemed to stretch out ahead of Charlie with no happiness and no love in sight. Caution and restraint were hardly necessary when the world was coming down around one's ears.

With full knowledge of the risks she was taking, she rolled away and removed her shift. Then she snuggled close to his back, pressing her body along the length of his. Slowly, she moved her hand down his side. His skin was soft and warm with hard muscles just below the surface that drew her touch as if by magic. Her fingers explored along his hip, down his thigh, and then to a place an unmarried woman should not even consider. What difference did it make now? Daniel was here with her for just one more night before she had to give him up forever.

Chapter Sixteen

January 1863
Havre de Grace, MD

The shop's bell tinkled merrily. Inside, the smell of leather was rich and aromatic, mingling with the tobacco scent. This was a man's shop. A place where he could go to buy the best in everything from leather wallets to hand-tooled saddles, not to mention pipe tobacco and cigars of the finest quality. Daniel inhaled the fragrances with appreciation.

"Hello, Dr. Reid, nice to see you again. How are your mother and father these days?"

Smiling, Daniel put his right hand out to greet the shopkeeper. "My parents are well, Mr. Patrick. How are Mrs. Patrick and all the little ones?"

"Fine, fine, thank you for asking, sir." The balding man nodded and took his hand in his strong, beefy fingers. "What can I help you with today, sir? A new saddle for that fine bay of yours?"

"Actually, what I need is something custom-made that calls for an expert touch and discreet handling such as only you can provide."

"That much is true, sir. I take care to give my customers only the best service possible." His amiable features broke into an even wider grin.

"As I thought," Daniel nodded with satisfaction. "Might we step into your back room to discuss this further?"

"Of course, of course." Mr. Patrick stepped over to the door beyond the laden counter and opened it wide, inviting him inside the private sanctuary.

Thirty minutes later, having accomplished his mission, Daniel stepped back out onto the boardwalk of his hometown. A blast of cold wind came whistling down the unpaved Havre de Grace Street, sending a chill down his neck. The wind off the Chesapeake Bay could be quite biting this time of year. He pulled up the collar of his black frock coat. His left hand stayed in his pocket. He had not bothered with a hat, and his freshly shorn blond hair did not ruffle greatly. Mother would box his frozen ears if she knew he had not worn a scarf in this cold.

He smiled at the thought. Even though he was a full-grown man now, she had fussed over him upon his return as if he were a child. Every night she had their cook prepare his favorite meals, over protests from Nora and Brad. If he didn't eat every bite, she would cluck and fuss about how thin he was.

Even Father, with his disapproval of Daniel's enlistment in the C.S.A. hanging between them, was extremely solicitous since he had returned, insisting only the best Baltimore doctors would treat his son's injuries.

Money was no object for the Reid family. Father had done very well in the shipping business. Martin Reid had large warehouses of goods coming down the Susquehanna River to be sold and shipped by train or water to any part of the country…except the South. Lincoln had placed an embargo on goods being sent to any part of Confederacy, which bode ill for the outcome of this war.

As Daniel walked to his next stop, he thought about the bounty the Federal troops had and how little the Confederate troops lived on. Pulling out his left hand, he placed it in his right and began the painful flexing of the wrist and fingers Will had instructed. He found it was better to do these exercises while his mind was at least partially distracted, in this case by walking. The doctors in Baltimore had confirmed the adequate mending of the bones in his forearm and had concurred with Will's diagnosis of nerve damage. They had pronounced the crippling of his left hand as permanent and scoffed when he told them of Will's exercises.

But Daniel believed Will would be proven correct. Already, only two weeks since the splint was removed, he could move his left thumb a tiny amount. Looking down at his hand as he walked toward the residential part of town, he concentrated hard and was rewarded with a slight flutter of his thumb. A burning pain ran from his elbow to his fingertips, but it was worth it.

He stopped as he reached the wrought iron gate, placed his left hand back in his pocket, and took a deep breath. What he was about to do could get him in big trouble, but he felt he had no choice. Lives were at stake, and there was no stopping until he had done everything in his power to help.

* * *

Placing another log on the fire, Charlie shivered. Coming home had been a stressful series of emotional ups and downs. She had been gone for over a year, and so much had changed.

205

Walking over to the window, she pushed aside the lace curtains and looked out. The moon, looming high over the mountains, shone brightly, casting a silvery glow over the acres of resting farmland. The mounded shapes of the haystacks in the fields reminded her of the happy days she and Josh spent playing and kissing in those haystacks at their joint family picnics.

Now Joshua Garrett was gone, buried so far away she could not even visit his grave. Unable to bear living among the constant reminders of him in their own little house, Charlie moved back in with her parents. Thankfully, she had found them both in good health, although, Mama's hair was totally gray now, and Papa had a careworn look about him that never disappeared.

To her surprise, she had come home to find her older brother, Eric, had returned from the war as well. His crutches leaned against the wall beside the fireplace now as he lay on the sofa pulled close to the heat. It wasn't so long ago she had offered to nurse Daniel back to health. Well, she was doing nursing, but it was her brother who needed her help. Between her, Mama, and Papa, they were doing all they could to bring Eric back to a state of health in mind and body.

"Charlie!" It was Eric. She turned from the window and walked over to where he lay. He looked up at her with such a look of anguish on his still boyish face that she wanted to cry.

"What is it, Eric?"

"My leg hurts something awful!"

She turned back the blanket covering his legs. "Do you want me to rub it for you?"

He shook his head violently. "No, it won't help. It hurts down by the ankle."

"You mean your right ankle hurts?" she asked, ready to rub the offending part for him.

"No, my left one." The shock must have been written all over her face. "I know," he said in a low voice. "It isn't even there, and it is killin' me!"

"I'll get you some tea to help relax you and ask Mama if she has any idea of what we can do," she responded cheerfully and whistled a tune as she went in search of her mother. The sick feeling in the pit of her stomach intensified as she headed toward the kitchen. How she wished she could talk to Daniel right now. Perhaps he would know what to do.

Dorothy Ashburn was in the kitchen staring at the rows of jars and sacks of flour stored there.

"Now, Mama, worrying about it won't make them multiply any."

Dorothy sighed. "I know, Charlotte, but I keep trying to think of some way to get more food so we can last through the winter."

"Papa went to town to sell Josh's saddle and his pocket watch, didn't he?"

"Yes, he will be back tomorrow," she paused, "…and I hate that he had to do that. The watch belonged to Josh's granddaddy."

"I know," Charlie answered softly, "but there is no son to give it to, Mama, so it might as well help keep us alive."

"Yes, and we have our guests to think of, too."

"Of course, we won't stop helping them, no matter

what."

"I am glad we agree. I was so afraid you and your brothers would disapprove of what we are doing. When I found that poor young girl, Sissy, hiding in our barn, Paul and I had to help her. It just seemed natural to keep on helping the ones that came after."

Reaching for her mother's chapped hands, Charlie pulled her out of the pantry and shut the door. "Well, we don't disapprove. I want to help as much as I can. I am sure when Scott comes home he will feel the same way."

The look of sadness, always present on Dorothy's face, deepened a little more at the thought of her youngest son still away fighting. "I hope so."

"Right now Eric needs us." Charlie put the teakettle on the wood stove and took some tea out of the tin. "He is having pain in his missing ankle."

"Oh, my! What can we possibly do about that?"

Charlie shrugged. "I haven't any idea, Mama. I was hoping you might know. Has this happened before?"

The gray head shook negatively. "No. Eric was only home for a few days before you arrived." Dorothy tapped a finger on her chin. "One of our latest guests is said to be a great healer. Why don't you go over and talk to her? Maybe she can help. I'll take the tea to Eric and try to distract him while you find out."

"All right, I'll go now."

Charlie put on her dark blue cloak, pulled the hood over her head, and went out the back way. To her right lay the cornfield with its forlorn rows of ragged dead stalks. As she walked, a chill wind blew up suddenly from the north, slapping her face with its cold hand.

Then an unexpected sound nearly made her scream aloud! With her heart pounding and her hand to her mouth, she stared out across the empty field, half expecting to see thousands of soldiers suddenly appear. The noise died down then, and all became still.

It is just your imagination running away with you, Charlotte Elizabeth Garrett!

Then the wind rose in a rush once more, lifting her cloak and flapping it wildly. This time she let out a small cry of fear. That sound again! The restless rustling of wind through the cornstalks bore an eerie resemblance to a sound she had heard many times…the cadence made by thousands of marching feet.

Memories of the cornfields at Antietam Creek and her lost comrades twisted Charlie's insides. Shivering, she pulled the cloak closer her and forced her feet to move faster. The bright moonlight helped her find the small log cabin she and Josh used to call home.

The little house was silent and dark in the pool of pale light. Its windows were barely visible between the overgrown bushes and vines. It looked exactly as Mama and Papa had meant it to look — abandoned.

Going directly to the back door, she knocked three times briskly, waited for a count of three, then knocked three more times and whistled. Slowly, cautiously, the door creaked open an inch. Two wary eyes looked back at her, then the face relaxed, and the door opened enough to allow her entrance.

Nodding, she stepped inside. Huddled together by the glow of the fireplace in the clean and tidy house was a family of eight — all of them escaped slaves.

Chapter Seventeen

Today he was putting his plan in motion for the first of what Daniel hoped would be many profitable trips. He told his family he was going to Baltimore to visit some of the friends from medical school and was planning to stay for a week or more to observe some of the latest medical techniques.

Pulling the sleeve of his new blue uniform jacket, Daniel adjusted the wool garment to cover the leather brace encasing his wrist and hand so it was barely visible.

"How do I look, old boy?" he asked as he mounted. "Like a Yankee captain, I hope?"

The horse snorted and swung his head from side to side.

"No? Well, it will have to do. Time to go." He clicked his tongue, and the two moved away from their hiding place behind his father's riverfront warehouse and headed toward Philadelphia.

As he rode north, he tried to go over the details of his plan and predict all possible outcomes, but thoughts of Charlotte Garrett kept intruding. He wondered how the lovely widow was faring on her farm without her husband. *Does she ever think of me as I think of her?* Even now he could feel her softness against his body when she had responded so sweetly to his embrace.

Many times over the past weeks as he lay abed, with his mother clucking about him, he had only been kept from plunging further into black despair by memories of Charlie. He had heard Mother whispering to Nora when he had stayed in bed day after day. Yes, he had heard her concern for his mental state. Nora had laid the blame at Lucy Masterson's door, believing Daniel's state of mind to be Lucy's doing.

"After all," Nora said, "nothing hurts worse than a broken heart."

Try as they might, Nora, Bradford, and Mother could not lighten the burden of sorrow gripping Daniel's soul. He grieved for the men killed in the Allegheny Mountains. He grieved for the men lost and maimed at Antietam, for the loss of his chosen calling, and for the loss of a woman...a woman who was *not* Lucy Masterson.

But it was Father alone who knew the true way of it. He was the one who had heard Daniel calling out in his nightmares of blood and death. It was Father who had demonstrated a depth of understanding his son had never known before. With his quiet composure and calm demeanor, he had kept the rest of the Reids away and stayed with Daniel, sometimes deep into the night.

Between Martin Reid's stalwart steadiness, the entire family's support, and memories of sweet little Charlie, Daniel had gradually emerged from the depths of his emotional ruin. A flicker of hope began to grow in his wounded heart.

But then something else began to trouble him that he could not shake. While Daniel was living in the lap of luxury with the best care and amenities money could buy, his comrades in the Confederate army were suffering, starving, and dying. The self-sacrifice each soldier was making...and the sacrifice Charlie had made weighed heavily on his mind. Could Daniel Reid just sit back and do nothing while others were giving so selflessly of themselves? The answer was no. Even if he could do nothing medically, he could do something as long as the rest of his body was hale and healthy.

So he rode to the place where he had attended the College of Physicians—the city of Philadelphia—where an uncertain outcome awaited. He was prepared and glad to be able to deal with his demons in the best way he knew…by taking matters into his own hands.

* * *

The snow had started out so prettily that day, with large, white lacey flakes falling gently to the ground. But by the time darkness had fallen, the storm had escalated. The wind threw stinging particles of ice into their faces. It was the perfect night for father and daughter to accomplish their task.

"I don't think we should have any trouble tonight, Papa. No one else will be about." Charlie handed the rifle up to her father sitting on the bench seat of the wagon.

"I quite agree. The best time to move is now. Patrollers were out by the Wilson place just two days ago. We can wait no longer."

She leaned over and handed the bundled sleeping baby into the waiting arms of his mother. Reaching down, she gave Reba a reassuring pat on the shoulder.

"Papa and I have done this several times before. As long as you remain quiet, Reba, no one will open the lid." She deliberately avoided using the term "coffin" since the runaway slaves were already nervous enough. There was no sense reminding her what the woman lay stretched out in, even though it was comfortably lined with quilts and pillows.

"I's not afeared of the slave chasers, Miss Charlotte, and I's not afeared o' this here box." She shuddered despite the brave face she wore. "Yo' is sure y'all aint't gonna jus' fergit us are ye'? I cain't stay here no longer than I has to."

The snow blew in Charlie's face and down her neck as she pulled the thick layer of blankets over mother and child. "We will get this done as quickly as possible, I promise. We should be at your next stop in two hours, three at the most. Remember, if the sleigh stops moving, cover your face with the blanket and lie as still as you can. The paregoric should keep Baby Moses quiet for the trip."

"Yes'm," Reba nodded and shifted the chubby baby against her side more comfortably. "Go ahead an' close the lid. I's ready."

As Charlie eased the lid down, she called out to Reba's husband, "We're going to leave. Peter, are you ready?" A muffled, "Yes'm," told her what she needed to know. The two coffins lay securely side-by-side in the wagon bed. Mother, child, and father were settled as comfortably as possible for the long, cold trip. The wagon wheels had been removed, and the runners were installed.

"It will be quieter to drive in the snow," Paul Ashburn commented cheerfully to his daughter as she climbed up beside him, shaking the snow from her hood.

"That's true, Papa, and we need all the help we can get."

He nodded, picked up the reins in his gnarled hands, and urged the horses forward. The wagon slid forward with a jerk.

* * *

After asking several soldiers for directions to the quartermaster's office, Daniel stood outside and took a deep breath of the frosty winter air. The air smelled of the city, not clean and clear like the open air he was used to. His left hand was casually positioned in his blue uniform's pocket, without the brace. Hopefully, his barely mobile hand would go unnoticed or, at the very least, no one would remark upon it. Even so, he was prepared to explain it as a battle injury that had reduced him to medical supply officer, which was close enough to the truth.

Looking around at his surroundings, he tried to ignore the sweat that trickled down his back. He licked his dry lips. Everywhere he looked there were Yankees. They walked and scurried in every direction. Some were on horseback, some carrying barrels, and most were armed with pistols or rifles with wicked-looking bayonets.

Blend in with them. Just relax and look like you belong. Don't think about being surrounded by the enemy!

There had to be thousands of them here…they seemed more numerous than the ants at the last Reid family picnic.

Just then a soldier approached leading a group of horses. As he watched the man walk closer, Daniel looked over the fat, sleek Union mounts. They were all in much better condition than the majority of the

Confederate horses.

In fact, one of the animals, a bay with a black tail and forelock, looked very much like Galileo, whom Daniel had lost at Antietam.

"Excuse me, Private!" he called when the soldier drew up beside him.

The man stopped and turned. "Yes, sir?" He saluted very properly. With only a moment's hesitation, Daniel returned the salute.

"Where are you going with those animals?" The bay turned to look at Daniel, the black forelock falling over the horse's forehead. It had to be him!

"These are just going to the holding area with all the extra horses."

"You say they are extra?"

"Yessir, we picked up some in Maryland from the Rebs."

The bay pawed the ground restlessly. It was Galileo! He was sure of it now!

"Is there any chance I could trade this one for that bay?" Daniel waved at the brown horse he had ridden from Sharpsburg several months earlier. "It's come up lame."

He turned to the animal, bent and picked up its front leg with his good hand. Shielding the view with his body, he managed to scoop up a rock and wedge it into the horse's shoe. Putting down the hoof, the animal immediately favored that leg.

"See," Daniel said and allowed the soldier to take a look.

"I see, sir. That animal is branded U.S.A, so there

should be no problem making the switch." He handed Galileo's reins to Daniel. "I'll unsaddle that one for you, if you have business to take care of. This one'll be here when you get done."

An hour later, Daniel was on his way out of the brick building with official papers in his hand. Two hours later he was looking at a wagon loaded to the bursting point. Galileo was tied to the back. Daniel couldn't suppress a smile. He had his old friend back.

"Looks like you have everything, sir," the soldier who had loaded the wagon was saying.

Daniel let his shoulders relax and struck a casual attitude, resting his hand on the back of the wagon. "You have done a fine job, Private. Thank you for all of your assistance."

The young, dark-haired man smiled and gave him a crisp salute, which Daniel returned. The soldier had two crooked teeth, which marred his friendly grin. Daniel hoped he would never encounter this particular Yankee in battle—in fact, many of the damn Bluecoats were far too nice for comfort. It would be so much easier to hate them and dehumanize them as evil…but they were just ordinary men.

Hours later, Daniel held the reins tightly between his teeth while he took the leather brace off his left hand and willed his fingers to respond. The left thumb moved stiffly, and he could open and close the whole hand fractionally. It was progress…painful, but progress nonetheless.

With a sigh of frustration, he replaced the leather brace and the gauntlet style gloves, picked up the reins again, and urged the horses on. Traveling at night in the midst of a snowstorm had not been in his plans, but here he was, driving a fully loaded wagon with U.S.A. painted on the side. He was pleased with the way this day had gone. No one questioned his forged requisition papers, and he had effortlessly obtained plenty of morphine, chloroform, quinine, paregoric, laudanum, calomel, and other medical supplies from the unsuspecting Federals, along with several barrels of salt pork for good measure.

Before taking on this adventure, Daniel had practiced ridding his speech of the traces of Virginia drawl he had picked up. His brother, Brad, teased him endlessly about his slower speech patterns, so it had been no great task to make the change.

The progress was slow for the two-horse team in the quickly deepening snow. Daniel considered his options — stop for the night and make camp or continue to Charlie's farm, his first stop with the goods. She would get the food and whatever medical supplies she needed, before he delivered the rest to the surgical corps. He longed so much to see her again. The memory of her beautiful face was burned into his mind…her sorrow at the loss of her husband, her joy at finding Clarence alive, and most of all…the glorious passion on her face for him.

Plodding along, with his thoughts far away from reality, Daniel did not hear the sounds of a disturbance until it had escalated to a high pitch. The team began tossing their heads in their anxiety.

Peering through the falling snow into the darkness, he could not see anything. Then he heard a scream!

"Go!" Slapping the reins, he urged the horses faster

toward the dark shapes he saw on the road ahead.

The next minute he was hauling on the reins and jumping off the wagon seat before the vehicle had come to a complete stop. Through the white curtain he could see the figure of a small woman struggling with a large man.

"Hey! Stop right now!" He plowed through the snow, the pistol in his hand. "Let her go!"

"Take your filthy hands off me!" The woman pushed ineffectively against the man's chest. *That voice…*

"I say again, sir, let the lady go, or you may find yourself on the receiving end of my gun!"

With a vicious kick at her assailant, the woman freed herself just as Daniel neared the duo. The hood fell back from her head and long, dark hair fell free, whipping around her face as she swung her head around.

"Papa, where are you?" she cried in a panic and turned wildly to face him. He found himself looking into the frightened face of Charlotte Garrett!

Chapter Eighteen

"What do you think you're doing?" The man growled at Daniel and leveled the rifle at his midsection. Charlie couldn't believe her eyes! What was Daniel doing here, and where was Papa? "You are interfering with official business, Mister. Hank and me are slave catchers. This woman is helping runaway slaves! She and her partner are under arrest."

Just then, another man came up, dragging Papa through the snow by the arm. "I only got this old one. The blacks got away. We'll have to get the hounds after them."

Daniel stiffened noticeably and cocked his pistol. "You plan to send dogs after human beings?" She heard the incredulity in his voice.

"You a soldier?" her attacker asked then pointed a gloved finger at her. "Just git on back to where you was goin', Soldier Boy. We got this woman here...she's the ringleader."

"Papa and I were just helping a family to safety, that's all."

"Do you know this soldier, Charlotte?" Papa had lost his hat in the melee, and his gray hair was covered with a dusting of white. She didn't get a chance to answer him.

"There is no way you are taking her anywhere." Daniel's voice was low and dangerous, unlike she had ever heard him before. "Forget any ideas you have. We can discuss this reasonably, friend." He lowered the gun and moved closer to Charlie.

The wind howled through the trees. Cold crystals stung her face. Her eyes watered and blurred. She wiped them with her glove and pulled her hood back over her head, shivering. He went to her and enfolded her in a big hug, burying her in the cape of his greatcoat. He felt wonderful! Wrapping her arms around his bulk, she leaned into him, still confused as to why Daniel was here and what was he going to do.

"Sir," Daniel said in a more casual tone now, "it is late and very cold. Is there some kind of agreement we can come to? Why don't we make camp for the night and see what we can work out? The snow is coming too thick and heavy now to travel any further this night."

He was right. The wind was blowing the icy flakes in solid sheets, making it difficult for Charlie to see the others. They were just dark shapes; the only one she could see was Daniel, precious Daniel here in her arms. But she had her father to consider.

"Papa!" She pulled Daniel with her toward the dark shapes trying to find her father. "Are you all right? Can you let him go, please?"

The man holding Paul Ashburn yanked the older man through the snow, closer to the group. "This ain't no good, Billy. I can't see nothing in this mess! What are we gonna do now?"

"I think the soldier might be right, Hank. We won't be doing no riding when I cain't see the hand in front o' mah face. Tie up the old man. That ought to keep the woman from runnin' away."

"No, you can't—"

"Shhh, honey," Daniel pulled her close to him again

putting a finger against her lips, then he bent and kissed her cold cheek. "It will be all right. Trust me."

The two slave catchers took her father, made him sit in the snow, and tied him to a nearby tree. For some reason they seemed to think Daniel was harmless and left him alone. Charlie took blankets from their wagon and, with Daniel's help, erected a crude shelter over where Papa sat.

She snuggled in beside her father and tucked the blankets close around his lean form. *What is Daniel doing with those two men over at his wagon?* She had seen them talking together when she retrieved the blankets from the coffins. *Why is he even out here in this storm?*

The darkness made it impossible to see more than a few feet in front of her. Peter would get Reba and the baby to the next safe house. She knew he would. Before the slave catchers arrived, Papa had been able to give him directions to the house only a mile away.

Charlie yawned. She was exhausted and cold. The events of the night sudden caught up with her, and she began to tremble. Her stomach felt queasy. They had come so close to getting the family captured or killed, not to mention getting themselves killed! Killing the enemy was one thing but getting her father in trouble or letting innocent people be put back into bondage or hurt was something else again.

Papa maneuvered one skinny arm out of the ropes and pulled her close. "Are you all right, Honey? You're shivering." She tried to answer him, but suddenly the world tilted and she felt herself sliding away into a gray void. "Hey, Soldier!" She heard Papa yell from somewhere far away. "My daughter needs some help over here!"

* * *

Damn! Daniel pocketed the bottle of laudanum and took off running through the snow. Mr. Ashburn's call made his heart leap into his throat. Had one of those idiots hurt Charlie?

He slid to his knees in front of father and daughter. Charlie was slumped against her father's side. Her eyes were closed, and her face almost as white as the weather. Putting two fingers against her neck, he counted the beats. A little fast, but strong—she had most likely fainted. This brave person, who had faced down bullets and bayonets, looked as fragile as the woman she was. Sliding his arms under her legs, he lifted her out of the snow. Her father held onto her arm, almost pulling the two of them down.

"Where are you taking her? Who are you anyway?"

"It's okay, sir. I'm Captain Reid. I'm a doctor, a surgeon with the Twenty-Fifth Virginia. I'm taking her to the wagon. I need to get her out of the snow and get her warmed up."

"Charlotte and Joshua were with the Twenty-Fifth!"

"Yes, sir. Don't worry."

With that, he turned and carried his precious burden to the Ashburn's wagon. He had seen the two coffins in the back. It was a pretty clever way to transport slaves. No one would think to look inside a coffin.

"Billy! Open one of those coffins for me!"

To his surprise, the larger, smellier of the two ruffians hurried over and threw open the pine lid, slinging snow into the air. Inside was lined with a beautiful yellow quilt and a fluffy pillow, still indented in the middle from the last occupant. Gently lifting her into the dry box, Daniel released her and brushed new fallen snow from her wet face with a corner of the quilt then pulled it over her.

Billy stood beside him, holding the lantern high, looking at Charlie. "She's one pretty lady, Captain."

"Yes, she is…and you will not touch her, understand?"

"Hey! I'm a married man. Don't go gettin' any wrong ideas! I'm only lookin' fer runaway slaves…that's mah job."

Daniel turned to look at the big man and softened his tone. "How about you and Hank go over to my wagon? I have coffee in a big metal tin. There's some salt pork in those barrels. I'll be glad to share it all with you fellas, if you'll build a fire and cook up the stuff."

A gleam came into Billy's eyes, and he placed the lantern on a box, nodding vigorously. "Good deal, Captain, seeing as we are on the same side, me and Hank can do that."

He wasn't so sure he wanted to be on the same side as those two, but there was nothing to be done about it right now. Spying a leather bag, he picked it up and placed it under Charlie's feet. The wet boots would have to come off. Using his right hand, he managed to get the laces untied and, forcing his uncooperative fingers together, he quickly removed her boots, cursing his lame hand under his breath.

Muttering and rubbing her cold feet to warm them,

he nearly jumped out of his skin when she spoke.

"Daniel," her voice was soft, sleepy…and sexy. "My feet are not the problem. It is my head that is light."

After propping her stockinged feet on the haversack, Daniel scrambled to the head of the coffin. She was struggling to sit up. "No, Charlie, in that you are mistaken. When the blood leaves one's head in a faint, the best way to restore consciousness is to elevate the feet, bringing the blood back where it belongs." With that, he gently pushed her back onto the pillow and leaned over her, shielding her from the quietly falling snow.

"My, sir, how you do turn a woman's head with such talk." She laughed, a sound that filled him with a rush of warmth. Her soft hand reached up and tenderly touched his cheek then moved down to his bristled jaw, tracing along his jawline.

Her green eyes sparkled in the dim light as he bent over her and brushed a dark lock from her forehead. "Are you feeling better now?"

"Yes, will you let me up now?"

"Not just yet, my dear," Daniel lowered his voice and nuzzled her ear. He had to keep the slave catchers from hearing him. "I want you to tell your father what I am going to do when you get a chance, but don't let Hank or Billy overhear you." He felt her nod her head and kiss his cheek. She grabbed his face and pulled him closer for a deeper kiss. Feeling the response of his body, he had to forcibly stop himself from groaning aloud at the sensations she was arousing. *How I have missed you, my love!*

"I would dearly love to continue this, sweetheart, but we have to talk. Here is my plan…"

* * *

The snow finally stopped, and the moonlight cast long confusing shadows amongst the bare winter trees. Charlie longed to have Daniel beside her, but he was lying on the opposite side of the fire with his hat over his eyes and his long legs stretched out toward the campfire. From where she lay, she could just make out something on his left hand. She had not had a chance to talk to him much. He said his arm was healed, and he was bringing supplies to the army, but that was all. But something was wrong with the way he was using that hand…she couldn't quite tell what the problem was in the darkness, but something was definitely wrong. He had been favoring his left and using his right hand for most everything.

Papa snored on beside her, oblivious to the cold and their tenuous circumstances. The slave catchers had untied him, deciding he was too old and frail to take off in the deep snow. She forced her eyes closed. Just because this was the first time she had seen Daniel in two months, and she didn't want to stop looking at him, was no reason to stay awake. Was it? Exhaustion seeped into her bones, but her mind was spinning with so many questions.

The letters U.S.A. were stenciled on the side of the wagon Daniel had been driving and on several of the wooden boxes and barrels stacked inside. Had he stolen the supplies from the enemy? If not, how else had he acquired them?

But the most important question was whether his plan would work. Lifting her lids, she peeked at Daniel again. How attractive he was! The time at home had done him well. The body she felt earlier under his coat was robust and solid and so…masculine. Images of him naked flashed through her imagination. The last time he had been injured and thin but still very attractive…oh, how he must look now!

The fire snapped and popped as the flames hit a pocket of sap. Everyone appeared to be sound asleep. Billy had left his partner to take the first watch, but loud snores came from the direction of the tree where Hank sat with his head slumped down on his chest.

Daniel's right hand came up and pushed his hat off his face. He was smiling — she could see the white of his teeth in the moonlit night. Startled, she watched him get to his feet.

"Charlie!" he called, "Wake your father. It is time to go!"

"Shhhh... They will hear you!" *Oh, Lord!* Her gaze flew to the slave catchers. They didn't move! "What?"

Daniel laughed…quite loudly. Papa sat up and looked around, blinking sleepily.

"Has something happened, Charlotte?"

"I don't know, Papa."

"Don't worry." Daniel laughed again and pulled a small brown bottle out of his pocket. "They won't be waking up any time soon. I gave them a little of this magic potion in their coffee tonight."

"You didn't tell me what you plan to do with them now." Charlie and her father came to stand beside him, looking down at the snoring men. He bent, picked up each one of the patroller's weapons and handed them to Papa.

"They cannot find out where you live. So the only possible course of action is to send you and your father home as fast as possible. I will take our two friends in the opposite direction."

"But when will I see you again?" Impulsively she took his hand in hers and, feeling the stiff leather brace, looked down in surprise. She had forgotten all about the leather he wore. He didn't pull his hand away, just followed her gaze. When he raised his face to hers again, his beautiful blue eyes were filled with pain.

"My arm is healed, but my hand has very little function, Charlie." He spoke quietly. "Despite treatment by the best doctors in the north, I will not be able to go back to my career as a surgeon…at least not yet. Perhaps not ever."

Her heart broke for him and the despair she heard in his voice. Silently, Papa turned away and began to break camp, leaving them alone.

Raising his hand slowly to her mouth, Charlie gently kissed each warm, but lifeless finger, one by one. But then, she felt his thumb move against her lips! She looked at Daniel's face. The sorrow was still there, but a tiny glimmer of hope seemed to lurk in the shadows of his eyes.

"Yes, there is a little improvement. I can move my thumb just a bit and my index finger." His face brightened. "I've been doing the exercises Will recommended, and it has been slow, but I couldn't move any fingers at all until about two weeks ago."

"That's wonderful! Then there is a chance you may eventually regain the use of your hand?"

"A chance. Yes, a chance, but I cannot know for sure…or how long it may take."

Unable to wait a moment longer, she moved closer and wrapped her arms around his waist. He returned the hug, squeezing her tight. His hands moved up and down her back then moved to her hair. "Your hair has grown long." He stoked it slowly, carefully. "It is so beautiful. I like it long."

Taking his good hand, he raised her face and bent his head to hers. His lips touched hers so softly and gently tears sprang to her eyes. "I've missed you, Daniel," she whispered.

"And I, you." He said against her mouth. His tongue ran over her upper lip, then the lower, igniting a fire in her belly that quickly spread through her whole body. A groan seemed to come from deep inside him. He deepened the kiss and pulled her more tightly against him.

Even through the coat and uniform underneath, she could feel the hard wall of muscle. Daniel's good hand moved inside her cloak, up to her breasts and cupped them gently.

With a gasp, Charlie ended the kiss abruptly and looked around. "My father!" she whispered urgently, pushing his hand away.

He grinned boyishly, making his eyes sparkle in the firelight. "I'll be good, truly, I just needed to remember what they felt like…and how nice and round they are."

Papa was still occupied over at the wagon while the slave catchers slept on, still snoring loudly. The wind whistled through the trees, sounding cold and lonely.

"Charlie." Daniel's quiet voice rumbled in her ear. "I need to ask you...what are you doing out here...you and your father...in the middle of the night? Were you helping runaway slaves like they said? Did you hide them in the coffins?"

How would he react when she told him the truth? Would he keep their secret, or did he believe the black people should be kept as property, as slaves? This was a subject she had never discussed with him.

Reaching up a hand, she pulled his head down so she could speak to him without being over heard. "In all truthfulness," she whispered, "yes, Papa and I were assisting our guests to move to their next destination."

"What does that mean? You are speaking in riddles."

"It means, yes. The answer to your question is 'yes.'" His ear was so close to her lips she couldn't help but take a little nibble of his lobe. He chuckled softly and then fell silent.

"Charlie." Daniel's breath created a fog in the cold, crisp air. He faced her, his face serious in the flickering light of the fire. Reaching out with his right hand, he grasped her upper arm and gave her a tiny shake. "You can't do that anymore. It is far too dangerous, and it is illegal. You've seen what can happen. The slave hunters don't treat abolitionists kindly. They don't hesitate to use force, even against women. You and your father are very lucky they didn't hang you on the spot!"

"Shhh," she warned, "you'll wake them up!"

"No chance, they got a good dose of my medicine...you're changing the subject."

"I won't change my mind. These people need our help. When I saw that little slave girl at the Gimble farm, I knew I couldn't turn my back and do nothing anymore. You should have seen her, Daniel. She was so precious and so trusting. She and her family just wanted to be free so she wouldn't be hurt anymore. They deserved to be free. They are people, just like us, and they need my help.

He shook his head, "I understand, but you and your father can't change the Southern way of life. The plantation owners depend on slave labor. Although I can't abide the idea of enslaving other human beings, I can't tolerate the idea that y-you..." His voice broke and he stopped, taking a steadying breath. "That you c-could be in danger."

"What about you? How can you speak of me doing something dangerous and illegal when you have a wagonload full of stolen supplies?"

She saw his eyes narrow. "How did you know they were stolen?"

She stamped her foot in irritation, but she just made a muffled squashing noise in the soft snow. "I am not blind or stupid, Captain Reid. I know a Union mark when I see it."

"That's different!"

"So you say. I say it is the same thing."

Why are we fighting like this, out in the snow in the middle of nowhere when Daniel is going to be leaving again?

"When will I see you again?" she asked once more, then touched his bristled jaw and wrapped her hand around the back of his neck, massaging lightly. The corded muscles of his neck were tight, an indication of the tense situation.

Turning his head back and forth, stretching his neck under her hand, he bent and rested his forehead against hers. They were so close she could hardly focus her eyes on his handsome face.

"I worry about you, Charlie."

"And I about you, Daniel."

He sighed deeply. "Take the food with you. I will take the two men far away and leave them someplace safe. Then I will be taking the medicine and supplies to our Confederate forces. I would like permission to visit with you and your family afterwards, if I may?"

Happiness lifted her spirits—she was going to see him again. "Of course, sir. How long do you think it will take to do what you need to do?"

He chuckled softly. "Charlie, you don't need to call me 'sir' anymore. You are no longer enlisted in the army…I am not your superior officer…I am—"

"—the man I love, Daniel Reid."

She felt him stiffen with surprise but was not sorry she said it.

"Oh, Charlie…you can't love me."

Hurt flooded her senses. Why didn't he love her? That had to be the reason he said that; wasn't it? Dropping her hands, she backed away and turned around so he wouldn't see the hot tears that sprang into her eyes.

"Wait…"

"No, no."

Shaking her head, she stumbled away, desperately heading toward the wagon, the agony of rejection wrapped around her heart. A gloved hand gently grabbed her shoulder, and she stopped short, her boots sliding in the soft snow. With a steadying arm wrapped around her waist, Daniel spun her around to face him. They had moved away from the fire, and his face was shrouded by the darkness.

"You misunderstand me. I have to fight this love I feel for you, and you must do the same. I cannot offer you a life or even the promise of a life together." Pulling her close, he pressed his lips to her forehead, then her cheeks, and her mouth as if he were starving. "No, my sweet, never believe I don't love you...I do." His voice was low and hoarse. "But we can't have a life together...not while the war threatens us all, and I-I cannot do what I was meant to do. I cannot perform surgery with this useless hand of mine." He held the leather-encased hand up and regarded it scornfully. "I cannot be a proper husband to you."

"But I do not care about all of that." Charlie looked up into the familiar face she could barely see. "I love you, and I want to be with you. We are good together. Do you not agree?"

"With all my heart—"

"Excuse me, Captain Reid." Papa gently took her arm and pulled her away. "We must be going before the patrollers awaken. What are you going to do with the men, sir?"

"Don't worry, Mr. Ashburn, when they awaken, they will have forgotten all about what happened here tonight." When he spoke again she could hear the longing in his voice. "Goodbye, Charlie, Mr. Ashburn…I hope we meet again soon."

No more words passed between the two of them as she watched the men transfer barrels of food to the Ashburn sleigh and wrestle the sleeping slave catchers into the Federal wagon. Papa turned the sleigh toward home. Charlie twisted around to watch Daniel ride in the opposite direction, disappearing into the darkness.

The snow began to fall again in small light flakes that swirled and danced like tiny white angels against a backdrop of midnight black. A wolf howled mournfully somewhere off in the distance—a sound that pierced her soul, letting sadness seep in. Daniel was gone again.

* * *

Daniel left the bordello with a smile on his face and a much lighter wagonload. The two slave hunters would have their hands full when they awakened to find themselves in Mama Rose's house surrounded by her girls and no way to pay for their supposed deeds. Mama would keep the two occupied for days working off their debt, or they would experience life behind bars in the local jail.

In return for treating her girls, several of whom had given birth to healthy babies with Daniel's assistance, Mama Rose took custody of the men with an unexpected glee. It turned out the madam was strongly against slavery and was all too happy to help keep the men out of circulation as long as she could.

Mr. Ashburn and Charlie would be able to return to their home unmolested and, hopefully, no one would know what they had done.

He yawned widely. The snow lay pristine and beautiful around him. On the horizon, the sun was just coming up, casting a pink sparkling sheen over the sugary white mounds. The horses' breath steamed in little clouds around their heads as they plodded on, pulling the Federal supply wagon. Galileo, trailing the wagon, snorted and tossed his head, the jingle of his bridle loud in the early morning quiet.

Rubbing his neck with his good hand, Daniel was more than ready to reach the Confederate hospital, turn over his supplies, and then pay a visit to Charlie's home. Mama Rose had fed him generously and supplied him with enough coffee to keep him awake for a few hours after leaving the house.

Flexing the uncooperative hand with the other hand to exercise it, he stared down at his fingers. They did not possess the dexterity to perform delicate surgery, but the hand could still be useful for such things as delivering babies and other less-intensive duties. Perhaps his days in the medical field were not completely over yet.

Occupied with his thoughts and drowsy from lack of sleep, he didn't notice the riders approaching until they were almost upon him. It was a group of Rebel cavalry soldiers, probably heading toward the latest campaign. The Twenty-Fifth had participated in the battle of Fredericksburg without him and were now assigned to Brigadier General John Imboden's command. Daniel would not know what his fate would be until he had reported back to Lovington Hospital.

"Whoa." He drew the team to a stop, allowing the

soldiers to draw near.

"Hello, Captain," the mounted officer greeted him with a salute. "Where are you headed?"

"Lovington, Lieutenant," he replied, returning the salute with a smile.

The soldiers surrounded the wagon, inspecting the contents with interest.

"Why are you alone, if you don't mind my asking, sir?"

"I've been out on medical leave and am returning with supplies."

Daniel stood and pushed open the front of his greatcoat to get his papers.

"HOLD IT! Don't move, Yankee!"

Startled, he raised his head slowly. He was looking down the barrel of two carbines!

"I'm not—"

"Sorry, sir, but your uniform and this wagon says differently."

Chapter Nineteen

Charlie watched Eric struggling down the steps of the front porch on his crutches and forced herself to let him manage by himself. So many young men were coming home from the war disfigured, maimed, or crippled in some way or another…or, like her beloved Josh, not coming home at all.

The March wind blew the snow about in drifts, while leaving the ground bare in other places. Brother and sister were both bundled up, heading for the barn. Eric insisted he could help milk the cows, even if he could do little else to help out. Papa was already out in the barn tending to the animals that remained after most were confiscated by the army. Food, including both cow and goat milk, was a precious commodity in these hard times. The barrels of salt pork Daniel had provided were a welcome addition to the diet of both the family and their periodic guests.

As usual, thoughts of Josh and Daniel came with feelings of sorrow, disappointment, and abandonment, alternating with worry. When they parted, Daniel had said he would come to see her…and now…over a month had passed, and still he had not appeared. Why hadn't he come as promised? Where was he and what had happened to him? She didn't speak of her fears to her brother; he had enough to deal with right now.

One of the crutches slipped on the ice, and Eric wobbled dangerously. Her hand shot out to grab his arm.

"I'm fine, Char, I can do this."

"I know you can, big brother, I just don't want you to have any excuse to get out of milking duty." She yawned widely, putting a hand over her mouth. "If I had to get out of my nice warm bed to do chores, you have got to help, too."

He grunted, concentrating on propelling himself along. The phantom leg continued to give Eric pain, and she found it helped to get his mind off the leg by keeping him busy.

"A new group of guests arrived last night."

Eric glanced at her and went back to watching his foot and crutches in the snow. "How many?"

"Only five this time."

"A family?"

"Not this time. This is a group of unrelated people— three men and two women. None are married to each other…or so they say. But they are all from the same plantation. They don't want to be split up."

"We'll make the trip together, you and me, Char. Papa's got a considerable bad cough. Those late night trips are hard on him in this weather."

Charlie opened the weathered barn door and held it for Eric to pass through into the warm, fragrant interior, then followed him inside. "If you think you are ready."

He chuckled. "Just make sure all I have to do is drive the wagon. No running around for me."

Immediately she began to imagine all sorts of situations where they might have to get out of the wagon and run. Thinking about the night they met up with Daniel had Charlie reconsidering. Perhaps Eric shouldn't be coming along on the next trip. If Papa shouldn't go, perhaps the guests could stay a while longer or she would take them alone.

* * *

As the Confederate guards escorted him into the overheated, stuffy room, Daniel looked around to see some familiar faces. John Dunn was the first one he saw. His bearded face was pinched with anxiety and sadness, a look that was mirrored on young Joseph Hill's face as well. All of the soldiers assembled were as clean and polished as they could get. He knew, without being told, that he was on trial here and now for his military career or, perhaps, for his life.

Being thought a traitor or a spy in times of war was no small matter.

He stiffened his back, yanked on the blue uniform jacket to straighten it and attempted to compose his thoughts and control his emotions. All it took was one look at the calm, relaxed demeanor of Will Mattingly, resplendent in a brand new gray uniform, and Daniel felt his confidence flow back. He had friends here, and they would help him the best they could, of that he had no doubt.

A soldier opened the squeaky gate of the pot-bellied stove in the middle of the room and fed another log into the waiting red-hot coals. At first it was a welcome heat, coming from the cold dampness of the tobacco warehouse. But, within minutes of arriving, Daniel was sweating under the blue wool.

Five hours later, he almost lost his voice from speaking so long in the smoky room, but he was not going to be found guilty. Only his impeccable record and his friends' testimony gave a kernel of doubt to the idea Daniel Reid was a traitor or a spy. Lieutenant Colonel Breckenridge heard his story. Despite the damning blue uniform, the commander decided he would remain a captain in the Confederate army, but he would be sent to the front line. There, under battle conditions, he would put his medical skills to the best use, and there would be no chance he could be involved in any kind of espionage.

Assuming Daniel had indeed smuggled the drugs and supplies from the Yankee supply depot, Breckenridge expressed the gratitude of C.S.A. for his efforts but issued a stern warning to be smarter and more careful in the future or face severe consequences.

"I believe that Captain Reid's record speaks for itself. Along with testimony from Captain Mattingly and the element of doubt in this matter of smuggling supplies, I do believe this subject is closed...my judgment stands." Breckenridge stood, walked over to Daniel, and reached across the table to shake his hand. "Good luck, son."

John and Joseph came up to Daniel, their relief evident as they clapped him on the back, welcoming him back to the Twenty-Fifth. He looked at Will, sitting beside him at the table. A broad, smug smile spread across his friend's boyish features as he nodded. Will was as pleased as a cat with his saucer of milk. Daniel couldn't help but smile in return.

Chapter Twenty

May 1863
Chancellorsville, Virginia

The bloodcurdling Rebel yell shattered the early spring evening. White-tailed deer, leaping gracefully over logs and bushes, fled for their lives in front of the attacking horde. The blurred gray forms of rabbits streaked past the larger animals, followed closely by a frightened family of sleek red foxes. With awe, Daniel watched his comrades heading toward the unsuspecting Federals hiding behind their breastworks on the Plank Road. Nothing was going to slow or stop these men, short of death. Their clothes and their very skin caught and ripped in the underbrush as they rushed headlong towards the enemy, bayonets ready.

Reaching for the pistol at his side, he drew it out without taking his eyes from the charge. Within moments, the air was filled with the sound of metal clashing, the rattle of gunfire, and the panicked screams of the horses. For a few minutes he wished he had become a fighting soldier rather than a medical officer. Hot blood rushed through his body. He was ready to join the fight. *Kill those damned invaders; kill Hooker and his Yankees!*

Before he knew it, his feet were moving forward. Then suddenly, his foot caught. He fell to his knees in the soft layer of fallen leaves. Turning, he looked back, angry at his clumsiness and anxious to join his fellow soldiers.

Lying on its side behind him was his surgeon's field companion kit. Realization and disappointment hit him like a physical blow. *I cannot fight with the lads! They need someone to patch them up and help keep them alive…and I am thus appointed. I gave my oath to this cause, and I will honor that oath.*

Daniel scrambled to his feet, sheathed his weapon, picked up the leather case, and headed quickly toward the place where the charge had begun. Men were already falling injured or dead. He could see them going down.

Normally, he would have stayed behind in the field hospital to care for the wounded, but today was different. General Jackson wanted to drive the enemy before him in a relentless push to the east, take the high ground at Taylor's farm, then keep them going down the Plank Road, eventually trapping Hooker's army with his forces to the right, left, and north.

As the men rolled over the Union soldiers, Daniel, Joseph Hill, and the litter-bearers would come behind them to pick up the pieces of the army. The distance over which the battle was spread made the presence of a field surgeon out among the men a necessity. A man could easily bleed to death before making it back to the hospital tent. Daniel and Will had discussed this at some length with the other surgeons who had assembled for the battle, and it was decided that Daniel was the best candidate for the job. His hand had not recovered enough mobility to allow him to do the more delicate task of surgery, but he had the knowledge needed to save lives out on the field.

Joseph was waiting at the hospital tent with a

knapsack full of bandage rolls and morphine. The morphine was among the pilfered Federal supplies Daniel had obtained a few months ago.

"Joseph, stick with me, and we can work quickly on the men that have a chance of surviving."

"Yes sir, Captain Reid. I would prefer to work together as well." Daniel could see the fear in the young man's face. "Don't worry. By the time we get to these men, the fighting will have moved on. Just keep your head down and listen for incoming artillery rounds."

Joseph's eyes widened. "Aren't you afraid?"

"Of course," he replied, "but the way I see it, when God wants to take you home, you will be going regardless of how or why."

"I guess so," Joseph said slowly.

"Time to join our comrades, son."

* * *

Spring planting time had arrived in Augusta County, Virginia, bringing with it long hours of hard work for the Ashburn family. Charlie and Dorothy walked behind the plow, dropping corn kernels in the rows and pushing the damp soil over the precious seeds.

Paul Ashburn walked behind the plow with a vigor Charlie had not seen in him since she returned from the army. The winter had been hard, but they had come through it with a few scars and still intact as a family.

A letter had come from Scott a month ago. Despite several near misses, Scott had survived the battles of Second Bull Run, Harper's Ferry, Sabine Pass, and Fredericksburg unhurt. He didn't speak of food shortages or worn shoes—the things Charlie knew plagued the Confederate forces. Scott spoke of the victories in battle and of his friends in the regiment. The upbeat tone of the letter, along with Eric's progress on his new wooden leg, and their continued success with all of their guests, had been a wonderful tonic for her parents.

She wished she felt as happy. It had taken a month, but a note finally had come from Daniel. He apologized, saying he would be unable to keep his promise of a visit, explaining that he had been sent back to active duty with the Twenty-Fifth. In his elegant handwriting, he said he would write her a longer letter when he could…but that letter had never come, and there had been no word of his whereabouts since.

The next day, Papa decided they would go into town to purchase supplies. Charlie asked around to see if anyone knew anything about the Twenty-Fifth Virginia Infantry. The tavern owner heard the regiment had gone to meet Hooker's troops. He didn't know any more than that.

"Thank you for telling me, Mr. Tucker." Her heart sank. *Daniel could be right in the thick of a major battle.* Fear for him and for Scott made her chest tighten. Charlie turned to leave.

"O' course, Mrs. Garrett. By the way, have y'all heard about the bleeding liberal hearts round here what are helping the blacks escape? Despicable, if y'all ask me…helpin' those people run away from folks who spent their hard-earned money jus' to get a little help runnin' their plantations."

She stopped and turned back, keeping her emotions in check. "Uh, no, I hadn't heard, sir."

"Well, don't you worry, Missus. Those breakin' the law are gonna be caught and strung up…y'all just wait and see."

"Um, I suppose so, Mr. Tucker…how?"

His beady little eyes widened with surprise at her question. "Why, the Home Guard is helping the slave catchers by going from house to house lookin' for any escaped blacks. Didn't y'all hear about that, neither?"

"No. Will they be coming out to our place do you think?"

A beefy hand came up to scratch his whiskered double chin thoughtfully. "Dunno. I suppose they'll go to everybody's house."

"Hmmm. Well, thank you again, sir." *Stay calm. Walk away normally, Charlie.* Casually, she walked across the floor, pushed open the tavern door and walked out into the sunshine with her heart pounding wildly in her chest. *Now what?*

* * *

"Don't give up on me, soldier!" Daniel yelled above the thudding of cannon fire. "You have to fight…you can survive this!"

The young soldier didn't seem to hear him. His brown eyes slowly glazed over as the shock of blood loss began to affect him. Yanking the strip of cloth tightly around the thigh, Daniel sprinkled carbolic over the wound and continued to wrap bandages until the leg was encased from crotch to foot.

"Joseph, get a litter for this one as soon as possible."

"I can't get him to drink, sir." Joseph knelt at the soldier's head, trying to force water laced with laudanum down the man's throat.

"Never mind. See if you can find someone to help you get him back to the hospital." Daniel stopped talking to cough as the smoke from the battle continued to drift into his lungs. Clearing his throat, he said, "I'm moving on to the next patient, Joseph. Do what you can to get some help."

"There are so many!"

Moans and cries for help were barely audible over another barrage of artillery fire.

"Just go!" He screamed then regretted it immediately as Joseph blinked, startled at his harshness, and wheeled away to carry out the order.

Just as the battle of Antietam overwhelmed and unnerved him, so did the amount of dead and dying men and horses lying in groups or alone out on the open fields and road. The carnage was incredible. Yankees and Confederates alike had been mowed down by canister shot and rifle fire.

As Daniel continued, he saw that a group of cavalrymen had been caught in a deadly volley, taking down close to thirty men and eighty horses in this fifty-yard stretch of road…and the majority of the casualties wore blue coats. The dilemma rose up in his throat again, and he choked on it…should he stop and try to save the life of his enemy when his own army was trying just as hard to kill them? Their pitiful cries for help in the aftermath of destruction here tore at his soul. *Wasn't it the duty of a doctor to save lives…all lives?*

But they were the enemy, the Northern Aggressors, the ones who had killed Charlie's husband and so many other Rebels. Steeling himself to look for Confederate soldiers only, Daniel reluctantly moved on until a tugging at his trouser hem halted him in midstep. Looking down, he met a Yankee drummer boy's pleading gaze, the freckles standing out in sharp contrast to his frightened pale face. "Can you help me, sir? Please?" The lad was lying under the body of a Federal, still clutching his drum strap tightly in his hand.

"H-he was trying to protect m-me." Tears streaked the boy's face.

Daniel's resolve shattered in an instant. Quickly pulling the body off, he knelt beside the boy. The small hand clutched at his arm desperately. "It hurts bad!"

"I know it does, son. I have something that will help." Taking the bottle out of his kit, he poured a small amount in a cup and added water from his canteen. "Here, drink this. It will help with the pain." A pair of skeptical blue eyes with lush blond lashes met his gaze. He smiled. "Don't worry. I am not going to poison you. I'm a doctor."

"But you're the enemy…and you talk funny."

A shadow of pain crossed Daniel's heart. This war was making children distrustful and stealing their innocence. Sending a ten-year old onto a battlefield to beat a drum was despicable.

"I do solemnly swear," Daniel made a crossing motion over his heart, "that I, Doctor Daniel Reid, will do nothing to harm…what is your name?"

"Gregory…Greg."

"…Will do nothing to harm Greg, so help me, God."

"Okay, then…I…guess…it will be…all right."

Daniel tipped the cup to the boy's lips. He gulped the liquid quickly and made a face.

"You didn't tell me it tasted so bad!"

"Sorry, you wouldn't have taken it if you'd known."

Daniel inspected the injury to the drummer boy's leg. It was a fairly deep gash but would heal. He breathed a sigh of relief—no amputation was needed. Looking at Greg's face, he saw the boy's eyelids getting heavy. Cutting away the boy's trousers, he opened his kit and, after flexing his left hand to loosen the muscles, quickly cleansed and sewed the wound. Then he wrapped the leg with clean bandages, packed up his supplies, and slung the strap over his shoulder. Bending down, he lifted the little blond-haired boy into his arms and began to jog in the direction of the house he saw in the distance.

* * *

A loud, demanding knocking at the front door startled Charlie as she placed a bowl of mashed potatoes in front of Eric. She jerked, nearly upsetting the bowl. Her brother's hand snaked out, setting the bowl right again.

"Papa's gone to answer the door, Sis." He looked up into her face. "You're more skitterish than a new-broke colt. Whatever is the problem?"

Three men dressed in Confederate gray uniforms stomped into the dining room on heavy feet followed by Papa, whose worried frown drew his silvery eyebrows together.

"That would be the problem," Charlie whispered.

"What is it you want, gentlemen?" Dorothy asked as

she smoothed her skirt and sat. "As you can see, we are about to have our meal."

"We are the Home Guard, Ma'am, and we have pledged to look out for the interests of the brave soldiers of Augusta County."

"I assume that includes my brother." Charlie moved behind Eric's chair and gripped his shoulder. "So why are you here in our house?"

The gray-bearded leader of the group stepped forward, removing his hat. "Mrs. Garrett, first, let me offer my sympathies on the loss of your husband."

Charlie nodded.

"Cut the malarkey, Joe!" his beefy companion growled, stepped around Joe, and planted both hands on the table. He glared at the family. "We have it on damn good authority you been harboring runaways here."

"Who has run away?" Dorothy asked mildly.

"The slaves that's who, you stupid old lady!"

Eric shot to his feet, holding the table for support. "Watch how you speak to my mother!"

"Whadda you gonna do about it, cripple?"

Papa grabbed at the big man's arm and attempted to pull him around. "Get out of my house! Now! I was willing to cooperate until you started insulting my wife and my son!"

Charlie listened to this exchange while slowly backing up, reaching behind her until she felt the revolver that normally sat on the sideboard. Gently sliding the gun off, she hid it in the folds of her skirt then moved beside Eric who stood quivering with rage.

"Eric," she whispered and nudged him with the butt

of the gun.

Without glancing down, he reached down, took the gun and brought it up swiftly. "You heard my father, you big oaf! Get out of this house...now!"

The one named Joe didn't look happy. "Come on, Jake. Now you've made things worse." He spread his hands wide in a gesture of apology. "Sorry, but we still have to look around. A group of runaways was seen heading this way last night. We have to check everyone in the area."

Eric gestured with the gun. "You'll have to come back some other time when you can send civilized human beings instead of big dumb gorillas!"

Now the tall, thin man who had not said a word up to this point gestured to his companions. "Let's go. We'll come back into this house later. Who lives in the small log cabin next to this one?"

Charlie shivered. The man's voice was cold, his face was unemotional, and his eyes were so flat she wondered if the devil himself was in their house. "That's my house," she said calmly.

He turned his black eyes on her. "Why are you here and not in your house?"

"I come over to my parents' house for dinner rather than eat alone if it is any of your business."

Joe spoke up. "We don't have to search her house. She is the widow of a war hero."

"Well now, I don't quite agree." Jake turned to scowl at Joe. "Mrs. Garrett, why don't you take us on over to your house and let us look around...unless y'all have somethin' to hide." He turned his cold eyes back on

Charlie. "I wants ta know why that house o' yours is all overgrown like."

"B-because…because…" her voice quivered. It was time to turn on her helpless act. She stumbled into a chair, put her head in her hands, and burst into loud, gulping sobs. "All right, all right," she cried without looking up. "I don't live there anymore," she raised her head to look pitifully at Joe, the man she thought she could influence. "I-I jus' cain't bear it. I can't walk into that house without thinking of Joshua. I m-miss him so much I could jus' die." She allowed the tears to pour down her face, not bothering to wipe them away. "M-mah husband is buried far away, and I c-can't even put flowers on his grave!" It was true. It was all true. The pain in her heart was awakened once more.

Dorothy moved to Charlie's side and wrapped a protective arm around her, glaring at the unwelcome guests. "You call yourselves 'Home Guard'? What are you supposed to be guarding? The women and children left behind in this war, that's who…and this is how you repay our Southern men? You insult their family and threaten their widows?"

"Come on. Let's leave them to their dinner, Jake." Joe gestured toward the door. The three men turned to leave, but Jake stopped at the door and looked back at Paul Ashburn with a malevolent glare.

"I'll be watching this house and all of you. You can count on it. This isn't over yet!"

* * *

"Hey! You git back here! Where you going with that Yankee! Leave him and help me!"

Daniel stumbled, almost falling over an abandoned cartridge box. He tightened his arms to avoid dropping the drowsy drummer boy. To his right, surrounded by bodies, was a Confederate soldier stretching a pleading hand toward Daniel. Blood ran down the side of the man's face and stained the front of his jacket.

"Captain! You can't be helping that boy! He's the enemy — kill him! Help me!"

Kill him? Kill a boy? Daniel couldn't believe his ears. Yet only a few hours ago he had been thirsty enough for the enemy's blood to take his own weapon in hand. It seemed wrong to abandon or kill this innocent boy...a boy who merely played a drum.

He looked down at the boy. "Greg, I've got to help some of my men here. I am going to hide you over there behind those bushes. I promise I will come back for you as soon as I can. You'll be all right until then."

The boy's sleepy eyes were suddenly full of both fear and confusion. "You promise you won't leave me there for good?"

"I promise on my grandma's bible, Greg. I swear it."

"Captain, will you come back before it gets dark, please? I-I don't like to be alone in the dark."

Clearing his tight throat, Daniel answered, "I'll do my best."

Then he carefully set the injured drummer boy in a thicket of bushes, gave him a canteen of water, and reluctantly left him alone, a small blue figure peering up at him with wide, frightened eyes.

All through the day, the fighting continued unabated as both sides pounded each other. Daniel and his assistant had no time to spare. Hooker's Federals had regrouped near the Chancellor House and moved their big guns to a ridge just south of the big house. The injured were everywhere. The noise and chaos was horrendous. As darkness began to cast a gloom over this place of untold human suffering, General Stonewall Jackson's attack began to lose momentum.

It was well after dark before Daniel was able to get away and return to the place where he had left the little drummer boy. In the darkness each thicket of bushes looked the same as the next. As he continued his quiet searching, he began to feel the anxiety rise in his chest. He had promised Greg he would come back for him and, though weary and liberally smeared with blood, he pressed on.

"Greg," he called softly, not wanting to draw attention and get shot. "Greg, answer me if you can hear me. This is Captain Reid. I helped you earlier today. Greg, where are you?"

Sporadic gunfire continued as Daniel crept quietly over the battleground, stumbling over corpses and hoping he wouldn't find anyone they had missed earlier. Stopping to check each soldier to make sure they were indeed already dead used up valuable time, but he couldn't live with himself unless he knew he had not left a living soul out here. His left hand ached and throbbed from overuse, and his empty stomach protested.

Stumbling over a full haversack, he grabbed it up and rummaged through it as he walked. It was obviously a Yankee's bag. Into his pocket went a small folding knife and into his mouth the piece of beef jerky he found inside. Several chunks of hardtack were also pushed into his pockets as he walked and looked around for the right clump of bushes. Placing the strap over his shoulder, he continued to search both for Greg...and for more food and drink. It seemed a ghoulish thing to do, but starvation was hardly a noble undertaking, and these soldiers didn't need their rations any longer. *It wasn't stealing...it wasn't stealing...* He repeated this to himself like a mantra and stumbled on through the hellish night.

Chapter Twenty-One

"Where have you been, Captain Reid?"

Daniel looked up from his work bandaging the soldier's stump of an arm.

"Hi, Will. I've been right here for hours." Will's normally friendly face now sported a tight-lipped grimace.

"I was talking of previously, before you came in here."

"Out on the battlefield, looking for survivors as ordered." He neglected to mention he was looking for one small survivor in particular…one he had not found, much to his sorrow. He prayed that Gregory, the little drummer boy, had found his way back to safety.

"As soon as you've finished with this patient, I need to see you in private." Will stepped up beside the operating table and lowered his voice. "General Jackson was hit tonight by our own troops."

Startled, Daniel met Will's gaze. "How bad is it?"

"We had to take his arm."

"Oh, God."

"Come by my tent as soon as you can."

"Yessir, Major Mattingly." Daniel forced the words out. He was exhausted.

Will smiled at Daniel. "Who would have thought I would be ordering you around…you look beat, my friend."

He glanced at Will. His friend's hair was sticking out in all directions, and he had dark circles under his eyes.

"You don't look so pert yourself, Major," he said, his speech slipping without his realization.

Suddenly, Will yawned widely and rubbed his eyes, lifting up his glasses. Turning heel, Will ducked out of the tent and disappeared into the darkness saying brusquely, "Just be there."

* * *

"We have to be extra careful now," Paul Ashburn warned as they prepared the guests and the wagon for the trip. Papa and Eric had converted the farm wagon into an enclosed peddler's wagon to help hide their guests. For weeks Papa had been fashioning secret compartments that were just the right size for a passenger.

No one would suspect that behind the bolts of colored cloth, shiny metal pots, and boxes of spoons, pocket combs, and tea bags, a small black child lay cocooned in a cleverly designed bed Charlie could not see for all the other paraphernalia. It was all just a false front. Pull a handle here or push a hidden door there, and the notions would slide away to reveal a comfortable resting spot.

"Just wiggle in there, Missouri." She held the hinged compartment open. The big man crawled in on his hands and knees, just barely fitting his broad shoulders through the opening. "Don't worry. It is bigger once you are inside. You'll be able to turn around to get out again," she called.

"Okay, Missus Garrett, Ah'm in." The muffled voice called back. "How's Iris doin'?"

"Fine, fine, Missouri." Another higher voice called

from behind the rack of cooking utensils.

Eric's dark, curly head appeared in the doorway. "Y'all ready back there, Char? Papa's itching to leave."

She smoothed her brightly colored dress and tied the yellow scarf under her chin. "I'm ready, Peddler Boy."

Holding a hand out to help her out of the wagon, Eric smiled. "Let's go, Peddler Girl."

* * *

A low rumble of thunder cascaded across Northern Virginia, sounding eerily like the now-silent cannons. Daniel rode hard in the torrential downpour that soaked through his blue uniform within minutes. It didn't really matter; he was already wet from fording the Rappahannock River as he headed back from where the defeated enemy had withdrawn. The Yankee forage cap he wore provided little protection. At first the soaking had been a welcome relief from the heat of the day, that is, while he still felt well. But, as nighttime air temperature began to drop, his body temperature began to rise.

The saddlebags were full to the bursting with morphine, chloroform, and other medical supplies. He was shocked when Will and Major General Samuel Jones asked him to don the Yankee uniform once more and cross enemy lines. Things had gotten to a critical level and once more, as at Antietam, the Confederate's medical supplies were exhausted. Something needed to be done, and Daniel was the one with the ability to rid himself of his accent and blend in with the Yankees.

Anyone who might have watched him riding brazenly into the enemy camp, asking for and receiving what he wanted, then riding away, would have thought he had nerves of steel.

This mission was even more deadly than the one he had undertaken before. In Philadelphia, the Yankees were complacent and not on guard against imminent attack. This time it was only a few days after the successful and horrific attack by his comrades. This time each pair of eyes viewed him with suspicion...or so it seemed to Daniel. No one in the Union army could recognize every face. There were just too many thousands of unfamiliar faces. He could have belonged to any northern regiment with his blue uniform and stolen U.S.A. saddle that Galileo wore.

Without stopping the horse, Daniel leaned over and lost his stomach contents. Sitting straight again, he wiped his mouth with his wet sleeve.

How much further was it to the abandoned cabin? He felt bad, really bad. A wave of dizziness made the dirt road in front of him tilt crazily. He had to get out of this uniform before he met up with any soldiers from his own side. Being mistaken for the enemy again was not going to happen. He concentrated on searching for the path leading to the small log cabin. All he could hear was the pounding of the rain on the leaves, the rolling thunder, and the crackling lightning, along with his own gasping breath. The sour taste of sickness lingered in his mouth, and the heat inside him increased. A chill snaked down his spine, and he began to shiver. He hoped the morphine powder wasn't getting wet.

* * *

The rain finally stopped by the time Eric drove the

wagon into the grove of trees that hid it from the main road. Dark, ominous clouds scuttled across the sky. Papa helped Iris and her husband out of their hiding places.

The five of them carried blankets, food, and other supplies as they trudged through the forest keeping a careful lookout for any intruders.

Papa slowly opened the door to the dilapidated log cabin. The small group walked inside. It smelled wet and musty and of old smoke. Iris clung tightly to Missouri's arm as they all waited for Paul Ashburn to light the lantern.

"Stop right there!" A deep, raspy voice came from somewhere in the musky darkness. Iris let out a scream. "Quiet! I have a gun," the voice continued. "Go ahead, Mister, light the lantern. I need to see who you are. But don't try anything."

"Okay, okay. We thought this place was empty," Eric said. Charlie wished she had gotten the rifle from the wagon instead of the blankets she held.

With a whiff of kerosene, the lantern flared to life, casting its light weakly into the depths of the small building. The man standing a few feet away from the group held a carbine rifle pointed menacingly in their direction. Charlie tore her eyes away from the black hole of the weapon to look at the tall figure of a soldier dressed in a gray uniform. She gasped.

"Daniel! I can't believe it's you!"

The muzzle of the gun went down. "Charlie? What are you doing here?"

Hesitantly, she stepped toward him. He looked awful. "What are you doing here? Why aren't you with the army?"

Suddenly, he bent over, grabbing his middle, and she rushed to put her arms around him.

"What's the matter?"

"Who is that, Charlie?" Eric's voice sounded angry. "How do you know him?"

"That's Captain Reid, Son." Papa answered for her. "He's a surgeon with the Twenty-Fifth Virginia, the same regiment Josh and Charlie were in."

She could feel the heat coming from Daniel's body right through the wool uniform. He pushed her hands away, staggered over to a blanket on the floor, and laid down. "I'm sick, Charlie. You had best not come near me."

She didn't care. She would risk anything to be with Daniel again. When she went toward him, she was suddenly jerked backwards.

"Eric! Let go of me!" She looked up to see her brother scowling darkly. "Whatever is the matter with you?"

"You heard him, Charlotte. The man is sick, so stay away!"

"But it's Daniel, you have to let me go to him!" she protested. She had to be near Daniel, to touch him.

"He's one of those surgeons!" Eric said. "One of the ones that cut off my leg without so much as a by-your-leave." Strong fingers bit into her arm.

Iris came creeping forward tentatively and pulled at Charlie's other arm gently. "Come on, Missus Garrett, leave da soldier alone now. Yo' brudder be right," she whispered. "Dat man be sick. No sense yo' getting sick, too."

Daniel waved a hand, "Stay away from me, Charlie. I don't want you near me." Then she watched him struggle to his feet. "In fact, I will leave."

Then he pointed to some clothing and a saddle lying on the dirt floor. "Just do me a favor and leave those alone. I'll be needing them later."

Picking up his gun, he shoved it into his holster then retrieved some bulging saddlebags, letting them drag as he wearily walked to the door. Papa and Missouri backed away, leaving him plenty of room.

Reaching the doorway, he stopped and turned back. The moonlight behind him cast a silvery halo around his blond head, leaving his face in shadow.

"Goodbye, Charlie. I love you," he looked from Eric to Papa and back to her, "and I would tell the world, if it would make a difference."

Stunned silence filled the room. Charlie broke away and ran to the door. She sobbed aloud as she rushed to reach her love before he rode out of her life once more.

* * *

It was so hard to get up and leave. His body didn't want to go and neither did his heart. As much as he disapproved of the danger she courted, he also admired Charlie and her family for their selfless acts.

But the fact remained he was ill and could infect others. They needed shelter for the night and, like a good soldier, Daniel would ride back to camp as he originally planned. The cabin was just a place to change Galileo's saddle and his uniform back to the ones that identified them both as C.S.A. Of course, that was before his insides had decided to rebel. *Dear Lord, it was so hot!*

Mounting the horse, he took out his handkerchief, and mopped his brow. He was sweating right through the wool jacket. Maybe his fever was breaking.

"Daniel! Daniel! Wait!"

Turning, he saw his angel running toward him. She wore a brightly colored skirt, her long dark hair tumbling free as her yellow scarf fluttered away.

Galileo pranced, sensing the agitation of his master.

"Charlie, please don't come near me." He held up a hand, but she didn't stop. She threw her arms around his thigh, holding tightly to the only part of him she could reach. Her face pressed into his leg. Reaching out, he touched the lovely silken tresses that shone in the moonlight.

"I don't care. Don't leave me again!

He pressed his stiffened left hand gently into those glorious locks. How soft they felt as he stroked her head. He missed her with an unbearable ache.

"I'm sorry, Charlie. I-I meant it when I said that I love you...I do. But once again, my love, we have met under less than ideal circumstances." As if to remind him, his stomach rolled over with nausea, and he had to swallow hard. "I have to go...this illness has been sweeping through our regiments, so I know how contagious it is."

Lifting his hand from her head, Daniel pulled her arm gently from his thigh. She looked up at him with tears spilling from her beautiful green eyes. Unable to resist, he brushed her cheeks with his fingertips, feeling the wetness. Turning her head, she kissed his lame hand,

Diane M. Wylie

sending a bolt of heat up his arm directly to his core.

"How is your hand?" she asked, holding it lightly in her warm hands and gently massaging his palm.

He nearly choked at the sensation those actions were causing in the rest of his anatomy, despite his fever and stomach cramps. "Better," he croaked. "I have to go. I have medical supplies that the men need badly."

"I know. I wish you could stay here...with me...I love you so much!" Her eyes pleaded with him to stay.

He pulled his hand away. A chill went up and down his spine signaling the start of another bout. Shaking his head, he urged Galileo forward into the night.

"Goodbye, Charlie. I do love you."

It had taken all of his resolve to ride away from Charlie once more. God, he was sick of doing that! All he wanted to do was lie down and hold her in his arms forever—was that too much to ask? In all the time he had known her, even when he had known her as a boy, Charlie was even-tempered, pleasant, and...oh, he could name her charms until the cows came home, and it wouldn't make a bit of difference.

He let Galileo have his head and just adjusted their direction a few times as needed. Laying his head on the horse's neck, he sank into a drowsy, feverish stupor...the kind that was filled with images of a dark-haired, green-eyed beauty. It was in that state, with the horse plodding along into the night, that the idea of marrying Charlie popped into his mind. Of course! Through a haze, he looked down at his left hand and slowly flexed it. The hand was gradually coming back. Will had been right, eventually all function would be restored. He would be able to practice medicine again and provide for a wife, assuming the Yankees didn't string him up.

With these thoughts running through his head, Daniel fell into a deep sleep.

The next thing he knew someone had grabbed him around the waist and pulled him off Galileo's back. Forcing his eyes open, he found himself looking straight into the concerned face of Major Mattingly.

"Will!" His voice came out in a hoarse croak.

With Daniel's arm around his shoulder and another soldier on the other side, Will began to drag him away.

"I got the medicine, Will."

"I know you did, my friend. Just relax—let's take him into the hospital tent, Private. Have you diagnosed your illness, Daniel? What are your symptoms besides this high fever?"

"Nausea, vomiting, all the same symptoms the whole camp's come down with. I've got Camp Fever."

He could hear Will mumbling and barking out some orders. "You did good, Danny, my boy...too damned many people crowded together...we'll get you through this, or I'll give back that blasted promotion...so little food it's no wonder...who wanted to be a major anyway..."

* * *

She knew she looked very nice in her green riding habit. Charlie wanted to look nice when she went into the army camp. She wanted to be able to turn on any womanly charms she possessed to find Captain Daniel Reid.

Since he left her at the cabin, thoughts of Daniel had

occupied her mind day and night. Sleep had been almost impossible...and when she did sleep, she dreamed of warm tubs of water, sleek soapy muscles, and a very naked Daniel Reid.

To sum it up, she was slowly going mad. The only cure for this madness was somewhere in the Confederate army, and she was determined to find him...and her brother, Scott, too, if possible.

So she coaxed Eric to ride with her to Winchester...to help her find Scott. Her brother didn't like surgeons, with good reason, and he made sure everyone knew it. No matter how much she told him about Daniel and her love for the captain, Eric simply scowled at her and grunted. So she changed her tactics. With Mama's support, she convinced him to come with her to try to get word of Scott. There was no reason why she couldn't ask after two people while she was there.

After riding for hours, they finally reached Winchester, where the population of sick and wounded soldiers outnumbered the healthy.

"Why don't we split up? You try the camp headquarters to see if you can find out where Scott's regiment is...and I'll ask at the hospital."

He gave her his usual answer, a grunt.

Studying the buildings, she also looked at each man who carried a gun. It was sometimes difficult to tell who was a soldier and who wasn't—they didn't all have uniforms, the army was too poor. The Federal blockades were strangling and starving the South and all of its inhabitants.

All of the soldiers were tattered, dirty, and thin. It

broke her heart. Somewhere her younger brother and her beloved were suffering the same conditions these men were forced to endure.

She looked at the painted sign hanging over the double doors—Lovington Military Hospital. Further down the street, beyond the city limits, she could see the acres of white army tents.

"Whoa."

Charlie turned to speak to her older brother. The sadness and anxiety he had on his boyish, clean-shaven face drove away any anger she might have felt for his rejection of Daniel. Eric's body had recovered with the love and care they had given him. But she wondered if he would ever recover mentally…would any of them ever recover emotionally from this war?

"Eric." Dismounting, she reached up and put her hand on his thigh. "Will you be all right?"

Shooting her a look, he shrugged, "Sure. I can do this. Time to find our little brother."

Immediately, her old friend *guilt* attacked Charlie. She wanted so badly to find Daniel that using the search for her baby brother was just an excuse to get her way. A hot flush rose up her neck, and she moved away, tying the horse to the rail and trying to hide her guilt from Eric.

"Come back and meet me here when you are finished, all right?"

He grunted his answer, turned his mount, and slowly rode away. Smoothing the wrinkles out of her jacket, she patted her hair and headed up the steps of the hospital.

* * *

Daniel stood by the window, looking out onto the green lawn and allowing his thoughts to drift aimlessly. He heard the soft tap of feminine footsteps enter the room. Curious to see who had come in, since women were not often in the wards, he turned.

A bolt of happiness ran through him when he saw the pretty little woman with the silky dark hair and luminous green eyes. She wore an outfit that matched the color of those eyes…then he saw her face. Charlie was radiant, the kind of radiance love could bring to a woman, he was sure of it.

Grinning, he held his arms out. With a glad squeak, she was in them in a thrice. Lifting her, he swung her around joyfully and kissed her full on the lips—in front of his patients!

"You are well?" she asked, laughing.

"Yes, my love, and you?" He knew he still had that silly grin on his face, but it wouldn't go away with this luscious woman in his arms.

"Very well, Daniel, now that I am with you again."

Setting her back on her feet, he lowered his head and kissed her again, softly, teasingly. Her body leaned into his. He felt her breasts pressing against him…and he remembered those breasts with their rosy pink nipples, all slick and soapy in his hand.

Pulling back slightly, she raised her head and smiled at him then looked at her shoes. "I remember the Gimble's house also." Her voice was soft and tentative, as if she were afraid to voice her thoughts.

Putting a hand under her chin, Daniel tilted her head up so he could see the love shining in those eyes…a love for him that was very humbling. "I will never forget," he said...and knew he never would. Suddenly, he knew it was the time...before something happened yet again to take her away from him. He dropped to one knee on the floor, holding both her hands in his. "I adore you. Will you marry me, Charlotte Garrett?"

The soldiers, who had been watching the tender scene with silent attention, cheered and applauded enthusiastically. A few of the men whistled.

* * *

Charlie looked around at these war-weary, bandaged men with missing arms or legs, sitting in wheeled chairs or lying down. They were all hurt in some way, but they were smiling...for them and their love.

How could she deny what had been in her heart for months? She thought of Joshua, gone for so long. But he was still with her; everyday she carried his love and wisdom inside her. She knew with absolute certainty that Joshua Garrett would agree...

"Yes! I love you with all my heart. I will marry you, Daniel Reid."

Chapter Twenty-Two

"What!"

Eric's face was beet red. He looked about as angry as she had ever seen.

"You heard me, brother." She smiled up at Daniel, who held her hand lightly. His handsome grin had slipped slightly with Eric's reaction. "Daniel and I are getting married…now…actually in about an hour."

"Oh, no you aren't, Charlotte Elizabeth Ashburn. You don't have Papa's permission…or mine." Daniel's hand tightened on hers.

"Eric," she forced a smile. "For one thing, my last name has not been Ashburn for some time, and you know it. For another thing, I don't need anyone's permission…I am old enough…and a widow, so I may do as I please." She glanced around. They were drawing curious stares from the people passing them in the street.

"What about Josh?" Eric demanded.

A stab of pain ripped through her heart. "Josh is gone," she whispered. "He has been gone for some time."

Eric's face twisted. "He was my friend, Char. How can you just replace him like that?"

"I-I'm not—"

Daniel stepped forward, putting his arm around her shoulders protectively. "Charlie is not replacing Joshua Garrett," he said, looking at Eric with so much kindness and understanding that a lump rose in her throat. "I will never expect her to stop loving him." He looked down at her. "I can share you with him, Charlie." Then he turned back to Eric. "Your sister has enough love in her to go around…enough love for all of us."

Something inside Charlie let go just then. Something that she didn't know would ever be released was gone…and suddenly she felt lighter, freer.

"So your middle name is Elizabeth," Daniel was saying. "That's a beautiful name." Then he let go of her and stepped up to Eric, holding his right hand out. "I don't know what it is y'all have against me, but I assure you I love your sister with all my heart. I will take good—"

Eric reached out and rudely slapped away his outstretched hand. Charlie gasped. Anger flashed in Daniel's normally calm blue eyes, and both hands curled into fists at his sides.

"I don't care. My sister isn't gonna marry a butcher like the one that cut off my leg."

What had happened to her kind, gentle brother? His face was an unrecognizable mask of anger and hostility. Charlie was so confused at this unexpected turn of events; she felt tears stinging her eyes.

"Why don't we take this conversation inside? Before we cause a scene."

"There ain't no way in hell I'm gonna go back inside that place of death! There's just more of the butchers like y'all in there…and soldiers y'all have turned into cripples like me!" By now Eric, his accent deepening with each word, was fairly screaming in Daniel's face and gesturing wildly about.

That was the final straw. "Eric Montigue Ashburn! How dare you speak to Daniel like that! I won't have it!"

Charlie stepped forward, reached out, and grabbed her brother's ear, twisting his lobe like Mama had done many times to them all when they misbehaved.

"Ow! Ow! Let go, Char!"

But she didn't let go; she pinched her fingernails into the fleshy ear lobe and began to walk toward the steps of the hospital, pulling Eric along with her. He didn't dare slap her hand away. Out of the corner of her eye she saw Daniel grinning widely, but to his credit, he didn't laugh.

* * *

A sullen Eric limped down the hall, following Daniel, with Charlie bringing up the rear. Daniel supposed she didn't want to give her brother any opportunity to get away before they had a chance to talk.

Coming to the door of a small examining room Daniel knew was empty, he turned the knob and went in. It was growing darker now as evening fell, casting long shadows on the stark chairs and table in the room. Lighting the kerosene lamp, he straightened and turned to his guests. A light breeze blew in through the open window, bringing with it the sounds and smells of the horses and people out on the street.

When he looked at his future brother-in-law, seated next to Charlie, he was surprised to see a sheen of perspiration and a grimace of pain on the ex-soldier's face. How well Daniel knew that look.

"Are you all right, Eric?" he asked, although already knew the answer. The man was pale, and he was rubbing his hand on his thigh above the artificial leg.

"Why should you care?"

So he wasn't going to stop being belligerent. Daniel

sighed. "I doubt you will believe me, but I am telling you the truth when I say that I loathe doing amputations…and so do most surgeons I know. It is not an easy thing to take off a man's leg or arm. But on the battlefield, it has been proven that it is the best way to save that man's life."

Tears stood in Eric's eyes, but he made no move to brush them away. The pain had to be bad.

"Is your missing foot hurting you?"

He watched the young man's eyes widen in surprise. "How did you know that—Charlotte tell you?"

"No, I didn't tell him," Charlie said. She was watching her brother with concern. Looking up at Daniel, she continued. "Eric's ankle…um…his missing ankle hurts him often."

Daniel nodded. Charlie had the most beautiful green eyes. It was so difficult to focus on anything else when she was around. "It is very common for patients to feel pain in their missing arm or leg long after the wound itself has healed."

"Is there anything that can be done for him, Daniel?"

She removed her bonnet. Several strands of dark hair had escaped from her carefully upswept style. He really wanted to pull out all of her hairpins and run his fingers through those silken tresses.

"It will take cooperation and trust on Eric's part, but there is something I can try. It has worked for quite a few of my patients."

The ex-soldier looked at him suspiciously and continued to rub his leg. Charlie leaned forward eagerly. "What is it, Daniel? Is it that trancelike state you learned in Sharpsburg?"

His darling was as smart as a whip. He couldn't wipe the grin off his face when he heard her speak. "Why, yes. Will you assist me?" Daniel turned to Eric. "Maybe you will be more trusting if your sister helps?"

The anger was fading from Eric Ashburn's eyes, and the tension was leaving his body. He sagged back in the chair and closed his eyes. "All right, Captain Reid. Though I don't really believe you can help me…if you can actually perform this miracle, I won't stand in the way of y'all marryin' Charlotte."

The proverbial gauntlet had been thrown, and Daniel fully intended to pick it up. He exchanged a look with his beloved. *This had better work.* "You have yourself a bargain, sir."

* * *

Charlie looked over at the man she married only a few minutes ago in a simple ceremony with only her reluctant brother, Eric, in attendance. The preacher said the same words she had heard at her wedding to Josh, but this time seemed so much more intimate and personal. She wanted to be with Daniel with an all-consuming urgency she had never felt before. Perhaps it was the horror of war and the chaos of their lives that lent itself to this kind of feeling. Whatever it was, she knew this was the right thing to do.

Now the two of them stood in the lobby of Winchester's Grand Hotel. He was signing the register. She looked at his bold signature. It read "Mr. and Mrs. Daniel Reid." She was Charlotte Elizabeth Reid now. That would take getting used to.

As soon as he finished signing, he turned and looked at her with a twinkle in his big blue eyes. He offered her his arm. "Share we retire to our room, Mrs. Reid?"

With a giggle, she made a little curtsy and took his arm. "By all means, Doctor Reid."

Minutes later, Daniel opened the door, then reached down, and swept her into his arms. She wrapped both arms around his neck, feeling the soft blond hair that curled slightly at the collar of his uniform. At eye level with him, she turned her head and captured his mouth with hers.

He kicked the door closed and walked deeper into the room with their lips still connected in the sweetest, most passionate kiss she had ever had.

Her need for him grew to a fever pitch in the blink of an eye. Slowly, slowly he let her body slide down the length of his. Charlie was having none of it. Too long she had burned for Daniel, and she wanted him NOW. Maybe it was unladylike of her, but…

She reached for his jacket and began, with shaking hands, to open it.

"What's your hurry, my love?" But his hands were unfastening her jacket in return.

"Shhhhh." She stopped long enough to place a finger against his lips. His tongue flicked out and licked her finger.

Both jackets hit the polished wooden floor. Now she worked on his shirt. As soon as it gaped open, she ran her hands inside over his warm, smooth muscles and sighed.

His right hand flipped open button after button on

her high-necked blouse. Then both of his hands were inside her clothing, burning right through her chemise as he cupped her breasts. She sighed again with pleasure.

Soon they were both naked from the waist up. Pulling her toward him, he ran his tongue gently over her lips. He buried a hand in her hair and stroked her back with the other hand. Gooseflesh broke out up and down her spine.

Feeling like a brazen hussy, Charlie reached for his belt buckle, unfastened it, and slid it free of his uniform trousers. *What was it about this man that drove her crazy like this?* She gasped as he stroked his thumbs over her taut nipples. Her hands shook as she worked on the buttons holding his pants together.

Ahhh, yes. She touched his smooth, lean ribs, followed the hollow of his hipbones, moved around to the curve of his back, and down to his warm, muscular buttocks. She squeezed.

He laughed.

She smiled up at him as she pushed his pants down. Bending her knees, she followed the trousers as they dropped, and removed every remaining item from his body, keeping her face upturned to watch his expression.

His eyes became smoky and heavy-lidded, but his mouth kept its upturned smile. His hands dropped to his sides, and he stood still, naked now…and glorious.

Slowly, she shed the rest of her own clothing, never taking her eyes from her new husband. Daniel stood, relaxed and loose-limbed, watching her every move with his blue, smoldering gaze.

"You are driving me crazy, Charlie," he whispered

huskily. "How I have missed you these many months."

Laughing, she took both of his hands and pulled him across the rug toward the big four-poster mahogany bed.

Side by side, they lay, sinking deep into luxurious softness. She feasted her eyes on his masculine form and watched his eyes move over her. As husband and wife they would have the time to learn each and every freckle and imperfection. Their lovemaking at the Gimble house had been tainted by her guilt and worry. Now, as his wife, she could enjoy Daniel freely and completely. Gently, she moved her fingertips over the long scar on his forearm where the bullet had plowed into his flesh and broken his arm. Taking his hand, she could feel the stiffness in it and began to massage the fingers and palm. Daniel laid his head down, closed his eyes, and groaned.

"I'm not hurting you, am I?"

"No, it feels wonderful, my love. My hand tends to ache when it gets stiff."

He moved on top of her, straddling her body. Slowly, leaning over, he put his warm hands on her cheeks. Lowering his head, his tongue flicked out to run teasingly over her lips. Tingles ran around inside her abdomen, and sweet tension began to grow.

She found him with her hands and stroked his smoothness until a moan escaped from deep inside his chest. His hands were far from inactive as his long fingers moved relentlessly over every inch of her, caressing, touching, and exploring until she fairly pulsed with desire.

"I need you, Daniel," she whispered into his ear then took his earlobe between her teeth. The coarse hair of his short beard rubbed against her cheek. The familiar scent of his soap soothed her senses, and she breathed deeply.

"God help me, Charlie, I would expire on the spot if you were to leave me now!"

He eased inside her, closely watching her face. Could he see the love for him shining there in her face? Could he tell she needed him, wanted him, and yearned for him with an all-consuming desire?

Moving against her, he filled her. A great feeling of completeness washed over Charlie. At this moment, all was right and wonderful. They had found each other in a time when so much was being lost. She welcomed him to her and each wrapped their arms tightly around the other. Faster, harder, higher they climbed until, with a wild burst of happiness, each was fulfilled by the other.

* * *

Once again he had to leave her. She sat on the bed, watching him pack his saddlebags.

"Special assignment? Why you? Why can't someone else do this, Daniel?"

Looking up, he smiled gently. "I wish someone else was assigned to do this, Charlie. I suppose I got myself into it by stealing those medical supplies the first time. Then Will was backed into a corner and needed morphine and more supplies after the battle at Chancellorville. Now our army is advancing into Pennsylvania in great force, and once more, we are in dire need of supplies…but I think you already knew that."

"Yes, I knew that. But why can't Major Mattingly go or someone else…anyone else."

"Honey, majors can't do things like this. They are too important...or at least they think they are. This time it was Major Vandergriff who has ordered me to go. Something about my lack of accent since I was raised in Maryland and my familiarity with Yankee procedures."

She opened her mouth to protest further but clamped it shut again when she saw his expression. He was a man of honor and commitment to duty, of that there was no doubt.

"Do you know where you will be going? Can I go with you?" She rose to follow him out of the room but turned back for a last look at the beautiful suite with its cool, pale green bed. Always, she would always remember this room and her first night as Mrs. Daniel Reid. Her new husband's voice called her attention back to the present.

"No, you can't go, you are not a soldier anymore. I have to find the Union army to get their supplies. So that is where I'm going...north."

* * *

June 1863

Dorothy Ashburn peered out at the night sky. "No moon tonight," she declared, "the clouds are too thick."

"Perfect." Charlie picked up the basket of food from the table. She was wearing a dark blue dress with long sleeves, despite the warmth of the summer night, to hide her pale skin. Eric and Papa came into the shadowy front room. They both wore dark, long sleeved shirts and dark trousers.

Paul gave Dorothy a peck on the cheek. "We'll be back before the cows come home, darlin'."

Three members of the Ashburn family boarded the peddler's wagon, and Eric drove it to Charlie's place. The tiny house was shrouded in darkness when she jumped to the ground and headed to the front door.

Holding the door open, she motioned the young couple silently toward the waiting wagon. Somewhere in the night a wolf howled mournfully. Shivers skittered up Charlie's spine, and suddenly, she had the strange feeling something was not right. Before she could call them back, she heard a movement in the lush green cornstalks near the house.

Silently a group of men materialized like ghosts from the field, moving quickly toward them!

"Hold it right there!" a deep voice shouted. "Don't do nothin' stupid. We want them slaves! Y'all are under arrest!"

"No!" Charlie screamed. She watched Abraham grab Delia's hand, and they began to run for the trees.

The world erupted into screams and gunshots. Dark figures ran toward the fleeing slaves. Torches sprang to blazing life. Suddenly, Papa was dragging her inside the house, his shotgun in his other hand.

"Where is Eric?" Charlie ran for her Springfield beside the fireplace.

But Papa didn't answer. He broke out the window and began shooting. Running to the other front window, Charlie broke it also and stuck her rifle out. Bullets whined and thunked, hitting all around the window and doors. The peddler's wagon careened away from the house. She watched the back doors swing open. Shiny pots fell out, rolling and banging.

Aiming, she took out a man shooting at Eric. Abraham suddenly jerked and fell to the ground, a victim of one of the slave hunters. Delia's scream split the night. With tears blurring her vision, Charlie watched the brave woman throw herself over her husband.

Gunshots continued their deadly clatter. Charlie reloaded while Papa continued to fire.

Smoke! Charlie sniffed again. She smelled smoke! A glow lit the sky to the left of the cabin.

"Papa, the house is on fire! Mama's inside!"

* * *

Pressing the horse's head into his chest, Daniel stroked Galileo's nose and whispered softly to the animal. A flick of the ears and a soft snort was the response, otherwise the horse stood still. The clatter and noise of a large Federal regiment moving down the road, just beyond the thick sheltering bushes, drowned out his soft words to his equine companion.

Though he wore Union blue, Daniel was not taking any unnecessary risks. The sheer number of men, horses, supply wagons, and caissons was staggering. He knew the road he had been traveling could accommodate at least four horses side by side, and yet he waited, hardly daring to move for close to two hours before the noise level from the army began to drop. The volume of the blue tide had slowed but not stopped.

They continued to wait. He looked at Galileo's face. The horse had closed his eyes and gone to sleep standing up, as horses do. He carefully released the animal and sat on the damp ground as quietly as possible.

As usual, Daniel's thoughts turned to Charlie. Their

quick marriage and short night together seemed like a dream. The reality of thousands of enemy soldiers marching by, on their way to kill more of his comrades, made anything that was good seem unrealistic.

The hideous war machine marched on, altering and eliminating the lives of perfectly nice people as it progressed. Somehow he had been lucky, finding his one true love in the midst of all the tragedy. He sent up a quick prayer that she and her family were safe. Their mission to save the runaway slaves had him scared for the entire Ashburn family. As her husband now, he would have to make her understand and stop her illegal activities. But stopping someone as headstrong as Charlie was not going to be an easy thing to do. He wished he had more time to convince her before being sent away.

A roving cloud of gnats zig-zagged their way in front of Daniel's face, threatening to fly up his nose. Frantically, he clamped his mouth shut and waved a hand, trying to shoo them away without making a sound. With his free hand, he pinched his nose closed, deciding to risk his other orifices to the whims of fate.

Then the sound of loud buzzing had him forgetting the gnats and looking around wildly. Too late! A loud horse shriek split the air, and Galileo threw his head around wildly, rearing on his hind legs. Quickly scrambling to his feet, Daniel grabbed for the reins, barely catching them before the horse bolted.

"Did you hear that? Is someone there?" The voices carried to where he was busy tussling with his horse.

Think quickly before you get captured!

Arranging his face into a nonchalant expression, he

sauntered out toward the road leading Galileo. "Hello, fellas!"

He was met with surprised stares, but no guns were pointing at him yet.

Daniel rubbed his belly and grimaced. "That supper went through me like greased lightning." He fell in beside a group of five Yankees and tried to look natural, as though he belonged there.

"Yup. Can be a real bear. Had me the same problem just the other day, sir," one of the men responded as they all continued down the road.

Dear Lord, don't let them ask me anything important that a Union captain should know.

"Still not feeling so well," he said.

"Not surprised, sir."

Tipping his hat, he mounted Galileo, bent his head as if he were ill, and let the horse walk slowly among the Bluecoats. For as far as he could see in front and behind him there were Union soldiers. He swallowed nervously and began to pray.

Chapter Twenty-Three

Charlie ran in the direction she had seen the peddler's wagon disappear while Paul Ashburn sprinted to the farmhouse. It wasn't until she was looking around in a near panic for her brother that she realized the shooting had stopped. The slavers were gone. But she could still hear Delia's keening cries, almost drowned out by the roar of the fire.

Spotting the wagon near the apple orchard, Charlie ran toward it. The team had stopped, and the animals were shifting anxiously in their traces, the smell of smoke drifting to their sensitive noses.

She found Eric lying on his side in the tall grass not far from the wagon wheels.

"Eric! Eric! Answer me!" She dropped to her knees beside him.

"Oh, Eric," Charlie sobbed. Gathering her brother into her arms, she began to sob even as she ran her hands over his body looking for signs of life. There were none. His heart didn't beat under her palm, nor did his chest rise and fall. First Josh, now Eric! Her tears fell on his pale, still face.

"No! No!" This could not be happening! But it was true. The light was gone from his green eyes, and his head lolled on his shoulders with an unnatural looseness. With a shaking hand, she lowered his eyelids so he looked asleep now. A small hole in the middle of his chest told the story. Blood barely oozed from the bullet wound directly over his heart. What a good heart he had, too. Sorrow squeezed her chest with its dark agony, so familiar to Charlie.

Brushing the hair from his face, she held him, rocking him in her arms, praying it was not true but knowing it was. Eric's beloved face was peaceful now. There would be no more pain in his missing leg, no more struggling with the false leg, no more of his affectionate teasing, no more, no more…

* * *

Riding among the masses of Yankees proved to be easier than Daniel expected, once he grew accustomed to the idea of being surrounded by his enemies. The infantry soldiers ignored him, as men are apt to do with officers. No one wanted to fraternize with an officer and be suspected of cozying up to gain an extra ration or lighter duty or some such advantage.

There was little he could do but go along. Before leaving on this mission, he had learned his own army was marching in a path parallel to his present course. Everyone seemed to be heading north, in the general direction of Pennsylvania.

"Gid up, boy." He moved his horse to the outside of the road and spurred him to a faster gait. It was time to locate the medical supply wagons. Perhaps he could steal an entire wagon this time instead of merely filling his saddlebags. Each moment he delayed meant another lad was suffering the lack of chloroform or worse, the lack of bromine.

Bromine was the new wonder drug Daniel learned about on his last trip to the northern army hospital tents. He had met a surgeon by the name of Middleton

Goldsmith after Chancellorville, right before the camp fever had begun.

Goldsmith was excited about his discovery and eager to speak of it to anyone who would listen. Daniel, who had also been doing some experimentation, was happy to risk spending time with a Union surgeon in the hopes of learning something valuable. The Federals had the best in medicine and new-fangled equipment…they had the resources and the money to get it.

"I'd be happy to explain my methods to you, Captain," Goldsmith had said with an excited grin, his eyes lighting up. "First dissect out any diseased tissue of a gangrenous wound." He handed Daniel a blue bottle and a syringe. "Then apply the bromine around the edges of the wound, fill the cavity with lint and soak it with a weak solution of bromine."

Goldsmith gestured eagerly as he talked. "Mind, it will seem as though nothing is happening for the next three to ten days, but you will find, my friend, that the recovery of the patient will be complete, and he will certainly survive. I have seen it happen again and again."

So Daniel had been all too happy to accept the gift of the blue bottle and syringe. At the first opportunity he tried the bromine on a patient at Lovington with a severe case of gangrene. To his joy, the drug had worked and worked well. He had wasted little time teaching the treatment to his colleagues.

But the precious stuff had run out. The embargo against medicines and equipment, forced upon the South by Washington, D.C., had been very effective. So he was here again, risking his neck in the hope he could help save others.

Carefully, he maneuvered Galileo steadily to the front of the Blue lines. He had to find those wagons.

* * *

There was little choice—they were forced to bury Eric and Abraham before the night was out. Charlie helped Papa dig the graves side by side in the Ashburn family cemetery. Mama had escaped the burning house unharmed. She and Abraham's wife, Delia, were now preparing the bodies for their final resting place.

Once they had gotten Eric and Abraham into her house, Charlie was glad to be able to help her father with the digging. The heartbreak of both women, in addition to her own misery, was almost too much to bear and remain sane.

"I am sorry to have to do this, Charlotte," Paul Ashburn huffed as he lifted another shovel full of soil. "This is a man's job, not the job for a woman."

"I have done a man's work before, Papa. I don't mind."

"I-I can't believe w-we lost Eric." Papa's voice was thick with tears. "H-he was barely home from the damned war. I don't know how Dorothy will get through this."

"M-mama is strong. She'll get by." Charlie sniffed. The light from the lantern cast eerie shadows from her grandparents' tombstones. Smoke hung heavy and acrid in the air from the burned farmhouse, making it difficult to see.

"Don't you think it odd that none of the neighbors came to help us, Papa? Why aren't Gabriel Kennedy or

Ralph Bradley here?"

Paul Ashburn's face fell even further. "I hadn't thought of that before." He cleared his throat and continued as he threw out another shovel full. "Eric told me he was sweet on Polly Bradley."

Charlie had to stop. She sat down suddenly and gave into tears again. "I-I know, he told me too. H-he wanted to ask her to m-marry him…but was afraid she wouldn't want a one-legged man."

"I don't blame the neighbors for not coming, Charlotte. We are breaking the law. They don't want to get involved with criminals like us."

Criminals? Is that what they were? Did Eric and Abraham deserve to die because they were criminals? Charlie didn't believe it for a minute. *We are just human beings helping others, as the good Lord wanted us to. How can we get punished for that?*

But agony had followed agony, and two more good men were lost…more lives ruined.

A warm breeze lifted her hair and rustled through the planted fields. An owl called to its mate somewhere deep in the forest, and another piece of her spirit disappeared.

* * *

Late June 1863
Gettysburg, Pennsylvania

Eating three meals a day was an unexpected bonus for Daniel. The pleasant feeling of having food in your stomach was not unappreciated. It had taken two days, but he finally located the main body of Federal medical supply wagons.

As he stood there, looking at the four fully stocked wagons and ten new ambulances, he had to force his gaping mouth closed. Standing here looking like an awe-struck greenhorn was not good.

"Hello," said a friendly New England-accented voice. "Are you a new surgeon? I haven't seen you before."

Turning, Daniel found himself facing a Union colonel. Quickly saluting the officer, he used the speech he had rehearsed, concentrating on speeding up his speech like a Northerner.

"Yes, sir. I'm Captain Smith from the Twelfth New Jersey, reporting." He fervently hoped he wasn't going to have to name any members of the New Jersey regiment. "Uh, I've not been in long, so I apologize that I don't know your name, nor very many of the men."

"That is quite all right, son." The colonel put his hand out. "Let me introduce myself...I am Colonel Anderson of the Seventeenth Maine."

Accepting the handshake, he tried to prepare for possible questions. The man was older, with a craggy, weather worn face and drooping brown mustache that reminded Daniel of one of the Twenty-Fifth Virginia's casualties, Ned Hagan. He tried not to stare at the crumbs lodged in that luxurious mustache.

"Nice to meet you, sir. If you don't mind, I would be interested in knowing what the situation is for medical supplies. We seem to be amassing tens of thousands of soldiers in this general area. Frankly, sir, it makes me nervous that we may run out of the necessary items."

"Would you like to see what bountiful wonders we

have at our disposal, Doctor Smith?"

"If it wouldn't take up too much of your time, sir."

With a dramatic flair, Colonel Anderson threw open the door to the specially appointed wagon, reached up, and pulled down a hinged section of wood that lowered to form a table. Now exposed were an assortment of handles affixed to compartment doors. With one hand, the officer pulled one knob and a tall, narrow shelf filled with neatly labeled brown bottles slid out. Behind another hinged door rested rolls of bandages in assorted widths. Again and again, Colonel Anderson pulled the handles to reveal the bounties that lay in drawers and on shelves, explaining the contents of each with a self-important grin.

"Nothing but the best for this army, son. We have, of course, chloroform, morphine, quinine, paregoric, laudanum, calomel, and bromine. As you can see we also have all assortments of ointments, creams, and instruments as well."

Daniel's excitement grew, and he swallowed hard. He was almost drooling over the medical treasure trove. With an effort, he forced the grin off his face. It would not do to appear over zealous. He needed to formulate a plan to steal this wagon. How he wished he had someone to help him drive away a second or even a third of these fantastic vehicles.

Then another thought gave him pause. If the Federals were this well stocked with medical supplies, how well stocked were they with guns, ammunition, cannons, and all other things needed for war? Their supply of soldiers also seemed endless. Daniel's heart sank. It didn't look good for the Confederates who were up against this big blue machine.

"Uncle Frederick! Uncle Frederick!" A young voice called.

Daniel was leaning in close to inspect the medical wagon's wonders and did not turn around. Behind him, the colonel laughed. A strange kind of thunk, thunk noise, accompanied by a small grunting reached Daniel's ears, but he continued to read labeled bottles with fascination.

"Captain Smith?" then came a subtle clearing of the throat. "Captain Smith?"

Oh, yes, that was his name, he had forgotten. He pulled his head out of the wagon and swung around.

Colonel Anderson was beaming with pride as he put his arm around a young boy dressed in a Yankee uniform and leaning on a pair of crutches. "I'd like you to meet my nephew. He's a drummer for the Twelfth. Poor lad got himself wounded at the engagement in Chancellorville recently. Say hello to Captain Smith, Gregory."

Daniel found himself face to face with a very surprised young boy, the one he had been searching for, but had never found...until now.

Chapter Twenty-Four

They had never traveled so far north before, but there was no choice. The Ashburn's farmhouse had been burned to the ground. Not one of the neighbors had come by to find out whether any of the Ashburns were alive. It was obvious they had been left on their own. It was time to leave the home Eric, Scott, and Charlie had grown up in and the home that they all loved.

Charlie picked up the bag of belongings and sadly locked the doors to her little house. She had hoped to live here with Daniel. Perhaps when the war was over...

But it was best not to dwell on what could have been. The reality of the situation was vastly altered now. Eric was dead. Her other brother and her husband were both somewhere to the north, fighting this hideous war. Their lives were in danger, and it was time to go.

Her quietly weeping mother and stoic father rode on the peddler wagon while Charlie followed behind on her horse. It was a long and solemn trip with little conversation among the family. From time to time they stopped to make a few sales to the households along the way. This helped remove suspicion and bring in a few pennies.

At night, Delia and the three other frightened runaways that had joined them on the journey, would come out of their hiding places to stretch their legs and walk along side the wagon when they traveled through isolated wilderness.

The shimmering Potomac River lay ahead. When

they crossed the river, they would be on Maryland soil…in the state where Daniel Reid had been born and had grown to a man.

Charlie unfolded the paper and read Daniel's instructions one last time. Then she picked up the stone she had put in her pocket for this purpose. Wrapping the paper around the smooth, cool weight, she stood up high in the stirrups and threw it with all of her might. It landed in the Potomac with a splash and carried its secrets to the muddy bottom.

Two days later, the group arrived in Harford County, Maryland. Following the directions her husband had given them, they rode down a dusty dirt road shielded on either side by majestic oaks, leafy maples, and thick bushes. Mosquitoes buzzed around Charlie's head. The dampness in the air told her they were very close to their destination.

Sighing, she pulled a handkerchief from her skirt pocket and wiped her face. She wondered if she could take a quick dip in the river when they arrived. Memories of the day she had first seen the half-naked Daniel among the many men bathing filled her mind. She yearned for some word of him. Perhaps his mother and father would know where he was.

Once again she worried about the reception she would get from the Reid family. She knew Daniel had written them of their marriage, almost a month ago now. But did they get the letter? Would they be glad their oldest son had married a common farm girl? She knew very little of his family. He had insisted they would all love her, but she knew they were town people, rich town people at that. She looked down at her clothing. Wet stains under her arms and down the front of her bodice made her grimace with embarrassment. *They'll hate me!*

"Mama, maybe we should forget about going to see the Reids," she called.

"No, Charlotte. We must go. We have come so far, it would not be polite to leave without meeting our new in-laws." Dorothy turned back and gave her daughter a small smile. "It will be all right. God will light the way for us."

The trees suddenly gave way to a clearing. There, down by the banks of the Susquehanna River, sat a gray stone mill house with its large, painted paddle wheel slowly turning. Several horses were hitched to a wooden railing in the front. A burly man was loading grain into a wagon, going inside the building and returning with sack after sack.

This was Rock Run Mill Daniel had told them about. Abolition-minded Quakers lived all around here. This narrow, rutted road leading to the mill was called Quaker Bottom Road according to his directions. This was supposed to be the "Land of Promise" for escaped slaves. Charlie sincerely hoped that it was.

Papa stopped the wagon under the shade of a huge oak tree. She dismounted gratefully, rubbing her sore bottom as she tied the horse firmly to a tree. Passing by the peddler's wagon, she rapped her knuckles on the side three times. This would let their guests know someone would be inside shortly to help them out of the hiding places.

"I will go inside and ask for Mr. Worthington,

Charlotte," Paul Ashburn said as he helped Dorothy down from the wagon. "Why don't you and Mama fix us all a nice dinner?" He glanced up at the sky. The light was becoming soft and muted. "The river is over yonder. I am hopeful the water will be drinkable."

The burly man she had seen loading the sacks approached with his hand outstretched in greeting.

"Hello, I'm William Worthington. Who might I have the pleasure of meeting?"

Papa took off his hat and shook hands with Mr. Worthington, his gray head bobbing up and down. "Nice to meet you, sir. I am Paul Ashburn, this is my wife, Dorothy, and my daughter, Charlotte."

A grin split the big man's face from ear to ear. "Peddlers are ye?"

"Why, yes, we are. We have traveled quite a distance to find you, Mr. Worthington. May I ask you, sir…might there be a place nearby where we could locate some sheep?"

Charlie watched the man's face change ever so slightly. His weathered face took on a more serious, almost reverent expression. He leaned closer to her father and said in a low voice. "There are already sheep in the barn, but there is room for more. They must be ready to be transported tonight."

* * *

The boat bobbing beside the wharf sat so low in the water of the Delaware River that Daniel vaguely wondered if it would sink before they reached their destination. Wearily he shifted his arms, trying to ease the dragging weight of the chains on his wrists.

How in the name of God have I come to deserve this? All he wanted to do was ease suffering by taking some of what the Union had in excess anyway. Was that so bad?

In the distance he could see the forbidding stone structure rising up from the flat, barren land around it. There were several rectangular outbuildings and lookout towers, but little else on the island to break the severity of the fort.

For a month Daniel had been going through a hellish nightmare, and it wasn't over yet. *Dear Lord, please let me see my wife again before I die.* They had been together one day as man and wife in the past thirty-two, and that fact alone would be enough to drive a man crazy. But the events that had transpired against him as soon as the little drummer boy opened his mouth to speak were beyond imagination.

"Hello, sir. What are you doing here? Aren't you a Reb?" Gregory Anderson had said innocently.

From that moment on, nothing Daniel said or did got him out of trouble. Colonel Anderson immediately ordered his horse confiscated and belongings searched.

Galileo reared and bellowed a protest at the Yankees jerking on his reins and rifling through the saddlebags.

"If you must take my horse, please give him to the boy, Colonel!" He was desperate. "Don't harm the animal! Please!"

The gray uniform was found and shouts of "Rebel spy!"

echoed through the camp.

Daniel was immediately seized. The Bluecoats jerked him roughly over to stand in front of the colonel. The officer glared at him with angry gray eyes.

"You insulted my intelligence and tried to play me for a fool, sir! Take him away and get the truth out of him. See what he knows, but don't kill him. Leave him fit for prison. I want him to rot there for a long, long time."

Though a tearful Gregory tried to plead with his uncle that Daniel had saved his life, it did little to ease his predicament.

"It's not your fault, Greg, not your fault!" He yelled to the weeping drummer boy over his shoulder as they dragged Daniel away.

The soldiers took him to a more remote area of the camp, away from prying eyes and ripped the blue uniform from him, leaving him with little more than a torn shirt and undergarments. Following orders, they had their revenge but stopped short of doing damage to his body that would prevent him from walking. He managed to inflict a few black eyes and bruises in the process. The Yankees were beyond reasoning. They tied him to a tree, after beating him nearly senseless, and left him there overnight to let the hordes of mosquitoes torture him further.

For two days he was tied to the tree, half-naked, injured, and humiliated. They brought him some food and water then harassed and hit him some more to divulge what he didn't even know.

On the third day, an officer happened by and ordered his Confederate uniform returned to him.

His break came on July 1st when word of a Confederate

295

attack began to filter through to the soldiers stationed where Daniel was located, south of Cemetery Hill near General Meade's headquarters.

They left Daniel where he was, next to a group of graves, bound hand and foot while preparations for battle went on all around him. Soldiers, horses, artillery, and wagons rattled and bustled past the captured Rebel.

The battle in the town of Gettysburg raged on for days, driving him mad with frustration at his helplessness. His people were out there, dying by the thousands, and he could do nothing to help. It wasn't long before more ragged Confederate prisoners joined him.

Word would reach him later, as he and the others were being sent to prison camps, that 160,000 men had fought this horrific battle that left close to 50,000 dead. General Lee had withdrawn to Virginia, having lost almost forty percent of his army. The South had suffered a tremendous blow.

Now, as Daniel gazed at the forbidding structure of Fort Delaware, he was filled with depression and fear, the likes of which he had never known. He had heard the whispered rumors of the cruelty inflicted on the prisoners who entered the massive stone fort with its high, thick, granite walls.

Would he ever see Charlie or his family again? So many men had died in this damnable war and, if the battles didn't kill them, living in this huge hellhole surely would.

"Daniel!" a female voice called urgently. "Daniel Reid, is that you? Dear God!"

Tearing his eyes away from the spectacle of fear looming out across the river, he turned wearily to see who had called his name.

Standing a few yards away was a group of fashionably dressed young ladies, looking like beautiful bright butterflies. They huddled together clutching each other's arms, staring at the dirty, tattered Confederate prisoners chained together. Their hands were full of packages they had obviously purchased at the little shops clustered near the wharf.

"Stay back, ladies!" one of the Yankee guards called, "You don't want to get their vermin on you!"

A golden-haired girl shook off her companions and stepped closer.

"Nora!" Daniel cried hoarsely.

She took a few hesitant steps toward him.

"No, don't go over there, Nora! They're filthy beasts!" another girl called anxiously.

Turning, Nora cried, "But Mary, it's my brother!" With that she overcame her fear and ran to him, tears running down her smooth, rosy cheeks and her yellow dress billowing about her ankles.

"Stop!" the guard yelled, his footsteps pounding on the wooden planks. He stepped in front of Daniel, blocking Nora's path.

She halted, one hand on her heart. "What have they done to you, Daniel? Where are you going? Why are you not doctoring in the hospital?" she sobbed, reaching toward him with her other hand outstretched.

It was no wonder Nora was shocked. He was a mess. The blows to his face had cut his lip and cheekbone and blackened one eye. A seam had split on one of his jacket sleeves, and he had a large tear in the knee of his filthy trousers. Three weeks of beard covered the lower part of his face, hiding more bruises.

The shackles wouldn't let him move his arms to hold his little sister, even if she could reach him.

"I'm all right, Nora," he lied. "They're sending me to prison, honey. Will you get word to Mother and Father…and my wife?"

"Get moving, you stinking Reb!"

The Yankee shoved him in the back with the rifle as the line began to move. Stumbling, chains rattling all around him, the line of prisoners shuffled toward the boat with Nora walking beside him.

"What will happen to you?"

Daniel's heart broke to hear the sorrow and desperation in her voice. "I don't know, Nora. Tell them I love them. Tell Charlie for me! I will always love her!"

In all his life, he had never felt more wretched then he did now, watching his sister trying to reach out to touch him with the Yankee blocking her attempts. With a roar of anger, he threw his shoulder into the guard, pushing him away. Nora gasped and threw her arms around him, still sobbing.

"Oh, Daniel! Father will get you out. Just stay safe, Brother!"

He felt her hand inside his jacket briefly before the guard reappeared. "Miss, I will ask you to please move away from the prisoner," he said angrily.

She stilled but didn't release him. "Let go, Nora," Daniel whispered. "Goodbye, my dearest."

Lifting her chin, she slowly let go of his arms and stepped back with a defiant look in her blue eyes. "You, sir, had better not harm my brother…or you will have to answer to my father."

A wicked grin slowly spread over the guard's wide, fleshy face. "We will see about that, little lady." The rifle butt shot out, quickly, catching Daniel solidly in the stomach. He doubled over with a grunt as the pain knifed through him.

"No!" Nora screamed.

The prisoner behind Daniel caught him by the arm and pulled him toward the waiting boat. "Come on, before he hits you again, fella."

As he climbed unsteadily into the rocking boat, Daniel stole a look back toward the shore. The yellow of Nora's dress made her easy to see through the mist in his eyes. He watched the lone figure of his sister until she was out of sight. The boat rose and sank on the choppy water. The stone fort loomed ahead.

Chapter Twenty-Five

A single boat drifted slowly down the Susquehanna River, the fisherman's pole angling into the sparkling surface. Charlie sat on the grassy bank, drew her legs up, and rested her crossed arms on her knees. Closing her eyes, she bent her head and buried her face in the soft gingham material of her dress sleeves. A warm summer breeze lifted the hair that had escaped from its chignon and tickled her neck. *Dear Daniel, where are you? I pray you are safe. Come home, my darling. Please come home. I need you so much.*

Goosebumps skittered down her spine despite the heat. She had to find out where he was before she went crazy with worry. But what could she do? Getting to her feet, she smoothed her skirt and headed back to the brightly painted peddler's wagon. As soon as their guests were ready to travel, she would convince Mama and Papa to seek out Daniel's home. Perhaps her in-laws could help ease her mind…maybe they knew where their son was.

The dark night held a strange combination of fear and excitement. Clouds blowing across the Maryland sky hid the moon from sight. The gentle sound of water lapping against the muddy shore was loud in Charlie's ears as they walked silently from the back door of the millhouse storeroom. For Charlie, saying farewell to Delia was the hardest of all the slaves they had helped in the months since she had returned home.

"We will always be sisters in a way." She leaned

close to whisper in Delia's ear. "Take care of yourself…and that baby. God speed, Delia."

The young black woman paused with one foot in the boat and one foot still on the bank and turned to grasp her hand warmly. "Yes'm, that be right. Neither of us'll ever forgets our mans so far from us." Both women had been forced to bury husbands far from where they would live. Abraham would never know this his wife was even now stepping into a boat bound for freedom.

In the darkness, Charlie could barely make out a faint smile on the other woman's tense face. "Yo gots yerself a new husband now…maybe someday ah'll have a new daddy fo' this here baby." She patted her still flat abdomen. "I gotsta thank you and yo' family fer helping me and mah baby to be free. Y'all will be in mah heart o' hearts forever," she said, placing a trembling hand over her heart. "Goodbye," she whispered and placed a tiny kiss on Charlie's cheek.

William Worthington stepped up beside the boat. "Time to leave." He helped Delia get on the boat and settle herself between the others as if she were a queen mounting her throne.

Charlie was glad to see it. Her faith in the mill owner grew. There was no doubt now that Worthington would take them safely across the Susquehanna River and on to freedom in Lancaster, Pennsylvania. Through tears of sorrow there was hope for the future. The child of Delia and Abraham would be born free—a dream that would come true.

* * *

The air was still and humid when Daniel stepped out

of the boat onto the mud that surrounded Fort Delaware. Mosquitoes immediately buzzed about his face, drawn to the blood on him. Chains clanked as all of the prisoners waved at the bugs in a futile attempt to save their skin.

Staring up at the massive pentagonal walls surrounded by a broad moat and green slime dykes, despair rose up to choke him as effectively as the thick air and insects. Escaping from this prison became his obsession from that moment on. Since the fort, with its thirty-two-foot high granite walls, sat on an island with the innocuous name of Pea Patch Island, he knew he would have to swim when the time came.

Being strong enough to swim meant he couldn't waste a lot of time planning before making an attempt. With each passing day, the lack of adequate food and the spread of illness would quickly steal way the strength he had.

"Hold still, you Rebel bastards, while I take off these chains." The Yankee sergeant came down the line rattling a ring of iron keys. "Remember, if you cause any trouble you'll get put right back into chains or worse. There are some damned nasty holding cells in the lower levels that we use for any fool who can't behave!"

The man next to Daniel gave a shudder of revulsion. "I bet they got rats down there," he mumbled, "I hate rats."

Disease, pests, and vermin! Damn! The battlefield actually sounded better. Holding his wrists out, Daniel was relieved when the irons dropped away.

Glancing around to see that no one was paying him any particular attention, he slipped his hand into his jacket pocket. His fingers traced the four pieces of candy—sticky peanut brittle—five gold dollars, and a tiny derringer, dropped into his pocket by Nora. The derringer was a gift from him the day Nora turned sixteen. His sister was such an independent young lady and took numerous trips with her many friends. Daniel felt better knowing she carried the tiny pistol with her wherever she went...and now...well, perhaps it would serve a purpose for him.

"This way!" The shouted command startled him from his thoughts. The guards were ushering the new prisoners over the drawbridge and into the fort. They made their way into the center parade ground of the fort. He was amazed at what he saw. Sutlers' stands were set up all around the dirt grounds. Most of the customers were Union soldiers, but a few ragged Confederate prisoners stood at the food vendor's tables.

"If any of you have any money...good U.S. money...you can purchase what you want."

Apparently they were being forced to live on reduced rations while food was within reach, but unattainable, unless you had money. Again he touched the coins in his pocket. They would have to be used sparingly and only when it was nearly time.

Taking a few steps deeper into the fort, Daniel was immediately swallowed up in the teaming crowd of unwashed prisoners that flowed around him, ignoring him completely. His stomach growled as he looked at the fresh summer tomatoes, juicy heads of lettuce, and plump green watermelons lying on the sutlers' tables. It was so tempting to spend the money now and fill his painfully empty belly. He shook his head. Not now. There was no way to say how long he would need to get out of here…and return to his beloved.

* * *

The brightly colored peddler's wagon drew more than a few stares as the Ashburn family rolled into the town of Havre de Grace.

"I think we should sell the wagon, Papa…we are drawing too much attention. The slave hunters may track us in this."

Paul Ashburn nodded. "In fact, Charlotte, I would prefer not to drive directly to the Reid home and implicate them in our business."

She shot an anxious glance at her father. Dorothy reached out and patted her daughter's nervous fingers. "Why don't we let you out here, Charlie? I know you wish to meet Daniel's family as soon as possible. Your father and I will see to lodging and selling off the rest of our goods and the wagon."

"Absolutely, child. We will come tomorrow to meet our new relatives."

Climbing down from the wagon, she waved farewell to her parents and walked down the tree-lined street. Many of the homes were large, sitting on large grassy lots with sculpted gardens that bloomed with late summer flowers. She wondered what kind of house the Reids lived in. The only thing Daniel had said about his family was that he had a younger sister and brother and that his father owned the general store and several warehouses.

That told her little. Storeowners could be wealthy or not, depending on how business went. Ahead was a large, green, Victorian style home with a wrought iron fence surrounding the garden.

An expensive carriage, pulled by matched grays rattled by, obviously in a hurry. It stopped suddenly in front of the Victorian. A young, blonde woman leaped from the carriage almost before it stopped. Her yellow summer dress swirled about her, nearly tripping her in her headlong rush to the door. Charlie heard the sobs and saw the anguish on the girl's face as she rushed by, totally ignoring Charlie's presence a few yards away on the sidewalk.

Charlie stopped dead and looked at the front of the house. The small gold-lettered sign beside the front door read "Reid" 906 South Union Street.

The windows of the house stood open to catch the summer breeze, allowing Charlie to hear the agonized words of the hysterical girl. She clutched the top of the iron post for support as her knees buckled at those words.

"Mama, Papa! I found him!" The girl's voice was filled with fear, "Daniel is a prisoner!"

* * *

Every day was a struggle against everything and everybody. Once more Daniel had to watch while a guard beat yet another prisoner for throwing the chamber pot contents out of the window onto the guard's head as he passed underneath.

When the beating was over, his fellow prisoners dragged the man's battered body inside the wooden barracks, and Daniel leaned over him.

"Stan, why can't you learn? I keep telling all of you

305

over and over not to do that!"

The man pried open one swelling eye and managed a bloody grin. "It's fun, Danny boy. 'Sides, I likes ta make y'all upset so's I kin hear that good ol' Southern twang come out in yer voice."

Daniel growled and applied a wet cloth to the raw bruises. "Stupid reason to get the tar beat out of you!" He straightened with a suddenness that had the prisoners around him stepping back. "I am giving y'all an order, like it or not! NO ONE is to dump chamber pot contents out the window…EVER! Not only does it get you punished, it draws disease ridden flies and vermin…I will empty the pot in the outhouse myself!"

"Hah, you cain't be givin' no orders," one of the soldiers surrounding them piped up. "You acts like an officer, but you ain't one. If'n ya were, you'd be inside them stone walls like the rest o' them." He paused for a breath. "But Dan's got a point there. One o' the boys said as how the guards like to shoot into a bunch o' prisoners just fer the fun of it. You ain't never gonna know when ol' Hamilton out there will git a notion to do more than rough ya up."

It took all of Daniel's strength to walk away from the men. There were times when he seriously doubted the mental powers of many of his fellow detainees. Some of them were downright idiots. *Why bring more suffering on yourself than you already had? Wasn't it bad enough to go around hungry all the time?* Even if you did get supper, there were undisciplined thieves among the Confederate prisoners called "flankers" that could swindle a man out of his food in no time flat.

Feeling the wooden floor bend under his boots as he walked to the door, Daniel wondered how long it would be before it all gave way and sank into the ever-present mud on this island. He stepped outside, immediately slipped sideways in the stinking slime, and had to grab the door jam for support. With a sucking noise, he pulled his left food out and gained his balance before letting go.

The smell hit him anew every time he walked outside. He kept hoping to get some fresh air to blow it away but was disappointed once again. For someone such as himself, who liked things clean, this place was an extra hell on earth.

Mud was tracked all over. It got on your boots, on your trousers, in your bed, and on the blankets…everywhere.

If the greenish brown, stinking mud wasn't bad enough, there were even worse torments. Every night when high tide came in, the ground flooded all around the fort and brought with it the miniscule beasties that multiplied in the standing water during the day. Dead fish and leaves, worms, larvae, tadpoles, and other putrescent things swarmed in the numerous puddles…decaying and stewing in the hot August sun until the smell was enough to make a man lose the little stomach contents he had.

The swarms of mosquitoes and other insect life thrived out here on their diet of Confederate and Yankee blood alike. They bred in the slimy puddles and in the wooden tanks set out to gather rain for the prisoners' drinking water. If the rain didn't fill the tanks often enough, the men were forced to go to drainage ditches or to the edge of the Delaware River to gather drinking water that was unfit for human consumption.

Gagging at the stench, Daniel pinched his nose as he slogged his way toward the huge stone fortress. Feeling in his trouser pocket, he closed his fingers around the precious coins. It was time to buy some fresh food...he could feel the lack of food dragging him down to a lethargic state. He found himself sitting, staring, and thinking of nothing too often...or even falling asleep in the middle of the day. If he was going to swim out of here, he had to spend some of the precious coins on food from the high-priced sutlers.

Chapter Twenty-Six

It had taken an entire month to finally implement this scheme…a month! Charlie paced nervously up and down the length of the bedroom in the Reid house where she had been living since Daniel's brother, Bradford, had discovered his sister-in-law in a sobbing heap by their front gate.

Upon learning she was Daniel's bride, he had scooped her up, carried her into the house, and deposited her on the sofa. Nora, Daniel's golden-haired sister, gave her chamomile tea laced with whiskey. After introductions were made all around, the entire Reid family launched into a meeting of the minds that lasted forty-eight hours straight before they broke to sleep.

Charlie was amazed by the non-stop bantering of ideas back and forth between Daniel's mother, father, sister, and brother over the course of those two days. Outsiders came and went as they were called upon for their services or assistance. She was exhausted when Harriet Reid, Daniel's vivacious mother, finally insisted Charlie retire.

Mama and Papa arrived the next day, and soon everyone was back into the discussion. Servants scurried in and out with food and drink. Coffee and tea was liberally applied to help keep them going…until finally a plan with some merit was agreed upon.

It has to work! We have to free Daniel from Fort Delaware! Rumors abounded as to the horrors of the place…and now they had heard smallpox was sweeping through the soldiers, killing them at a rapid rate.

Charlie put up a hand to her shorn locks and grimaced. Once more she wore the outfit of a young boy, complete with a hat and spectacles. What would Daniel say when he saw her? She promised once—a lifetime ago—that she would never again disguise herself and…here she was.

Her pacing took her back in front of the mirror. Stopping, she studied her appearance carefully. The white linen shirt with full sleeves and generous cut, topped by a simple brown vest hid her bound breasts. The glasses and cap lay on a side table, ready and waiting. She turned and inspected her rear end. Mother had expertly altered the trousers to disguise the womanly shape under them. A thick band of padding around the waistband gave her a boxy figure and the appearance of a slightly overweight young lad who had not lost his baby fat.

"Are you ready, sister?" A masculine voice called out from outside the closed door.

"Ready, Brad."

Donning the hat and glasses, she opened the heavy oak door and stepped out onto the deep pile carpet in the hall.

Daniel's younger brother stepped back in surprise. "Why, I can't believe it!" His blue eyes, so like his brother's, were wide. He turned and called down the hall. "Nora, come here, you have got to see this! Now I know why our brother was so easily fooled!"

With a rustling of crinoline, Nora emerged from her bedroom and approached. Her eyes flew wide at the sight of Charlie as well. "Charlotte, dear, is that really you?"

"Of course, it is. You helped me with this outfit, Nora, don't you remember?"

"Yes, silly, I only said that because I was surprised at how much you really do look like a young boy…a very pretty young boy, though." She turned to her brother. "Don't you think she looks a lot like young Henry Roget? The dark hair and her fine features make her look like the French baker's son. Very convenient, don't you think?"

Bradford Reid nodded vigorously in agreement, "Absolutely, Char, you do look like the baker's boy. Mother will be pleased with the results. Have your parents ever seen you in disguise before?"

"Actually, no, they have not. I didn't change into my soldier's uniform until I had already left home." She looked at Brad anxiously. "Has your father been able to get any news from Fort Delaware?"

He took her elbow and steered her toward the stairs. He was dressed casually in the same type of white shirt and brown trousers that Charlie wore. "Nothing new. But we are all ready to take our places. Remember, you are not to speak unless you absolutely have to. I am afraid that Southern accent and sweet woman's voice will give you away."

* * *

Only two nickels and one penny left and still there had been no opportunity for escape. Daniel debated once more whether to spend the precious money. He sat on a muddy log and stared across the river at the fertile cornfields on the New Jersey shore. A single horseman rode slowly through the tall green vegetation, reminding him of the horse he had lost. Galileo had been such a great horse too...the animal was one more thing the damned Yankees had stolen from him.

It was late in August now, and he knew his time was running out. If he waited much longer, the water of the Delaware would turn cold and show no mercy if he tried to swim away from Pea Patch Island.

His decision was made. He would buy the food he needed to bolster his strength and, within a few days, make his attempt. If it brought him a bullet in the back, so be it. Dying by the enemy's hand quickly was better than the slower agony of starvation or, even worse, of smallpox.

It had been hard to keep from offering medical assistance to the men, but, if the Yankees knew he was both an officer and a surgeon, they would move him inside the fortress walls and there would be no chance of escape. Besides, there was little he could do for them anyway with no supplies to work with. Let the Yankee doctors deal with it...they had caused the problem in the first place.

Daniel pulled his aching left hand from under his jacket and began to work the stiffened joints and muscles with his right hand. Since coming here, the injury to his hand had flared up again, leaving it stiffened and sore. This was just one more thing to bring his spirits even lower.

God, how he missed Charlie! He would jump into that water right now, despite the rifles of the twenty guards that patrolled directly behind him, if he knew she was waiting on the opposite shore for him.

Wearily, he hauled his body off the log. Supper tonight would be just the same as it had been every night — slimy, rusty bacon; soup swimming with white worms and pea bugs; a thin slice of salt pork or a mouthful of fresh beef. Sometimes they were lucky enough to get a potato…those nights, when the fresh beef and potato came on the same night, were a reason to celebrate.

Daniel tugged up his tattered uniform trousers. They were getting looser and looser on him, threatening to fall off, despite the belt cinched as tightly around his waist as it would allow. He heaved a sigh and slogged through the mud toward the pentagonal walls.

* * *

Waiting and watching for a glimpse of her husband among the thousands of dirty, ragged soldiers was pure hell. For over a week, she and Bradford had come by boat each day with the other sutlers to this massive fort. Once more they stood side-by-side and offered the Frenchman's baked goods for sale to the starving prisoners.

More than once, she had tried to slip a roll to a hollow-eyed man, only to be angrily admonished by Brad. "Don't do that," he warned. "If the guards catch us giving away food, we'll be told to leave and not come back! You must take money for our goods, even a copper penny will do."

Pushing her glasses up on her nose, Charlie leaned behind the table to get the cloth sack holding the small loaves of day-old bread. She had just begun to dump the loaves into the large basket on the wooden table when she noticed how still Brad had become, despite the customer in a filthy Confederate uniform directly in front of the table.

She stopped shoveling the loaves out of the sack and looked at the scratched metal belt buckle in front of her. The letters C.S.A., for the Confederate States of America, were still clearly visible, though dirt was caked in the point of the letter A. Slowly she raised her head and joy surged through her in a rush.

Daniel! The only thing that moved was her heart as it pounded furiously in her chest. Dear Lord, she wanted to throw her body across this table into his arms and kiss him! But she didn't move. Her beloved husband's beautiful blue eyes slowly filled with tears, but he didn't move. Neither did Brad or Charlie. Then Brad cleared his throat.

"What will you have today, soldier? We have some nice wheat bread…only one day old." Brad had to clear his throat again.

Charlie drank in the sight of Daniel. He was alive—dirty and thin, but alive. The beard covering his cheeks was shaggy, and his blond hair was in the same condition. Mud was splattered on his boots and trousers. But his eyes were clear and bright and they spoke volumes to her. She could see the love in them, the happiness at the sight of her and his brother, although his face remained expressionless and flat.

"Will this be enough, sir?" He opened a shaking hand to reveal a nickel.

"Certainly," Brad said briskly and took Daniel's

hand in both of his to collect the money. He held his brother's hand briefly before releasing it then dropped three cents into his open hand. "Give him a loaf, Charlie. Charlie's a good helper, but he doesn't speak much."

Daniel nodded slowly and turned expectantly toward his wife. A Yankee guard strolled past the table watching the transaction carefully. She swallowed hard and prayed she wouldn't burst into tears. Reaching into her pocket, she retrieved the note and slipped it under the loaf as she passed it to Daniel in a single, well-practiced movement.

Only the slightest twitch of his eyebrow told her that he felt the presence of the paper. Both hands shook slightly as he reached for the bread, touching the tips of her fingers lightly as the food and message exchanged hands.

"We'll be here again tomorrow, make sure you tell your friends that our bread is the best around, and our prices are fair, even for Rebs." Brad informed his customer easily, finally shifting into his usual relaxed stance.

The strain Daniel was under was obvious. He looked down at the bread then up at his wife and brother again. It seemed as though he wanted to say something, but was unsure of his words.

"Sure wish I had a knife to cut this bread. It would be better than tearing it." He finally spoke in a hoarse voice that made him seem slow-witted, and Charlie felt her heart break. Giving them a polite nod, he stood in front of the table for another moment, then turned slowly and walked away, melting into the teaming crowd. She saw the unnatural rigidity of his back and the stiff movements of his legs, quite unlike his usual easy grace.

Please, God, she prayed. *Let him come back again tomorrow.*

* * *

Jumping down from the horse and tossing the reins over the iron hitching post, Charlie dashed up the steps, across the painted porch, and into the big house as fast as her legs could carry her.

"Mr. Reid, Mrs. Reid, Nora! We saw him! We saw Daniel today!"

At her call, the family came quickly. Nora rushed down to the parlor in a flurry of skirts. Martin Reid and his wife, Harriet, came in from the dining room with excitement on their faces.

"Charlotte, that is such good news!" Harriet took hold of her hands and pumped them up and down. Tears streamed down Charlie's face uncontrollably, and she pulled a hand free to dash them away. "Why are you crying, my dear…" Daniel's mother stopped for a moment then gasped, "…Is my son ill?"

Brad's boots resounded on the hard wood floors as he quickly joined them.

Charlie shook her head, unable to speak, removing her glasses and her hat then dropping into a chair.

"Mother, Dan's a bit thin, but he is fine. Charlie managed to pass him the note. I am positive he will come back tomorrow, and we can find out more!" Brad beamed at them as if he had personally accomplished this miracle.

"Wonderful! The sooner we get him out of there, the

better. I fear the weather may turn cold any time now, and that will bode ill for a swim." With a look of fatherly concern in his kindly brown eyes, Martin turned his attention to Charlie. Seeing his expression, she straightened and wiped her wet cheeks with her hands.

"What is it, Mr. Reid? Has something happened?"

"Yes, my dear. My lawyer returned from Augusta County today." Coming to stand in front of Charlie, he reached down and covered one of her hands with his large hand. "He discovered what you already suspected, that your family is still wanted by the authorities for helping the runaways...there is a reward posted for anyone who turns you in."

She gasped. "I thought they would still be looking for us, but I didn't dream they would pay money for our return. We—we only wanted to help people in trouble...now we have a price on our heads!"

Martin shook his head slowly. "I am afraid that is not all." He turned to his wife. "Harriet, would you please get Charlotte a glass of wine? I fear she will need it."

"No." Charlie held up a hand. "Mrs. Reid, I don't need any wine, thank you. Tell me what else the lawyer learned, please."

"Mr. Templeton, our lawyer, met a man by the name of Bradley, a Mr. Ralph Bradley in the local tavern. The man was drunk and spreading tales about your father."

"What kind of tales?" Her voice wavered, and her palms grew damp.

"Are you sure you wouldn't like a drink, Charlotte? Perhaps something stronger than wine?"

Charlie was getting more upset by the minute. She gritted her teeth. "Just tell me, please, sir."

He took a deep breath. "Mr. Bradley is telling people Paul Ashburn murdered his eldest son, Eric, in a fit of rage when he found out Eric raped one of the runaway slaves."

Chapter Twenty-Seven

Finding some place private when you were sharing an island with twelve thousand prisoners was next to impossible. The only place Daniel could find to be alone was the outhouse, so that is where he went. Opening the door, he stepped inside, hearing the frantic scurrying of tiny mouse feet. A huge spider ambled slowly off the latch handle. With a shudder, he let it leave before taking hold of the piece of wood to latch the door shut. He took the note out of his pocket. This outhouse was positioned directly above the river, allowing waste to be washed away by the moving water.

His hands shook as he unfolded the tiny piece of paper. They had come for him! Somehow, Charlie had gotten together with his brother and come for him. This time, he had not been fooled for a second by her disguise. The weakness in his body could not stop the quickening of his pulse and the tightening of his loins the moment he realized just who was standing on the opposite side of that bakery table. His stomach growled, and he tore another bite out of the small loaf.

Leave it to Brad to have figured out a way to get onto the island. Daniel smiled. Setting themselves up as sutlers was ingenious. Finally, angling the paper to get the best light through the cracks in the ramshackle wooden building, he read the note.

Dearest Daniel,

We are so happy to have found you again. When next we meet, we hope you will have discovered a way off the island. We have obtained the services of a good boatman and can pick you up during the night at a point you designate. Communicate your needs when we see you again. We love you and miss you. We will get you home again.

Your Loving Family

Tearing off a piece of bread with his teeth, he chewed and thought. There had to be a way to escape during the night, when there were less guards about. Somehow he had to get into the river without being detected and swim out to a meeting place.

The river always flowed toward the sea…south…the best place on earth. He didn't have the strength to battle the current, nor did he have any desire to go any further to the north…but how was he to get off this island? Drumming his fingers on the wooden platform of the privy, he pondered the dilemma.

Suddenly, he stood up and shoved the paper and bread into his pocket with the tiny derringer. In the darkness of the outhouse, it was difficult to see well, but he had been in and out of this tiny three-by-four foot structure so often that he knew what it looked like.

Slipping his fingers under the edge of the privy top, he pulled up on the wooden planks. Nothing moved. With his gentle surgeon's sense of touch, he moved his fingers blindly along the top surface of the platform, feeling the lengthwise boards and each nail head. Five nails held it down along the closest edge, four down the left side, six nails across the back, and four more nails held it attached along the right side.

A cool breeze came up between the planks, stinking of sewage and river water. That meant only this platform, made up of four lengthwise boards held together by crosspieces and nailed around the edges, stood between him and the Delaware River beneath.

"Hey, you almost done in there?" an irritated voice called out.

"Yes, sorry!" he called back. If he had some way to get those nails out, then…

"Soldier, you'd better get your sorry Rebel self out of that outhouse now!"

Daniel opened the door, allowing the daylight to come in. He took one last glance behind him to confirm what his fingers had felt. *I can do it!*

Then he stepped out to allow the dancing man go in. "Watch out for the spiders!"

"Yeah, yeah," the man grumbled, pushing past him.

* * *

Mr. Reid sent for Charlie's parents and told them over dinner what the lawyer learned during his trip to Virginia.

"You don't believe that, do you, Martin?" Paul Ashburn asked. The sorrow on her father's face made Charlie's heart ache for him. "I loved Eric, as much as I do Charlotte and her younger brother, Scott. Eric would never attack a slave woman…and I would never—"

"I know that," Martin Reid said. "I know you are not a murderer…and a son of yours would never do what Bradley is saying."

Charlie shook her head sadly. "Eric was in love with Ralph Bradley's daughter, Polly. Ralph's son, John, and

Eric were best friends their entire lives." She pushed the untouched food around on her plate. "I just don't understand how Mr. Bradley could say such a thing. He knew Eric his whole life."

There was no response from her mother or mother-in-law to this conversation. Charlie looked down the long, heavily laden dining room table at the two.

Harriet Reid sat at the end of the table, her blond hair perfectly coiffed and her gown a beautiful shade of blue. Dorothy Ashburn wore her homespun calico dress…the one Charlie knew was her best dress. But the women, so different in appearance and personality, were united in their love for their children. Their heads were bent together as they talked, paying no attention to anyone else. Occasionally, one of the women would take a sip of wine or a bite of the delicious meal prepared by the Reid's cook.

"What are the two of you discussing so seriously, my dear?" Paul asked, noticing the direction of Charlie's stare.

"Oh, we are just discussing the problem at home and the situation with Daniel, just like the rest of you, Paul." Dorothy smiled at her husband with a look, which Charlie knew meant, "This is none of your business."

Dorothy's gaze fell on Charlie's plate, which still held most of its original contents. "Charlotte, dear, you haven't touched your dinner. Do you feel all right?"

"Actually, I have a headache, Mother." She looked down the table at Nora, Brad, and the four parents. "I think I shall retire for the night."

With an understanding nod, Harriet Reid spoke,

"Certainly, my dear, if that is your wish. However, you will not hear the plan Dorothy and I have developed to solve all these problems."

* * *

The stinking contents of the bucket slopped against the sides, threatening to spill. Daniel slowed his pace through the mud and concentrated on where he placed his feet.

The Yankee guard passing by paid him no mind…and why should he? Every night for two months Daniel had performed this duty. Since the night Stan had been beaten for dumping the bucket's contents on the head of the guard, he had taken over the chore of emptying the evening chamber pot contents. The night guards were glad enough to be saved further humiliation at the hands of the Rebels who delighted in that type of harassment.

Entering the little outhouse, he dumped the bucket's load down the hole and worked on another nail with the little pocketknife his courageous wife smuggled to him in the loaf of bread.

Following the instructions in the first note, Daniel had asked for a small knife. With regret he further wrote that, after receiving the knife, he would not return to the sutler's tables for a few days to prevent suspicion.

It had been agony to stay away from the fort's parade grounds, knowing his wife and brother were there, continuing the charade. Day after long day, he kept his distance until returning at the promised time.

For a long time that day, he had watched his two loved ones from a distance, soaking up the sight of them.

Diane M. Wylie

Charlie's silky dark locks were short again under the boy's cap she wore. Then he watched her turn her head and spit. He barely suppressed a chuckle when he saw the startled look on Brad's face. *My darling wife still remembers the lessons learned in the army.*

Slipping the edge of the knife under the nail with as little noise as possible, Daniel worked it all the way around, wiggling the blade to coax the nail from its bed. He only had precious minutes to work before the guard would become suspicious. Pretending that one had diarrhea could only last so many times before you would be stuck in the hospital, which was something he wanted to avoid at all costs.

He would have liked to include some of the other soldiers in his escape plan, but now he couldn't trust a single one of them. Things had turned ugly among the prisoners. Men were turning their comrades in to the Yankees for real and fictitious transgressions in return for rations. All it took was a sideways glance at the wrong person, and he was telling a guard that you were planning to escape. Then, without a chance to explain yourself, you were tossed in the dark, dank, subterranean stone rooms of Fort Delaware, and your betrayer was getting a piece of unspoiled meat.

Prying the nail up gently, Daniel kept his left hand cupped over the top of it, just in case. He had lost one nail in the darkness that way and didn't want to lose another. Testing it with his fingers, he felt it give up its hold on the damp, swollen wood.

Tiny insect feet tickled the sensitive skin on the side of his neck, and he shuddered, brushing it away.

324

Stopping for a moment, he waited to see if he would feel the sting of a spider bite. One poor fellow was bitten by a spider a few weeks ago in this very outhouse. His leg had developed horrifying sores, and the man had fallen deathly ill. The Yankees had taken him away to the hospital and he had yet to return.

Daniel sighed softly with relief. No needle-like bite was forthcoming. *Perhaps it wasn't a spider.* Quickly he reamed out the hole with his knifepoint and slid the nail back into the hole. It came up again easily with his fingertips.

Someone banged on the door, making him jump.

"Hey...you inside the outhouse!" a voice called. "You better get out here...NOW!"

Opening his mouth, Daniel made a loud retching noise, waited a moment then staggered out, empty bucket in hand.

He could barely make out the figure of the Union guard with a rifle pointed at his belly. Ignoring the man, he staggered past, wiping his mouth on his sleeve. "Sick," he murmured and kept walking unsteadily toward the barracks. No bullet hit him in the back. Sweat trickled down from his armpits. *Stayed too long, better be more careful next time.*

* * *

Charlie watched the dark water of the Delaware River slide away beneath the boat as the men at the oars strained against the current. She shivered. The air was growing cool. Looking toward Pea Patch Island, she saw the massive forbidding stone structure jutting up from the flat surroundings like a great monster rising from a calm ocean surface.

Dark clouds scuttled across the sky. A storm was brewing. The sutlers wouldn't stay long if the rains came. The thought of spending another day without even seeing Daniel made tears sting her eyes. She blinked them back and reached under her glasses to rub at her eyes.

How much longer would he need to complete his plan? She hoped it wouldn't be much longer…she didn't think she could bear coming to this horrid place for many more days.

"Come on, Charlie. No time to be daydreaming, my lad." Brad's cheerful voice cut into her thoughts.

Nodding without speaking, she rose, slung the bag of breads and rolls over her shoulder, and followed her brother-in-law's broad back, climbing out of the boat.

She was still sorting the breads and rolls into their groups when the prisoners began to line up to buy food. No matter how many times she saw her countrymen in their tattered, filthy butternut and gray, it still evoked anger toward the well-fed, well-clothed Yankees that guarded them.

"My assistant will give you what you want, gentlemen. There's plenty for all." Brad repeated the words he used over and over during the course of each long day. Charlie would pass the prisoner what he asked for or pointed to, and Brad would collect their coins.

Sometimes, she would give them two for the price of one, warning them with a look and a nod to keep quiet. She would be rewarded with a quick, sad smile of gratitude.

"Could I have two rolls, please," a familiar voice asked quietly. "This is my last coin."

A tingle ran through her body as soon as the first word hit her ears. Casually looking up, she saw it was indeed her husband speaking. A faint smile touched his lips, and he nodded so slightly to her that she almost missed it.

"I'll take your coins, sir," Brad spoke up. "Charlie will give you the rolls."

Not daring to smile back at Daniel, Charlie reached for two plump golden rolls and placed them in his outstretched hands.

"Thank you." His voice washed over her, melting her insides. He turned to his brother, knowing Charlie could not speak to him. "Might be a thunderstorm tonight."

Brad bobbed his head agreeably. "Not a fit night for man nor beast tonight."

"Move along now!" a harsh voice broke in. The guard came up and gave Daniel a hard shove with his rifle butt. He went sprawling to his knees in the dirt, dropping his rolls. Charlie watched in mute horror. The Yankee gave Daniel a hard kick in the ribs. Two starving Rebels grabbed up the rolls and disappeared into the crowd.

"See here, sir, the man didn't do anything!" Brad protested, beginning to move around the table. Charlie grabbed his arm, pulling him back.

"The damn filthy Rebs are all slow. They move too slow." The big booted foot pulled back and hit Daniel in the lower back as he lay on his side. She watched him arch in pain, but he didn't make a sound.

Picking up two more rolls, she eased around the end of the table, keeping her head down and shuffling her feet in the dirt. Slowly, bowing slightly to the Yankee, she moved to Daniel's side and crouched beside him, holding out the rolls. She longed to wrap her arms around him and help him to his feet. Then she wanted to take her Springfield rifle and blow a hole in that guard.

With effort, he struggled to his feet, keeping his eyes on Charlie. She saw the frustration in his blue eyes and a flash of barely controlled anger, before the submissive shutters came down. He accepted the rolls silently, turned, and staggered away into the watching crowd.

Chapter Twenty-Eight

A brilliant bolt of lightning lit up the sky. Seconds later, the crash of thunder split the air. It was the perfect night. Daniel waited until the men in his barracks were snoring, and the rain was pounding hard. It drummed against the wooden roof, finding entrance points and dripping in on the sleepers.

He heard O'Reilly curse the rain and settle back to sleep, a little closer to the man next to him. Rising as he had every night, Daniel used the chamber pot, dumped its contents into the bucket and opened the door.

The wind threatened to tear the door out of his hand, and he had to struggle to close it again. He stepped out into deeper mud than usual. Immediately, he was soaked to the skin. The guards were not likely to be patrolling as often.

Another flash lit up the guard towers. He saw a soldier, dressed in his dark greatcoat, standing on the platform. Hunching his shoulders against the biting wind and stinging rain, he slogged through the mud with his bucket.

His ribs and back ached with a dull throb. After the punishment today, he had returned to the barracks to find his side had turned a purplish black from the bruising, but no ribs were broken. He wasn't so sure about how his kidneys had fared but knew they were still working.

Laboring with the outhouse door against the wind, Daniel slammed it shut. After dumping the bucket and its contents down the hole, he quickly pulled up the platform top. It came up easily, nails dangling from their positions. Propping the platform against the back wall, he could hear the river rushing by, but could see nothing but blackness below.

Pulling off his boots, he dropped each one into the water, knowing they would be swept away quickly by the current. Then he shrugged out of his jacket. Taking the little derringer out of his pocket, he looked at it for a moment. It would be useless to take it with him. The water would ruin it in a heartbeat. He bent over and pushed the tiny gun into the corner. Perhaps it would be of use to someone else. Sitting on the side, he turned around, put his legs into the hole, pushed off, and lowered his body into the cold water. Rain continued to pound the roof of the little outhouse drowning out the gasp he couldn't hold back when he went in.

He shoved the jacket under water, reached up and lowered the platform back into position over his head. The darkness was complete now. Daniel prayed there was nothing to trap him under the structure, took a deep breath, and pushed down into the watery unknown.

Lungs nearly bursting, he came up to the surface as quickly as he could. Gulping for air quietly was hard, and he struggled to control his breathing. Treading water, he shook the wet hair from his eyes and looked around. A few trees and bushes protruded from the muddy bank into the water, close enough to reach, so he paddled closer and grabbed a branch for a few moments' rest and to get his bearings.

As his eyes adjusted to the dim light, he realized the

rain had let up just a tiny bit, and was now just a steady pitter-pat on the river's surface. Straining to see, he could not discern the New Jersey coastline on the opposite shore — everything was a black void in that direction. Turning toward the shoreline, he tried to figure out how far he had come downstream of the outhouse. His heart skipped a few beats when he realized where he was.

Looming vertically above him was the dark stonewall of the pentagonal Fort Delaware. Protruding ominously from three tiers of gun ports were weapons that could take out a ship and erase a man from the face of the earth. If anyone happened to look directly down from those gun ports, Daniel would be a sitting duck.

With his heart still pounding furiously in his chest, he began to move as silently as possible, pulling himself along using tree branches, swimming in short, slow strokes when needed and staying as close as possible to the bank.

After taking this course of action for an hour, Daniel was finally about a mile away from Pea Patch Island. Taking a deep breath, he decided to swim toward the middle of the river channel using longer strokes. He kicked out with both legs. Pain shot up his left leg! He went under the water rolling in agony. His foot had hit something hidden just under the surface of the river, wrenching his ankle sideways from the force.

Please don't let it be broken! Grabbing for his ankle, he rolled onto his back, letting the current carry him and felt along his bare foot and ankle gently. He could feel it swelling already, despite the cold water.

There was nothing to be done about it now. With a

weary sigh, he rolled back onto his stomach and began to swim again. Fatigue and pain were his only companions now as he set out through the inky blackness with stiffening muscles and an empty stomach.

* * *

Five miles down river, two small boats fought the wind and rain. Charlie held fast to the side of the boat while her father and the hired boatman used the oars to pull the vessel through the waters of the Delaware River. She could see the lantern winking in the distance as the boat containing Mr. Reid and Brad bobbed up and down.

Each boat moved back and forth along their section of the river searching. Three hours later, the wind died down, the rain had stopped, and the moon shone brightly on the restless water. Still there was no sign of Daniel. She was cold, tired, and extremely anxious. *Had he been able to get out? Did he get caught in the act? Perhaps he had been shot...or...*she didn't want to think about it...

Staring out over the water's surface intently, she could see nothing but water.

"Do you see anything, Papa?" she whispered.

"Not yet, Charlotte." He was sitting beside her and reached over to pat her knee. "If he doesn't show up tonight, you'll return to the fort in the morning to see what happened. Perhaps he was unable to get away." Paul Ashburn spoke quietly, just as reluctant as she to break the silence.

Silvery light tipped each wave cap before it dropped away into darkness. Straining to see, Charlie's breath stopped in her throat. There...a dark thing floated in the water about forty yards away.

"Over there, sir! I see something!" She tugged at the boatman's sleeve and pointed.

"Yes." He and Paul pulled at the oars, turning the boat to move toward the object that bobbed up and down with the motion of the water.

They pulled up beside it. It was a man! She could see his arms wrapped tightly around a log and his head resting on its sodden surface.

Leaning over the side, Paul and the boatman grabbed the man's arms and together they wrestled him into the boat. Charlie reached out to pull his head and shoulders into her lap.

It was Daniel! His eyes were closed, his face pale and still in the dim light. Quickly she bent over him, putting her fingers to the side of his cold neck as he had taught her to do so long ago at Antietam. In those few split seconds, she knew a fear so deep and so wide that it threatened to swallow her whole. The heartbeat was slow but steady.

"He's alive!"

Chapter Twenty-Nine

Yankees rode up and down the streets of Port Penn, knocking on each door, looking, they said, for twenty escaped Confederate prisoners from Fort Delaware only five miles upriver.

Charlie and Nora watched through the window as the group, who had just marched through the small house, mounted their horses and rode away.

"They won't be back," Brad's confident voice behind them said as the Bluecoats disappeared. "This house father rented is so far from everything they won't bother...it is the perfect place to hide."

Turning quickly, Charlie pulled aside the rag rug, and Brad yanked open the trap door to the hidden cellar. In minutes, Martin Reid appeared below with his arm wrapped around his oldest son, supporting him.

Three pairs of arms reached down to help Daniel up the rickety steps. He smiled at them gratefully and hobbled into the small kitchen. "Thank you, everyone."

Brad and Nora got on either side of their brother and helped him into the sitting room where he sank onto the stuffed sofa, stretching his bandaged leg out as Charlie sat beside him.

"Damned sunken logs." He muttered a few more curse words before closing his eyes for a moment, missing the raised eyebrows from his sister. "I can't believe I sprained my ankle."

"I can't believe you escaped through an outhouse," Nora laughed, "and that nineteen other men apparently followed you out."

Martin Reid entered the room with a smile on his jovial face. "Your mother will be sorry she wasn't here to pamper you again, my boy. You know how she loves to do that."

Daniel groaned theatrically. "I know she does, Father." He turned his head and reached out a hand toward Charlie. She took it, relishing the warmth of his fingers as they curled possessively around hers. "But I have a wife to pamper me now."

"Have you heard from Mrs. Reid? How are she and Mother doing?" It worried Charlie immensely that her mother and Harriet Reid had gone back to Augusta County, even though they were escorted by the Reid's lawyer, Mr. Templeton.

"Why, yes, I just got a letter from her today." Martin took a paper out of his pocket and began to read it aloud to the room.

Dearest Martin and Our Family,

Dorothy and I send our love to you all. We hope you are well and have rescued our son. It is only because of my confidence in you that I left to take on this project. Dorothy and I have talked to Mrs. Bradley about her husband. The lady was most kind and apologetic regarding her husband's malicious gossiping. As a result, all allegations of wrongdoing have been dropped.

We have some wonderful news to tell you! While we were staying at Charlotte's house, a member of her family came by to visit. Lieutenant Scott Ashburn dropped in, accompanied by a

Miss Polly Bradley and her brother, John. It seems the three met while visiting Eric's grave before coming up to the house.

We were quite a while sorting out the details for young Scott, but he sends Charlotte and Daniel his congratulations and his love. Dorothy was very cheered by her son's visit and the outcome of our trip. It helped her deal with the sale of her family property here in Virginia, which Mr. Templeton has arranged for a nice sum, considering there is still a war in progress.

After the sale has been completed, we will meet up with Mr. Ashburn, who is making all the arrangements for the wagon train trip. Mr. Templeton assures us there is plenty of rich land available out in the western part of our country for a reasonable price.

The youngest Ashburn was excited at the prospect of joining his family when the war is over. He said he would love to be a cowboy. That made us all laugh, especially Miss Polly, who had been having a hard time with her grief over Eric's loss. She is a pretty little thing. It is a shame her father is a drunken sort.

Martin, you must try to send word as soon as you obtain Daniel's release. We are praying for his safe return. We hope to return to Maryland soon

.

Love to Everyone,
Harriett and Dorothy

"Scott is safe and alive!" Happiness swept through Charlie in a warm rush. Squeezing her husband's hand, she raised it to her face and touched his palm to her cheek. She was so thankful to have them both alive and well…too much grief and loss had struck her family…she could not have been able to stand more.

"I am so happy to hear your brother is all right, Charlie," Nora said cheerily. Most of Daniel's family had adopted her nickname. She liked it. Hearing that name reminded her of the time she spent in the Confederate army…a time she never wanted to forget. "It was a good idea that your mother had…going West is the safest way to keep out of the clutches of the slave catchers."

Charlie looked around the room at the three Reids in this tiny riverside house they had used since they plucked Daniel from the river. They were an intelligent and hearty bunch. Working together, they had rescued Daniel. The echo of family ran in their blood and bodies. All three children had their mother's blue eyes that were as clear as a Virginia sky on a crisp fall day like today.

Those intense blue eyes were resting on her now. She sensed his gaze and squeezed his hand, feeling the returning strength in his grip. Her entire body tingled at the long ago memory of his sleek muscular legs entwined with hers, strong arms holding her close …

"Darling…" Her husband was speaking to her. "I was just telling everyone I think I am doing well enough for them to return home, don't you agree?" He winked.

She smiled and nodded. "Oh, yes, and don't forget, Daniel is a doctor, so he would know."

"Absolutely. I can't thank you enough for pulling me through this ordeal and helping me escape from that prison." His shudder of revulsion ran through the hand she still held.

"We have talked about it and decided Charlie will

accompany me when I leave here. I don't know where we will be going, but it will be better that we stay together for her protection, now that her family is heading west. But we are fine now. What I mean to say is—"

"—But, what my husband is trying to say is—"

"—Yes, what I am trying to say is…Charlie and I did not have an opportunity for a honeymoon period when we were first married and…"

Brad held up a hand. "Say no more, brother. We are as good as gone."

Nora turned a pretty shade of pink, opened her mouth, and then closed it again. She smiled and tried again. "I am just so happy for you both!"

"Quite, quite," Mr. Reid said, nodding. "By all means, let us pack our things and take our leave, children. I have a business to attend to."

Brad and Nora turned and left the room, arguing over who had last seen the luggage, but Martin moved closer to the sofa and sat next to his son. "I was so afraid I had lost you, Dan," he whispered.

"I'll leave you two alone to talk," Charlie volunteered, letting go of Daniel's hand.

Martin swallowed and visibly straightened. "No, stay." His voice was stronger now. "I just have one more thing to tell Daniel before I go pack my things." Reaching into his jacket, he extracted a piece of paper. "Do you remember telling me how wonderful that stuff you called 'bromine' was?"

"Yes, that is what I primarily wanted to steal from the Yankees. The amount of medical supplies they have is considerable. What I wouldn't give to see some of that for our boys."

"Although I am not generally a Southern sympathizer," Mr. Reid said, "I do believe in human life, just like my son." He handed Daniel the paper. "This is the order for a shipment of bromine. I bought as much as I could put my hands on. It is being delivered to your friend, Major Will Mattingly, at Lovington Hospital in Virginia later this week."

* *

Slowly savoring the swell of her hip and the valley of her waist, Daniel touched his wife as he had only done in his dreams for months. The hardships and horrors of swimming the cold Delaware River to freedom were a thing of the past now.

He pushed such thoughts from his mind, knowing full well they would return to haunt him in his sleep. This was time to be spent with Charlie, his brave, beautiful, and very naked, little wife.

With a long, sweet sigh, she rolled over to face him. Reaching out a hand, he ran his fingers over her silky dark tresses. Even the short style suited her, though he preferred it long enough to lie enticingly along the curve of her creamy breasts.

"I missed you s-so much, Daniel." He heard the tears in her voice.

Placing a finger against her soft lips, he shook his head. "Shhh, my love. Let us not talk of such things…nothing sad or somber."

She stroked his outstretched arm. He felt his body respond even to that simple touch. He thought of them together like this so many times in the past months. The need to hold her grew strong, and he gave into it, pulling her close. This was so right, so perfectly, spectacularly right.

With effort, he controlled his body and buried his face in her hair, smelling her soft scent of lavender. Her shoulder, so close to his lips, beckoned, and he kissed his way down the side of her neck to that rounded joint. With a soft sigh, he felt her relax in his arms and was surprised she had not been relaxed before.

"Charlie…Charlie…do you still want me? Do you still need me after all this time?" He felt the hurt rise up in his chest. "A-am I a stranger to you now?"

"No, you are no stranger. You are my Daniel, my heart, my home, my love." This time she put a finger up to his lips. "Have you forgotten your own words? Let us speak of nothing sad or somber, you said!" She laughed then, a bright and silvery sound in the moonlit darkness, and bent her head to kiss his lips.

Moist and hot, her tongue darted out and delved deeply into his mouth. It lit him up from head to toe as if he had been set on fire! She must have felt him throbbing back to life between them because she let out a soft chuckle. "You are splendid, indeed," she teased, and he felt wanted once more.

Rolling onto his back, taking her with him, he urged her up his body until his mouth was right where he wanted it. Lifting his head, he licked the sweet tip of her breast until it tightened into a hard pea. Then he switched to the opposite breast and did the same thing, all the while running his hands lightly from the arch of her spine and up her back.

"So soft," he murmured, "so wonderful."

She straddled his hips and ran her hands down his sides. He did what he had wanted to do for so long, kissing and stroking every inch of her luscious body, feeling her respond with muted groans and soft hissing breaths. Slowly, gently he swirled his finger, feeling her grow swollen and wet with desire.

Her hands were not idle. She, too, explored the contours of his body, touching and caressing him everywhere.

His wife gave no indication that she felt differently for him now than she had in the past. She was responsive, sensuous, and...absolutely wonderful, fulfilling his dreams and easing all doubts.

Chapter Thirty

"What in the hell do you mean? LEAVE?" Will shouted so loudly that the windows of the hospital rattled, and Charlie jerked with surprise.

Daniel watched his wife smooth her skirt over her knees. Her green eyes were wide with anxiety when they met his. She had never heard Will yell before. He winked at her reassuringly and stood up from the chair in front of Major Mattingly's scarred wooden desk.

"Is this about your hand? I have seen you use that hand without any problem."

"No," He looked down and flexed his left hand. It was indeed fully functional now. "My hand is just fine. I told you, Will, I am sick to death of all the killing. I have had enough of it to last a lifetime," he said, placing both palms on the desk and leaning toward his friend. "My enlistment period is up in two months. I intend to take advantage of that fact."

"But you can't abandon us, Dan. You know our army needs all the surgeons, hell, all the soldiers we can get." Will's hand ran through his hair, making the ends stick out in all directions.

"I know that. Don't you think this decision has been hard for me?" Straightening, Daniel turned to pace the tiny office, stopping to stare out of the window. Beyond the window, the cold November wind blew down the streets of Winchester, lifting ladies' skirts. He watched a young drummer boy chasing his cap as it was swept away, his drum banging against his legs as he ran.

Images of a little Yankee drummer boy injured and scared served to reinforce Daniel's agonizing decision.

"Since Lincoln decided to make this an issue of slavery, I have had a hard time committing myself to this Cause."

Will's eyes narrowed. "Are you planning to jump to the other side, Captain Reid? If so, I could have you arrested right now as a traitor."

Daniel sighed and walked to place his hands gently on his wife's shoulders. She was his source of strength, and he needed it now. Charlie put a hand on his and squeezed gently.

"I love the South and all of its people, Will, you know that…and I mean ALL its people, no matter their skin color. But I also have many friends in Maryland and in the northern states. I cannot go on taking up arms against them."

"But as a surgeon you are not taking up arms." Will jumped to his feet and pounded his fist on the desk. "Listen, I understand you have been through a lot. But you are fully recovered now—"

"STOP!" Daniel held up a hand. "My mind is made up, Major. However, I do have a compromise for you that should benefit the Confederate army." He watched Will's struggle as he opened his mouth to speak than closed it again. His friend would hear him out.

"If you will not fight this, and allow me to finish out my enlistment term so that I may be honorably discharged, I will agree to work in any hospital you choose for as long as you choose. In return, you could contact the authorities and have all charges against my wife and her family disappear, if you were so inclined." Pausing, he held his hand out to Will, ready to shake hands on the deal already. "I will not wear this uniform again, but I vow to perform my duties as a civilian surgeon, for those in need, to the best of my ability."

Looking down at the hand offered to him, Will sighed. "You know I could force you to remain in the army?"

Daniel kept his hand out. His gaze held his friend's. "Yes, I do. But you and I both know it would serve no good purpose. My wife would lose her husband by her side, my child would lose its father, and you…you would lose the best friend you ever had."

Will looked at Charlie, and she nodded, her face breaking into a wide smile. Daniel saw the transition from army major to best friend as Will's boyish face broke into a grin, and his eyes twinkled merrily behind his thick glasses.

"Father? You hornswaggled me, Captain Reid. Now you've gone and plum argued me out of all my arguments, haven't you?"

Will fell silent then, pushing his glasses up his nose and looking at Daniel for a long moment. Then he nodded and held his hand out to Daniel. The two friends clasped hands tightly across the desk, smiling idiotically at each other.

"Welcome to Lovington Hospital, Doctor Reid and Mrs. Reid." Daniel was pulled into a bear hug right over the scarred piece of furniture. "I do believe we will have to set you up in the civilians' housing." Will stepped over to the office door and opened it to peer out. "I'll have my assistant, Sergeant Stoner, show you what we have available."

"Stoner?" Charlie asked.

"Yes, here he comes now."

Through the open door stepped an older fellow with a graying beard, cut short and neat.

"Clarence!" Daniel and Charlie cried out together then all three of them were laughing and shaking hands.

"What are you doing here?" Charlie asked, a shimmer of tears in her eyes.

With her hands still clasped in his gnarled ones, Clarence grinned, revealing a missing front tooth. "It got to be too much for an ol' fart like me…marchin' all over creation. Major Mattingly got me an easy job with him. I help train more sharpshooters from time to time, too."

Then Clarence noticed Daniel for the first time, and his gaze grew suspicious. "What are y'all doing with the captain here, Charlie?"

Daniel chuckled. "We're married now, Sergeant Stoner…and very happy together." Charlie's smile looked as wide as his own as she nodded in agreement.

"Well, Mr. and Mrs. Reid, is it?" Clarence said. He chuckled and held Charlie at arms length to look her over. "And y'all is gonna be a mama…that's some pumpkins for sure…some pumpkins!"

Daniel had to agree as he watched his wife's face, radiant with joy and impending motherhood, it surely was. Yes, it surely was.

Diane M. Wylie

Author's Note

It is estimated that somewhere between five hundred and a thousand women disguised themselves as men to enlist and fight as full-fledged soldiers during the American Civil War. Some women joined for the money, some followed lovers or husbands, and some joined out of true patriotic duty. But they all served with dedication, spirit, and bravery amid the chaos and horror of a war that cost more American lives than any other war in our nation's history.

Diane M. Wylie

Acknowledgements

A special thank you goes to:

Ed Wylie for being my lover, my friend, and husband through thick and thin. Being married to a romance writer isn't all that bad, is it?

Susan Auer for reading Secrets and Sacrifices and offering her insight, suggestions, and support.

LaVerne Wylie for being the best mother-in-law anyone could ask for.

Dolores, Karen, Lillian, Diane C., Angela, Kathryn, and Alice for your love and support throughout the years since college and beyond.

Maryland Romance Writers for providing me with an education in the romance industry and friendship.

Bill Zaspel for your expertise in the Civil War Period.

The ladies of TA Instruments for your lunchtime companionship and for listening to me talk about my books.

The men and women of the United States Military, past and present, for doing your best for us.

Vintage Romance Publishing offers the finest in historical romance, inspirational, non-fiction, poetry, and books for children. Visit us on the web at www.vrpublishing.com for more history, more adventure and more titles.

Printed in the United States
76870LV00001B/1-9

9 780978 536855